Aron Beauregard's
PLAYGROUND

ISBN: 9798353703464

Cover & Interior Art by Anton Rosovsky

Cover wrap design by Aron Beauregard

Edited by Patrick C. Harrison III & Kristopher
Triana

Printed in the USA

WARNING:
This book contains scenes and subject matter
that are disgusting and disturbing; easily
offended people are not the intended audience.

JOIN MY MAGGOT MAILING LIST NOW
FOR EXCLUSIVE OFFERS AND UPDATES
BY EMAILING:
AronBeauregardHorror@gmail.com

FOR SIGNED BOOKS, MERCHANDISE,
AND EXCLUSIVE ITEMS VISIT:

www.ABHorror.com

DEDICATION

For those once youthful spirits that have now grown old
and cracked, but still remember the carefree days when we
took to the playground on a hot summer's day with our
minds unshackled. When our innocent friends played
beside us with beaming smiles as bright as the sun, and the
many problems of life weren't for us to deal with yet.
For the days that felt like they would last forever…

I love you, Kenney.

ACKNOWLEDGMENTS

An extra special thanks to Kristopher Triana for reviewing this massive manuscript and offering his thoughts and robust writing experience to make *Playground* the most polished and high-quality final product possible.

An extra special thanks to Brian Keene for all he's done for the Extreme Horror & Splatterpunk Horror genres to keep the path open and relevant for future generations.

Additionally, Mr. Keene's classic, coming-of-age horror tale *Ghoul* was a point of reference for *Playground.* I've never written so many child characters in a novel previously, and the realism and detail of Mr. Keene's characters in *Ghoul* helped me remember what it was like to be a kid again.

WARNING

THIS BOOK CONTAINS SCENES OF GRAPHIC
VIOLENCE INVOLVING CHILDREN.

PLAYGROUND

A leather leash extended from Caroline Clarke's hand to her little boy. Her narrowed eyes rested on her son Donnie, who sat a short distance in front of her, sluggishly swaying on a swing. His smooth, pale face was flat, absent of any discernable emotion.

Caroline cupped her free hand, protecting her cigarette from the raindrops. The warmth rising to her fingers was welcome on the uncharacteristically chilly evening. She snuck a quick but deep drag and did her best to keep the tobacco dry.

Rock Stanley watched them from the entrance of the park. The thick wrinkles stretching over his gigantic head added a puzzled glare to his grizzled appearance. The droplets fell at a rate that would've sent any sensible parent heading for their car. Yet, there, with her tiny boy, Caroline remained.

In a way, Rock felt a measure of relief at the sight. While he was looking for a parent with at least two children, securing another participant would be better than none. He was glad he'd decided to check the playgrounds on such a dreary afternoon. Surprisingly, the improbable gamble had the potential to payoff.

Rock clenched a brochure in his big hand that read: 'HELPING HEARTS.' It displayed various information about the charity that helped underprivileged children gain access to modern playground equipment. It also had an area with cut lines that surrounded a single ticket for family entry embedded on the final page.

Not wanting it to get soaked, he slipped the informational material back into his pocket. He'd always hated approaching people. His towering height and bulky frame always seemed to intimidate them. Additionally, his social ineptitude was a hurdle. Rock had a lack of experience that no amount of practice could make up for. Despite his many faults, the motivation that awaited him back home turned him into a miracle-maker at times. Hopefully, he could come through again as he had before. But there was something else that was still on his mind besides securing a reservation.

He's not a fucking dog, Rock thought.

Rock squinted his eyes. The more he focused on the toddler tether attached to the child's back, the more it bothered him. In his mind, it was the physical manifestation of restriction itself. Just the sight of such a domineering tool filled him with ire. As the rain pattered down on Rock's faded flat cap, he clenched his teeth.

The boy looked just old enough to attend school. He didn't require the weight of such an oppressive invention dragging him down, siphoning the urge to explore and roam freely from his soul. Rock expected such a crass contraption might mutate the child's spirit into something more predictive and robotic.

He knew it all too well.

As Rock watched the boy sit on the swing, he already appeared halfway there. Most children in his position would be rocking back and forth, testing the limits and heights they could push themselves to, exploring acceleration with a youthful vigor to borderline dangerous speeds.

Donnie looked dead.

It was as if his mother was pushing a tiny corpse along for a ride in the downpour.

It sickened Rock. He didn't know if he could watch it anymore. But just as he considered taking a step toward them, Donnie's pace changed.

Caroline took one last mighty pull of her Parliament before she gave Donnie a hard push in the spine. The force sent him upward and left him rocking.

"You've gotta do some of the work too!" Caroline scolded. "I can't do everything for you! Kick your feet forward!"

Doing as he was told, the young Donnie picked up speed. Caroline stepped to the side, ensuring he could rock backward and gain momentum. She continued to push him, and with each completed motion, the leash stretched further and further.

Rock watched with discomfort and anger infecting his chest. The scene was difficult to take in.

Then, suddenly, when Donnie reached the pinnacle of his forward motion, Caroline violently tugged the leash backward.

The power of the purposely ill-timed jerk caused the unsuspecting boy to flip backward. The yank was just strong enough to turn his body half a revolution. After the four-foot drop, Donnie landed headfirst in the muddy sand. The sickening thud of his body hitting the gunky beach grains was highly unsettling. Rock could hear it from where he stood. He cringed.

His eyes flared. It was all too familiar.

"Get up!" Caroline screamed. "You have to hold on! Didn't I tell you to fucking hold on?!"

As the dizzied boy rolled off his back and sat up, Rock saw the mass of wet sand that matted his hair and clung to his face. It was beginning to make sense why she took her child to the playground in the pouring rain.

A flurry of vicious imagery invaded Rock's head. He'd never felt such a strong urge to hurt someone. Inflicting violence wasn't a deed that typically crossed his mind, but he had no control over the psychological jolts.

The terrible things he might do under the right set of circumstances seemed unending. But as attractive as the horrible ideas were, Rock understood they weren't possible. That dreary day wasn't about him.

No day was.

Life, and the dynamic between Rock and the pair of strangers he studied, were far more complex than an idea so simple.

"Clean yourself off, *now!*" Caroline yelled.

She slapped the back of Donnie's head. The force behind the strike was so hard that sand flew from the boy's hair. Rock looked away. He couldn't watch it any longer. Instead, he focused on interrupting it.

Walking toward the swings, he extracted the brochure from his pocket.

ONCE IN A LIFETIME

"So, he just handed it to you?" Tom Grimley asked.

He took his eye off the road to gaze at his wife. Molly was smiling.

"I couldn't believe it!" Molly replied. "Well, Macomber has gone to total crap over the last few years. I had to fish out broken glass from the sand the last time I took the kids. I didn't even want to bring them again, but they love that place. The swings are all busted up too. I think there's a couple of junkies living behind the bleachers back in the woods. Maybe that's why he was there? Throwing a bone to families that have to use that sad excuse for a playground. That's what it seemed like, anyway."

"Yeah, maybe."

"Who cares why? I mean, this place looks amazing! And three-thousand dollars just to have our kids test out an ultramodern playground for a few hours? It'd be a treat for the kids too! It's a no-brainer! I swear, when he explained it, I felt like Charlie finding the golden ticket."

Pushing her black hair aside, Molly looked down at the ticket embedded in the vibrant brochure, unable to contain her excitement. The play spaces highlighted in the various snaps on the pamphlet were nothing short of exhilarating—

tall, twisting slides; sturdy swings; clean sandbox; cushy seesaw; multicolored merry-go-round; balloon house with ball pit; and a massive stretch of monkey bars were just a few of the alluring sights.

The area surrounding the pamphlet's adolescent toys was filled with what looked like the softest sand and was encircled by the greenest grass. It was a space of pure magnificence, a visual that would cause the heart of any child to thrash.

Molly wasn't even going to be the one playing, but she could barely contain herself. Her eagerness was mostly unselfish—she wanted the best for her children. But at the same time, the money felt like gravy. Gravy being laid on so thick it could drown them.

The Grimleys would be happy to drown in it.

While their bank balances were less than desirable, the payout wasn't the only reason Molly wanted to take the trip. Showing her little hell-spawns a good time was always a top priority. Finding ways to have fun despite their fiscal fiasco was a challenge she welcomed.

The Grimleys were never rich but were able to live with relative comfort for the last several years. However, their content mediocrity suddenly vanished several months ago when Tom lost his job at Electric Boat.

The firing was outside of Tom's control. Company cutbacks came because of an executive-level fixed pricing scandal. The EB stock tanked. Even now, the company's survival wasn't guaranteed, especially given the public outrage.

The company quickly cleaned house at a leadership level, but the reverberations of the scandal were felt by the little guys too. Tom still wondered if it was best that he'd been forced to move on. Either way, as a result of his exodus, money was tighter than ever.

"It just…" Tom began.

"What?" Molly asked.

"It just sounds too good to be true."

"I'd say the same if that thousand-dollar retainer wasn't sitting in our bank account right now. But you saw the balance. I damn well know you saw it."

"But isn't that kind of weird too? I mean, who just gives someone a thousand fucking dollars at a playground? C'mon sweetie, you know as well as I do, we have shit luck."

"Yeah, but just because you win the lottery doesn't mean you'll win every time you play."

"It's still hard to believe."

"Well, hopefully, it sinks in when we're another two grand towards the black and the kids are having the time of their lives."

Tom furrowed his brow in deep thought. It wasn't the first time he'd discussed it with Molly.

"Yeah," he said. "I guess you're right."

"Thank God! I was starting to think you didn't want to go anymore."

"Don't worry. Everything you said makes sense. I know I tend to overthink stuff a little sometimes."

"A little?"

Molly rolled her eyes jokingly and returned to the pamphlet.

Tom found his smile again. He understood he was a pain at times, but he thought it brought balance between them. Molly was far more daring and spontaneous, as opposed to his tightly measured approach.

"Oh, look," Molly said. "There's more! I didn't even see this part before."

She touched her slender finger to the text at the back page and keyed in on the writing positioned under the header 'OUR GOAL.'

"Geraldine Borden aims to implement one state-of-the-art playground in 1995 somewhere in the New England area. After a review of potential candidates, a less fortunate region will be selected, and the grand play space will be presented as a surprise to the chosen representee's city and the lucky children who reside within it."

Molly shrieked with delight.

"That's why they didn't want us to talk about it! This— This is some kind of *super* exclusive thing! Oh my God, imagine if we got selected? If they built it next year, right in Pawtucket?! We'd be set!"

"Relax. You *always* do this," Tom replied, a melancholic tinge weighing down his vernacular.

"Do what?"

"No matter what the odds are, you always think the best things are gonna happen to you."

"Well, *you* happened to me, didn't you?"

Tom remained silent.

"Didn't you?" she persisted.

She tickled his side and gave him a loveable smile. Molly felt Tom twitch and squinted her eyes. She leaned into his stubbly cheek and planted a proper peck on his face.

Tom let out a chuckle. "You always were a charmer."

"And you're as sweet as strawberry shortcake."

The sign for Exit 13 appeared and Tom flicked his turn signal on cue. His hand fell onto Molly's tan thigh and he squeezed it twice.

"We're almost at your sister's," Molly tittered excitedly, placing her hands over Tom's. "The kids are gonna be so surprised when we get there."

Molly stared gleefully out the passenger window, looking at the beautiful sunny sky. Tom glanced at the brochure in her hand, back to racking his brain.

"Geraldine Borden?" he asked. "Where have I heard that name before?"

"Well, she's obviously a state philanthropist of some sort. I'm not surprised if you've heard of her."

"I thought you said it was a guy that talked to you in the park, though. Didn't you?"

"Yeah, he was a big fella. Thought he might be trouble at first, but once he started talking, I realized he was just a gentle giant. He said he was a representative for the charity. He was really timid, especially for a man of his size. But I'm glad he finally mustered up the courage to give me this. It might very well change our lives."

Tom rolled his eyes and huffed as if to say, 'There you go again.'

Molly acknowledged his comical mannerism with a grin of her own.

"What?" Molly asked. "At least for a day anyway."

THE FALSE IDOL

Greg Matthews pulled the Dodge Caravan into the black tar driveway, slowing it to a halt beside a massive maple tree. He looked over to the passenger seat at his son, Kip. Greg reached behind him and lifted a red clay-colored baseball glove forward. He smacked it into Kip's belly.

The mitt looked pristine and shined, like a piece of equipment you might see in the Little League World Series.

"She's already oiled up for you," Greg said, "but it's up to you to break her in. You can start today."

There was a look on Kip's face like if he could've used his mouth to make a motorboat noise, he would've. Instead, he thanked his dad with little enthusiasm.

Greg was reading his body language loud and clear.

"What the hell is it with you?" Greg asked his son. "Not only am I getting you top-of-the-line equipment, but I spend all my free-time training you, and that's all you have to say?"

"What? I said thank you."

"You said it like I took a shit in your cereal."

Kip tried to suppress a giggle. He'd never heard his dad use that one before. Greg smacked his hand against the dashboard. The loud *slam* caught Kip off guard. His arms immediately rattled.

"I'm not fuckin' around, Kip! I'd have figured by now you'd realize this is serious business! Do you wanna go pro, or dilly-dally around here fightin' for peanuts the rest of your life?"

"I wanna go pro."

Kip spoke the words like he was reciting a religious verse that had been beaten into his brain. He was conditioned to conform, to win.

"Well, why don't you fuckin' act like it then?" Greg asked, lifting the brown bottle of Budweiser up from the cup holder.

He took a huge swig, polished the contents off, and threw the empty bottle to the backseat with the others. The hollow container clanged as glass struck glass—he'd blown through several over the course of their drive.

"You know," Greg said, "when I was your age, I'd have given my left nut to have a father that gave a shit about what I was doing. When I finished high school, I had offers available from some of the top farm teams in the country, and scholarship offers for college football *and* basketball. I was a goddamn prodigy! A fuckin' three-sport athlete!"

Kip hated how his father screamed when he had too much to drink. It was uncomfortable and frightening all at the same time.

Greg went on. "You think that cocksucker ever said boo to me? You think he ever gave me any pointers along the way? If you did, you'd be wrong. And if it wasn't for my knee going out at Boston College, it wouldn't have mattered. He wouldn't have had a choice. My face would've been all over the TV."

The passionate speech was one Kip's father had gotten a lot of practice at. He recited it like a normal person might the lyrics of their favorite song. It was an obsession. Kip had never met his grandpa—he'd died before he was born—but the way his dad talked, Kip imagined him to be a real son-of-a-bitch.

"So, you should be grateful I'm on the sidelines for you,' Greg said. "I could be out with my buddies, having a beer. I could be doing so many things that I actually enjoy. But instead, I'm grinding it out with you. Teaching you the traits that are gonna make you a millionaire one day. But you won't leave your dad out in the dark once you make it, will ya, kid?"

Greg slapped Kip on the shoulder, trying to liven the boy up a little.

"Course not, Dad."

"That-a-boy. The proof is in the pudding. Just look at your brother, CJ. You listen to me, and you'll be just like him in no time."

Kip didn't respond but looked into his dad's glazed-over eyes and smiled with a nod. The grin was so theatrical it could've reeled in an Oscar.

"Alright, kid, let's get to it then."

Greg hopped out of the van and slid the back door open, reaching inside, and retrieving the black and green, metal Easton baseball bat. It had its share of scuffs, compliments of the two muddied baseballs he lifted with it.

What sounded like a knife grinding against a stone wheel suddenly invaded Greg's ear. The beer flowing through his system made him slow to react, but just as Kip exited the car, he looked to the street curb.

Greg's oldest son, Bobby, entered his line of vision. A massive, Chinese-style dragon was imprinted atop his yellow skateboard. He was sliding sideways in a 50/50 grind position. The momentum he'd gathered prior to his ollie was enough that it impressively brought him down the remainder of the street curb.

Bobby hopped his heavy frame off his board as he reached the driveway and kicked down hard against the back of the skateboard. The wood jumped up to him and he grabbed hold of the front axle like it was second nature.

Greg didn't seem to find Bobby's feat impressive. The snotty, unimpressed look on his face crinkled into a glare that was more angry than anything.

Bobby had seen the look before. It seemed these days it was the only look he saw from his old man anymore. Bobby wasn't usually so soft and welcoming with others, but for his father, he'd do whatever he could to stay on his good side.

"Good morning, Dad," Bobby said.

He forced himself to smile but nervousness warped his grin.

Greg narrowed his eyes at him. "Is it?"

"It's, uh, pretty nice out, I guess."

"Good day for baseball. I don't know about *that* shit though," Greg said, bobbing his head toward the board in his son's hand.

"Yeah."

Greg stepped beside Kip, who quietly watched on.

"You see, Kip," Greg said, "if you get fixated on something like this X-Games horseshit your brother's always babbling about, you'll end up broke."

"They're making it into a sport next year, Dad. Like, a legit competition—"

"I don't give a damn what you say. Ain't no bicycle, skateboard, or—or roller skates, no matter where you use 'em, that'll ever pay the bills. That's a fact. Ain't no one that's gonna tell me otherwise. If you got something to say about it, just don't. You know how Nike says *just do it*? Well, for you it's *just don't*, 'cause I don't wanna hear it. Understood?"

Bobby's face turned a deeper shade of red, traveling outside of the normal range that, as a bigger kid, manifested when he was skateboarding.

"Are you fat *and* fuckin' stupid?" Greg asked his eldest son. "I said, *understood*?"

Bobby nodded his flaming face. In his eyes laid the personal pain of being a disappointment.

"Well," his father said, "you'll have to excuse us. Your brother and I have real stuff to work on now."

14

Greg approached the gate leading to the backyard. Kip remained in place, looking at his big brother, and mouthed the words 'don't listen to him.' As the gate came open, Greg pressed his fingers to his bottom lip. His loud, obnoxious whistle ripped the air.

"Let's go!" Greg ordered.

In the eye contact exchanged between Kip and Bobby, there wasn't an ounce of bad blood. They were each at the mercy of the same grouchy guardian. Kip didn't know why his dad was the way he was, and neither did Bobby. They had both just been dealt a shit hand.

But they weren't the only ones.

***

Tanya set the paper down on the countertop and pushed it towards her mother, her eyes like those of a puppy dog that had just gotten into the trash. She hadn't done anything wrong, but she was anxious. Tanya had been dreading the conversation they were on the cusp of having for days.

The document in front of her didn't just hold ink on the page, it held her heart too.

"Sixty dollars? Are you crazy?" Lacey asked, a snarl of repugnance plastered across her face. "Do you think we're rich or something?"

"It was the only one I could find," Tanya begged. "I checked the phonebook and all of the papers. I—I even wrote them and told them about our situation. The price is normally one hundred, but they said for us—"

"A hundred dollars?!"

Lacey's pretty, blonde head quickly tensed up as if it might launch like a rocket right off her shoulders at any moment.

The agony engraved on Tanya's face was out of a horror movie. Her mother's heated reaction was the equivalent of pulling her tiny heart out and stabbing it on the table a thousand times over.

Tanya's thin bottom lip crumpled inward like a three-leaf clover. Four leaves wouldn't have been suitable for a child of such an unfortunate ilk.

"But I love swimming, Mom. I know I can make you and even Dad proud. I just need a chance. Please."

Lacey chewed on the idea. "I know when the pool at the YMCA closed, it broke your heart, but maybe it'll open back up again, eventually. The membership at the Y was affordable. But this kind of advanced class it's—it's just too much. Do you have any idea how much Hamburger Helper that would buy?"

Tanya begged her with her eyes this time, the sadness and frustration creating a dark window.

"Please, Mom," she whispered.

"I'm sorry, but I just don't think it's worth it."

A big tear fell over Tanya's eyelashes and down her face.

"C'mon," Lacey said. "Don't cry, honey. I didn't get to do everything I wanted at your age either. You know that, right?"

Tanya looked down at the table.

Lacey pushed the paper back to her daughter. "Listen, in a few years, you'll forget about all this anyway. You'll be busy thinking about boys and finding yourself a looker like I did with your daddy. Maybe once a couple more years pass, we can afford a cheerleading outfit for you. If not, you can always use my old ones."

"I hate cheerleading!" Tanya cried.

"But you've never tried it."

"I know what it is. I wanna swim!"

Tanya folded her arms.

"Now don't get snippy with me," her mother said.

"I'm sorry. I just—I just really, really, really, *really,* want to do this. When have I ever asked you or Dad for anything?"

Tanya wanted to ask why Kip and CJ got to do what they wanted while she couldn't but knew that wouldn't be fair. The driving force behind the extreme baseball fandom in this house wasn't her brothers. That was all Dad.

"Cheer is *a lot* more common for girls than swim," Lacey said.

"Mom."

Tanya's growl wasn't going to be enough to convince her mother. She wiped the tear from her cheek and did what she did best: analyzed the situation.

As a straight-A student, she was sharp enough to realize her approach was off-kilter. Grown beyond her years, Tanya forced herself to turn off the emotional aspects of all she strove to attain. She took a deep breath and reassessed the scenario, then readied her refined tactics.

It was obvious—she was asking the wrong person.

"Okay," Tanya said. "I respect your opinion, but will you please ask Dad too? I just want him to know how much it means to me, even if we can't afford it."

Tanya knew her dad's personality all too well. She knew he'd see swim as a competitive sport and cheerleading as nothing more than a sideline attraction. While there were cheerleading competitions, it still most definitely was *not* a sport. As far as Tanya was concerned, it was just a way for pretty girls to showboat.

Since winning was practically embedded in her father's DNA, Tanya figured her last shot at getting to swim lived and died with his opinion.

Lacey looked at her daughter and couldn't help but smile. While she didn't enjoy how Tanya continued to push back, she was impressed with how eloquently she phrased her question. Tanya displayed a methodical grace and kind-hearted intelligence that had failed to find either of her parents. It was like all the decent genetics had skipped a generation on both sides.

"Okay, honey," Lacey said. "I'll bring it up to your father. Just don't get your hopes up though."

"Thank you. Oh, and I was going to surprise you, but I may as well give it to you now."

Tanya reached under the table and pulled a small box

from her pocket and set the square, zebra-pattern box on the table in front of Lacey. The hot-pink lettering on the box read: *Fantasia Accessories*.

"What's this?" Lacey asked.

"It was supposed to be a thank-you gift for letting me join the swim team."

Lacey pulled the box toward her and grabbed the top.

"But even if I don't get to join the team, I still want you to have it," Tanya explained.

Tanya figured things might not work out in her favor. She got the gift in advance to butter her mom up as best she could.

When the top came off the box, Lacey's eyes widened. "Oh my God, I love it!"

While Lacey was genuinely enthralled, some confusion arrived seconds after her initial declaration.

"What is it exactly?"

The round bracelet with the zebra pattern overlapped inside itself a few times over. Lacey plucked the gift out of the box and raised it in front of her face.

"It's a slap bracelet!" Tanya said. "C'mon, Mom, they're everywhere." She snatched the bracelet out of her mother's hand and straightened it out the bracelet. "You flatten them out like this before you use them."

"Wait a second, slap bracelet? Aren't those the things that got recalled for cutting people?"

Tanya drove the bracelet down over her mother's wrist and watched it wrap around it. The zebra and hot-pink design fit her like a glove.

"You're fine, aren't you?" Tanya asked.

Lacey's eyes widened again. "Are you crazy?!"

"Mom, it's fine. That story is just an urban legend. Don't you think if they *actually* hurt someone they wouldn't be for sale anymore?"

It wasn't the first time Lacey felt out of her league exchanging dialogue with her daughter. What she said made sense. Plus, the sound and feel of the snapping bracelet circling her wrist like a gentle snake were so satisfying she couldn't help but remove the bracelet and straighten it out again.

But as she did so, Lacey also got a look at her watch. "Shoot! We need to get going! Otherwise, we're gonna be late!"

Slap!

Lacey swiftly banged the bracelet against her wrist again and let it curl around her. "I need you to go upstairs and get your brothers. Tell them to come down right away."

"Okay, but you promise, right?"

"Promise what now?"

"You promise you'll ask Dad about swim class?"

Lacey grinned and looked back at her fancy, new accessory. "I think that's the least I can do for you."

***

CJ's excited glare fell upon the colorful, inky pages of his comic book with absolute adoration. The Savage Dragon's chest and face were sliced up pretty good after his fight with the rat man, but CJ saw it as a thing of beauty.

Most of the Marvel and DC comics with their pretty art and childish superheroes didn't do it for him. CJ preferred Image Comics. They never skimped on the blood and broke all the boundaries. Although he was just short of being twelve years old, he'd already acquired a taste for adult content. Thankfully, his parents saw comics as a childish distraction. If they actually took the time to crack one open and saw the bloody chainsaws, boobs, and guts, they might be compelled to change their opinions.

The hefty stack of comics that sat on his bedside included many issues of *The Savage Dragon*, *Spawn*, *The Maxx*, a variety of old EC Comics reprints, and Kevin Eastman's *Teenage Mutant Ninja Turtles*.

The comics were his window to elsewhere. They let him escape from the pressures that confronted him daily and without fail. He saw a future within them, a place and time of peace. His favorite activity was listening to his Walkman and losing himself in the illustrations and dark stories. The only problem was, CJ wasn't the one who decided how he utilized his time.

The play button popped up, momentarily interrupting The Savage Dragon's carnage. He extracted the cassette—Cypress Hill's *Black Sunday*—and flipped it to the other side. But before he could hit the play button and re-immerse himself into the bloodshed and stoner lyrics, his father's voice bled in from the open window.

"If you're gonna reach your potential, then you've gotta practice more than just a couple hours! That's two errors already! Now hustle back out there and don't give me any lip!"

CJ quietly slipped his headphones off and positioned himself at the window. He crept forward and peered around the corner. In the backyard, his little brother, Kip, was huffing and puffing.

"But how come CJ and Bobby don't gotta be out here?" Kip whined to their father. "It's not fair."

"Yeah, well, I got news for you, kid: *life* ain't fair." Greg windmilled the bat, stretching his wrist. "Bobby ain't out here 'cause he's a dud. A shit athlete. No matter what he says, that stupid fuckin' skateboard is pointless. That's a *hobby*. That ain't no sport. And CJ gets three hours to himself on weekends. Maybe you will too someday—if you can learn how to field a simple ground ball, for Christ's sake. If you wanna get what he gets, then you'll play as good as he does. It's that simple."

Kip slapped his new baseball mitt against his leg in frustration and backed toward the fence. His father tapped the ball toward him at a decent pace, and Kip scooped up the one-hopper.

"Or, *I* can just be a dud too, like Bobby, right?" Kip asked.

He tossed the ball back in his father's direction.

CJ smiled momentarily, but his grin quickly faded. His kid brother was smart, but CJ understood the miserable truth behind the question. He knew that whether or not Kip was as good at playing baseball as *he* was, Dad was still going to ride him hard either way. Kip wasn't going to be hanging out with friends, reading comics, or thinking about girls. He would be confined to their modest backyard, fetching balls like a dog. And it wouldn't be because he wanted to, but because he had to, so Dad could feel a little closer to achieving the on-field success he'd never found for himself.

"Nice try, but *I'm* the one who has the eye for talent," Greg told Kip.

He knocked Kip's gentle pitch back with far more power than the last and drilled the ball at his son to make a statement. Constantly asserting his dominance kept the boys under his thumb.

"You're only a dud if I say so," Greg continued.

The line drive went right at Kip's face. He was just able to get his glove up and avoid getting beaned, but when the ball smacked into the palm of his mitt, a sharp, stinging sensation ran up his arm.

"Ouch!" Kip cried.

A sour cringe found Greg. "C'mon, don't be a sissy. Did I tell you to take a break yet? Send it back!"

The visuals unfolding before CJ's eyes were all too familiar.

"The pros don't feel pain," Greg said. "Now shake it off and send it back."

Three short knocks pulled CJ's attention away from the sad display.

"CJ?" Tanya asked from behind the door.

"Yeah?"

"Can I come in for a second?"

CJ walked over to the door and pulled it open.

His sister stood in front of him, smiling excitedly. They usually didn't get much time together because of his full-time focus on baseball, a truth that saddened CJ.

"What's up?" he asked.

"You almost ready? Mom says that we've gotta get going now if we're gonna make it to that playground on time."

"Oh crap! I completely forgot about that!" CJ grinned.

He'd been so lost in the tranquility of his music and comics that it had slipped his mind. Relief fell over him. He wouldn't have to drag himself out back for another one of Dad's famous late afternoon practices. Instead, he might actually have some fun. He imagined the activities at the playground would be *far* more exciting than the endless, repetitious drills he'd otherwise be forced into.

"Dang," his sister said, "I don't know how you could forget after seeing those pictures, but today's the day. And *remember*, you promised we'd seesaw!"

"Oh, we'll seesaw alright. I'll send you right to the moon and back," CJ said.

A laugh escaped him. He recalled the last few times they went. He'd vaulted her so high into the air that her butt flew several inches off the seat before smacking back down.

"No! None of the launch me in the air five feet stuff! You're gonna give me a heart attack!"

Tanya punched him in the arm softly, still maintaining her cheesy grin.

CJ knew Tanya liked acting as if she hated it when he messed with her, but that wasn't the case. He wouldn't have done it to her if it truly bothered her. It was just one of those things she screamed and acted upset about but secretly loved.

"Okay, I won't," he said, winking.

"Seriously though, I'm looking forward to hanging out today. I'm so glad we get to do this!"

"Me too."

"But I really hope they have a seesaw. I've never heard of an ultramodern playground, have you? What's that even mean?"

"I don't know, but they've gotta have one. What's a playground without—"

22

Suddenly their mother yelled from the bottom of the stairs. "Tanya! I told you to get CJ and come downstairs! We need to go, *now!* We're not supposed to be late! And tell Bobby to move his ass too!"

Tanya crinkled her face in annoyance and silently mimicked her mother's mini-rant.

A grin came over CJ's face. For the first time in a while, he just knew it was going to be a good day. With all the fun they had lined up in front of them, how could it not be?

GENTLE GIANT

Rock Stanley stared at Geraldine Borden like she was a black hole, a gaping portal of darkness ready to devour him without a moment's notice. His eyes felt just as heavy as the weight that he carried on his stout shoulders. The terror encapsulated in his pupils wasn't anything new. The fear and uncertainty had been stapled to them long ago.

The old hag's glare burrowed into him with the speed and ease of a laser beam. The discomfort that was transmitted left him fidgety. Rock reached up, removing his weathered flat cap, unsure how to respond.

"It's a simple question," Geraldine said. "How many were we supposed to have?"

Rock held the cap firmly in one hand and used his remaining sausage fingers to scratch the disheveled follicles on the top of his skull. The words still weren't coming.

"Answer me, you idiot! How many?!" Geraldine's aged vocal cords screeched.

"Nine?" Rock finally managed to blurt out.

Rock's uncertain tone didn't ooze intelligence, nor did his timorous nature fit such an intimidating presence. At six-foot-three and just under two-hundred-eighty pounds, he didn't have to take shit from anyone. Yet, he did.

"Well, I'll be damned!" Geraldine said. "It speaks! Then help me understand, why did you approach a single parent with only one child yesterday?! Furthermore, you waited until now—hours before they arrive—to tell me!"

"Y—You said that I shouldn't bother you unless—"

"Not another word! You'll never be worth a damn!" Geraldine placed her hand over her mouth, adjusting her dentures. Anger left them on the verge of sliding out. "This is why you'll never be a Borden! Why you'll never be worthy of my fortune! All I ever wanted was another deserving generation to continue once I'm gone! Is that *really* too much to ask?!"

Rock's depression and angst only boiled harder with each cutting remark. He'd never been good enough. Not good enough for his blood parents, and certainly not good enough for his adopted mother. Geraldine was never shy about letting him know he hadn't earned acceptance. He was an outcast, an idiot, a habitual failure—an uncommon man in the sense that, even while in the presence of others, Rock Stanley was still alone.

"If my ovaries weren't barren, I would've had someone capable!" Geraldine said. "But instead, I had to wait almost two years just to get custody of a useless, sorry excuse like you! They didn't even give me a female! Even when you were just a child, I knew you'd be shit! I didn't get *this* successful," she swirled her finger around at the collection of valuables in the stunning room, "by *not* having an eye for failure. I saw you, boy. I saw you coming unglued a mile away. I should've known better than to expect anything less. I should've known better than to believe I could somehow change you."

She turned her back on Rock and looked up at the oil painting of herself that hung above the fireplace. It was a recent rendition that captured all her wrinkles and the oversized, hazelnut mole on her left cheek sprouting several inky hairs she'd neglected to trim. The vivid illustration outlined the compounded hatred and disgust she'd harbored for decades, a lifetime of disappointment trapped in her eyes. While Geraldine's hair may have been a blend of yin and yang, her soul was the former—black as night. And within that sinister space laid the fuel to propel anything her corrupt mind could conjure.

Outside of the parlor, which was nearly the size of a high school gymnasium, the echo of footsteps approached, pausing at the doorway.

Just beyond the threshold, in his elegant brown slacks, white collared shirt, and brunet vest, stood Adolpho Fuchs. The curled brow above his left eye indicated a bit of concern.

"What's all zhe fuss?" Fuchs asked, his German roots shining through as he spoke.

Geraldine squawked. "There's only going to be eight now, thanks to this goddamn putz!"

Rock's squared face and boxy jaw sank lower as he hung his head and clasped the edges of his flat cap with each of his bulky hands. His attire was a far cry from the aristocratic garments worn by Geraldine and Fuchs. The worn-out long-sleeve had small holes developing over his elbows, and his leather belt was hanging on by a thread.

The lack of respectable clothing wasn't the result of financial limitations. Rock simply hadn't *earned* the right to high fashion. The way Geraldine talked, he probably never would. Unless of course, Rock was being unleashed to seek out candidates for the playground. In that case, Geraldine had a special outfit she allowed him to don. No family was going to trust riffraff.

"And? Is eight not enough?" Fuchs inquired.

"Nine is the number of children my mother had," Geraldine said. "And her mother…and I just…" She paused. There was a quiver in her bottom lip that she struggled to subdue. "I just wanted to know what it was like to be her for a day. Just a day."

The German couldn't help but chuckle.

Geraldine glowered. "What's so funny, Mr. Fuchs?"

"Nothing, my lady," Fuchs replied, the amusement dissolving off his face.

"When my mother fell ill, out of all my siblings, it was *me* that stayed by her side! When all the others left, I stayed. I deserved this."

Even Fuchs, who had been around Geraldine for many decades now, wasn't so much shocked by her outlandish standards, but more by the rare display of emotion she'd offered them a window to.

"I'm sorry, I wasn't aware," Fuchs replied.

The emotion saturating her cadence quickly evaporated when she thought about what came next.

"We've had several *individual* children come and play here in the past," she said. "The low number amounted to the safest approach. But, as you both know, today is special. Today we take a risk! Today is about the family!"

The madness in Geraldine's eyes flared. It wasn't so much about family as it was about *the* family, the one she'd always wanted but was incapable of creating. It was about molding an extension of her own genetics into what she saw fit, about having an intimate connection with the mind she aspired to groom.

Geraldine still had Rock, but as he'd grown, his company was nothing like she'd envisioned. She would never look down on the rest of the world *with* Rock. She could only look down *on* Rock, along with the rest of the world.

If Geraldine had gotten *the family* she desired, there was a chance none of the day's events would even be necessary, that her corrupt mind would've been occupied elsewhere, and the vindictive philosophy it housed might've never come to be.

But that wasn't the case.

"These lowly peasants wallow in filth and poverty, yet, ironically, they've created something even my wealth can't buy, the thing I wanted most, something even a brilliant mind such as yours couldn't give me, Mr. Fuchs." Geraldine turned to Rock. "These heathen parents have potential in their seeds. Generational potential! Their pathetic, utterly pointless legacies can be furthered by simply existing, by being graced with bodies that function properly. It's not the result of action! They didn't *earn* anything! They didn't *do* anything! It's dumb luck! But that luck runs out today. That unwarranted opportunity shall come to an end."

"Zhat it will," Fuchs said.

The German brandished a warped smile that conveyed he was every bit as sick and in line with the ideas Geraldine put forth.

Geraldine put her eyes on Fuchs once again. She mirrored his grin until another thought wormed into her brain and stunted it.

"That's if this numbskull can be effective for one day," she said. "It's probably too much to ask, though."

Geraldine fixed her glare back on Rock. He hung his head and his hands began to shake. As his cap bobbed up and down, Rock tried to imagine he wasn't there. As beautiful as The Borden Estate was, to him it was a prison built of gold. None of the castle's luxuries could make it worth his stay.

Rock lived inside an echo chamber. The rage-laced rants Geraldine regurgitated with cunning consistency ensured there would always be resounding reminders of his inferiority. The points were always punctual, so he could never forget.

He was a failure.

He was a lesser human.

He would never be good enough.

It was not just how Geraldine saw Rock, but also how Rock saw himself.

"Zhe boy will never be perfect," Fuchs said, "but he has secured you eight. We must be grateful for those efforts, otherwise, we risk ruining zhe festivities. You mustn't let one bad apple spoil zhe bunch, my lady. You should still have some joy, for today will be far different zhan any other zhat we've ever witnessed."

Geraldine glared at the old man and let the words Fuchs offered simmer in her brain. A smile crept over her haggard face. "Maybe you're right. It's not perfect, but I suppose we'll just have to make the best of it." She turned herself back in Rock's direction. "Go to my room. It's time we dress you properly before our guests arrive."

FUN AS FAR AS THE EYE CAN SEE

"Settle down," Tom demanded using his best disciplinarian voice. "I know you're excited, but unless the two of you relax, we'll turn this car right around. I'm serious, no more screaming. Is that clear?"

"Yeesh, chill out, Dad," Sadie replied.

"Yeah, we're just playing," Samantha said.

Sadie leaned into her and let out a girlish giggle.

Isaac pushed his bulky glasses up his nose and sat staring out the window. He peered over the edge of the cliff, watching the stunning waves hypnotically flow. Even the road leading to their wondrous destination was fancy. Something incredible was approaching, and he wasn't about to let his sisters fuck that up for him.

He usually preferred to keep to himself, but in this instant, he needed to speak up. At ten-years-old, Isaac still had much to learn and was fully aware of that. But for his age, he was far ahead of the majority of his peers. He wasn't egotistical about it; quite the contrary. However, as he often did, Isaac used sound reasoning to plead his case to his father.

"How is it fair to punish *all* of us because Sam and Sadie wanna be brats?"

"Hey!" Sadie yipped.

While Tom kept his focus on the road, Molly took the initiative. She craned her neck around to Isaac and let out a sigh.

"I suppose if that happened, we'd just have to do something *extra* special for you in the future," Molly said bouncing her eyebrows.

"We'll be good," Sam begged.

"Yeah," Sadie chimed in.

"After seeing the pictures that you showed us of this place," Isaac said, "there's no way you could one-up it. I'd still be losing out."

"It sounds like your sisters are going to behave, right?" Tom interjected, glaring at Sadie and Sam in the rearview.

They noticed the stare of chastisement and nodded at him accordingly.

"You shouldn't have anything to worry about, buddy," Tom assured him. "Besides, I think it's just up ahead."

Tall, ebony gates pointed toward the slow-drifting cluster of clouds floating above. The towering steel spears seemed higher than necessary. The preview of the immaculate patch visible through the gates of the property was breathtaking. The medieval architecture ripped from a children's fable.

The placement of the estate at the end of the sequestered cliff-walk created another inordinate coating of privacy. Along with the location, the sheer altitude of the massive stone walls layered in front of the steel fencing could've kept a colossus at bay.

The girls screeched in unison. "We're here! We're here!"

Isaac crinkled his face in annoyance. His sisters knew how to squeak out pitches that always got under his skin. They knew it did. That's exactly why they did it.

While Sam was a year older than Sadie, most people believed them to be twins. It wasn't the case, but it spoke to their kinship and bond. Their personalities were in stark contrast to their older brother—Sadie in particular.

She might've only been seven years old, but she didn't let that stop her from squaring off with Isaac. She'd been known to assault him, both verbally and physically. She was a firecracker, and once her fuse was lit, Isaac knew he was in for a battle.

Sam was no angel either but never seemed to initiate the torment. Despite being born first, she followed Sadie's lead. If Sadie was mean, Sam was mean.

The mimic of brazen behavior was most likely the reason people believed them to be twins. Also, they both had a similar dainty stature and were blessed with the same shimmering blonde hair. The easiest way to tell them apart was their hairstyles. Sam's hair was normally held back in a ponytail while Sadie had pigtails.

Most people who encountered the sisters for the first time perceived them as innocent. But looks could be deceiving, and often were.

"How the hell does this work?" Tom asked.

"Good question," Molly replied, scanning the brochure.

"These gates are so huge," Isaac mumbled.

"Your ears are huge," Sadie sniped.

She reached around Sam and flicked the wide, awkward cartilage that leaped off the side of her brother's face. Her harassment was stealthy enough to avoid garnering parental attention.

A slight rush of blush manifested on Isaac's cheeks—his sister knew how to hurt him.

It wasn't enough that he was scrawny and unathletic, or that he was shy as a chipmunk. He already got fucked with in school for having strange ears, but Sadie wanted to turn the screw even further. She wasn't the type to avoid people's sensitivities—she preferred to exploit them, to publicly tar and feather them. It wasn't just Isaac. She'd done it to her peers, strangers, and friends. At just seven years old, Sadie's name rang closer to her personality. She was a psychological sadist.

As the family wagon crept to a stop, Tom rolled down

the window of his driver's side door. He gawked at the small speaker with a single white button staring back at him.

"I guess I'll just push the button," Tom shrugged.

Molly nodded at him in approval.

The crackle of the speaker suddenly erupted with an elderly man's German accent. "Hello, name, please?"

"Ah, it's Tom—Tom Grimley."

"Wonderful. Zhe gates ahead are opening now. Follow zhe path all the way up to zhe main entrance and we shall be with you very shortly."

"Alright, sounds good!"

A loud metallic unlocking sound rang out, followed by the electronic hum of the gate gliding backward. The Grimley family sat wide-eyed as Tom pushed down on the accelerator.

IMPROMPTU ENCOURAGEMENT

Rock stared into the mirror, the collective pain pooling in his glazed eyes. Geraldine lurked creepily behind him and slipped the raggedy coat off his torso. Her hands lingered longer than necessary on his muscular frame, familiar with his physique. She caressed Rock as she disrobed him.

"Oooof, my word," Geraldine said. "When's the last time you bathed? You're most certainly going to need to take a shower. I can't have you smelling so foul in front of our guests. Even if you're not above them, you need to act like it. Get this undershirt off."

Rock hesitated. An unavoidable, rotten reminder was looming. One he wasn't ready to confront again. It was the reason his funk had become so swollen that it leaked into his battered garments.

Geraldine scrunched her face.

"Take it off, I said!"

The cutting command caused Rock to jump.

Geraldine's hands remained resting on the back of his arms. She quivered as the warmth spread through her. Feeling the physical manifestation of his fear contact her phalanges excited Geraldine. It enticed her.

Rock pulled the white undershirt over his muscular

frame and dropped it onto the floor.

Geraldine peered around the wall of man in front of her, gazing into the standing mirror, feeding on the agony bouncing back from Rock's pupils.

The melancholic muscleman eyed the reflective glass, still unable to believe it was real. He was the past, present, and future in a single glimpse.

Suddenly, his senses were overwhelmed, and visceral flashes of the encounter crept back into his head. The scent of cooked flesh found his nasal cavity again. The sound of searing skin crackled its way into his eardrums. He felt the itchy ropes binding his wrists, and the rigidness of the wooden chair he was tied to. The soreness in his throat flared from the desperate screams relentlessly ravaging it.

Rock's eyes dropped as they took in the reddish-violet skin that bubbled back toward him. The eternally inflamed tissue puffed upward, discolored by the unforgiving heat of the branding iron Geraldine had held all those years ago.

At that time, Rock was just a throwaway, an unwanted and undeveloped teenager. She'd been harsh and wicked to him, but he'd never expected things to escalate in the manner they had. He never imagined such an irreversible event would transpire.

Through that old, adolescent lens, Geraldine looked a bit different in his mind. Her skin was smoother, and her hair had more color, but her tongue was still as sharp as ever. The verbal lashings hadn't changed with time. They remained her most punishing tool, one that haunted Rock as steadily as Geraldine's hand the moment she pressed the scalding iron into his chest.

Over.

And over.

And over.

Rock recalled how Geraldine had screamed while his flesh had flared from the blistering heat.

"Why did you look at her?!" she'd said. "I saw you!"

Just a short distance away from where he'd sat, Wanda,

the then live-in maid, lay motionless on the floor. A growing outline of garnet gruesomeness had infected the carpet. The soaked flooring her cracked head lay upon would be the site of Wanda's final thoughts.

The battered brain tissue littered around her malformed head was a ghastly image that had burned itself into Rock. It was the picture of all potential fear. The violent amalgamation of inner cranial tissues, skeletal fragments, and Geraldine's rage. An incident that left an impression of such depth on him that it would last a lifetime.

Rock remembered the nonchalant nature of the only other living adult in the room, the straight face Fuchs wore as he watched the madness unfold, sitting casually on the sofa by the fireplace. The gory murder was far from the most difficult thing Fuchs had seen. It looked like just another evening for him as he puffed away on his pipe, watching the branding irons in the fire grow a lighter shade of ginger.

"You'd better take a damn good look at her now!" Geraldine bellowed. "Because it's the last time you'll ever fucking see her! It's the last time you'll ever see anyone!"

Geraldine's grim words weren't exactly accurate. Rock would see her again, for he would be tasked with turning Wanda's body into fertilizer.

Her carcass was hefty.

The generous portions of garbled-up tissue allowed the insects to eat well that evening. After the deed was done, Rock peered over the land, trying to lose himself in the soothing sound of the ocean waves. In his heart, he hoped the garden's insects would never eat so well again.

It wouldn't be the last time Rock heard the hungry hum of the industrial-grade wood chipper. More meat would be tenderized, and more bones would be mangled. The device continued to gain relevance as his twisted relationship with Geraldine unraveled.

Wanda's departure left a void in the housework, but no replacement was hired. Geraldine's jealousy kept new personalities from entering the fold. Instead, she forced Rock to absorb all of Wanda's duties, in addition to the ones he already managed.

Geraldine's delusional belief that there was a sexual interest between Rock and the help would never be corrected. His punishment remained permanently in effect, and those living within the walls of The Borden Estate continued their push to total societal isolation.

Rock trembled with disgust, breaking out of his dream-like state as Geraldine's pruned paws glided upward over the unalterable letters scorched into his skin.

"You're mine, remember?" she whispered seductively.

The discolored letters weren't perfectly aligned, but they were close enough to understand the four-letter word that had been singed into Rock's soul.

As Rock stared into the mirror and read the ghastly font that comprised the word 'MINE,' a single tear fell down his bristly cheek.

"And you'll be mine forever," Geraldine said.

She laid down on the bed behind them and delicately tugged Rock's hand.

The conservative dress Geraldine wore became the opposite when she arched her rickety back, and pulled the onyx-toned sartorial up over her hips.

As Geraldine stared at his solemn expression and the permanent label she'd administered beneath it, she only grew more eager to feel his tongue inside her. She pulled her moist panties down, allowing her fermented beaver to peek out from below. The scent was just as ungodly as the sight. Rock stared at the stretchy skin abound with wrinkles. The slick and sudsy sap leaking out from her floppy hole glistened in the daylight. When Geraldine got juicy, she manufactured a rancid odor all her own, one that made Rock sick to his stomach each time he encountered it.

The fetid aroma floundered about, triggering a flashback to the many awful pastimes Rock had been forced into. The sourish scent stunk of outdated dairy, spoiled seafood, and asparagus-tainted urine. The monstrous melody that was Geraldine's cave brought Rock to his knees.

As Rock looked at the moldy meat, he heard Geraldine's ravings in his head. *The chemicals in those soaps and shampoos shorten the average lifespan. That's why you'll need to stay clean and why I need to maintain my natural oils.* Rock had watched Geraldine grow conspiratorial in her old age. It was like she sensed death looming, but her bottomless wealth could only extend her life so far.

"What are you waiting for?" Geraldine asked.

She pulled her leg backward, exposing her cunt and asshole. The playful passion in her voice was starting to dry up. Impatience—*anger*—could return at any moment.

As the sickening crack of her hip popping resounded through Rock's skull, he knew it was best to begin. A woman of Geraldine's age shouldn't have been so flexible, but she'd put Rock up to the task with such regularity that the yoga-like stretch had become an amateur task.

He'd heard her bone clear as a church bell. It rang most times just before he was presented with his most appalling chore. With an inner disturbance beating around his bowels, he wished it was over, but wishes weren't for people like him. They were for those who celebrated birthdays, and those who aspired to accomplish great things in their lifetimes. They were for normal people that hadn't disappointed everyone they'd come into contact with.

Rock unhinged his jaw and tried to accumulate saliva. Anxiety had dried his mouth to dust. He stared at the faded meat littered with spiky, gray hair. There were patches of scratchy, old skin infected with flaking, dead cells. Not to mention a mortifying, rash-like irritation that encompassed her entire cunt. There were also other areas afflicted with random discoloration—flesh dominated by something that looked fungal in origin.

Geraldine harbored countless battle scars from the experimentation Fuchs had put her through. The molecules of other men had left her altered. She'd made many sacrifices en route to achieving an impossible dream.

"Do it!" she barked.

As Geraldine waited for Rock to dive in, she glared deeply into her reflection in the standing mirror.

Rock finally consented, sticking his boxy face between her feminine snakebite. As his tongue registered her tart taint, he did his best not to vomit. He couldn't prevent it totally, but the minuscule, acidic wave that crept up his esophagus proved useful.

He swashed it around his palate, allowing his dry mouth a measure of relief before he went full-bore eating her clit. It was a trick he'd learned some time ago, using his own revulsion to his benefit. As Rock nibbled on the rosy micro-penis, he allowed the clear vomit to dribble over her pussy and down her ass crack.

"Oh, yes!" Geraldine roared.

Her cries signified how alive she felt.

She arched her head back and used her free hand to latch onto the hairs growing from her mole. She twisted the elongated follicles with each lap Rock took, then refocused her gaze on her worn reflection. She became lost in herself as she wailed out and tugged the sharp mole-hairs, taking joy in the subtle, stinging pain.

Rock accelerated, using the technique he'd gained from their prior encounters. He tried his damndest to make her cum as quickly as possible. He didn't want to be eating her ass and cunt any longer than the bare minimum.

He kicked into an even higher gear, accelerating his perverse actions, doing his best to remember what made her moist. Rock's jaw began to ache alongside his heart. He used his fattest finger to gather spit and puke, then gently massage the skin between each of her holes.

"Fuck," she cried. "Don't stop! Don't you fucking—"

Geraldine's sentence was cut off by her own lust-laced excitement. Her eyes widened to capacity as ecstasy overwhelmed her, and her ghastly head whipped side to side with such jubilation that it caused her bottom dentures to eject from her mouth.

A hearty wad of drool leaked from her gummy mouth in the heat of the passion. Geraldine didn't let the slip spoil her moment. She cradled Rock's face with her thighs and pulled it deeper into her pussy. Then she dug her pointy nails into the back of his head and came like a hurricane.

HOUSE OF THE BLIND

Geraldine lay alone on her silky gold sheets, the ecstasy slithering through her wrinkled system a fleeting one. Upon being penetrated with the smarting sting of boredom again, she crawled her way back out of bed.

She hadn't bothered to put her teeth back in or wipe her slimy vaginal leakage dry. She was too focused on the door at the far end of her bedroom. Her cunt dribbled onto the hardwoods as she closed in on the knob.

She'd found her enthusiasm again.

As Geraldine twisted her wet, liver-spotted hand and pulled the door open, a different world presented itself. One that often preoccupied her wicked mind. A place that no one else but her could possibly understand.

The reflective surfaces stretched from the floors to the walls to the ceiling. Not an inch was left uncovered. Light fixtures dangled from the reflective ceiling in the narrow, rat maze of mirrors.

Parts of it felt like a funhouse, the architecture of the room having so many numerous paths that crossed over each other. But the images the room projected didn't stretch Geraldine's physique in childish or exaggerated manners. She'd designed the area so she could gaze upon the most granular, ornate details of the body she was obsessed with. The only vessel that could propel her heart to race and bring back the legendary memories.

Geraldine was the oyster of her own eye.

Having a perpetually unsatisfied sex drive took work, but however unorthodox the measures, she aimed to quench her thirst. Geraldine knew she'd never be able to have herself the way she craved, but she'd done everything to make the experience as close to her unusual fantasies as possible.

The shiny hallways looked like the exterior of a diseased cactus. The countless, multicolored pricks of pleasure extended outward, calling to her.

Some were long.

Some were wide.

Some were soft.

Some were hard.

The dildos were suctioned to the glass mirrors within the hallways. She could slow her haggard frame in front of whichever one struck her fancy and adjust it to the appropriate height and angle.

She turned her back to the wall and looked at her slender, worn reflection.

"Just the girl I was looking for," she said with a smirk.

The orange rubber cock littered with stout veins of nightcrawler-sized dimensions immediately made her lips pucker. A crusted, hormonal residue still hung in gunky flakes on the pumpkin-toned shaft from one of her previous sessions. She was ready to reintroduce the dried remains into her soggy cavern.

The dildo drew closer to her slobbering slit and Geraldine's stretchy parts quivered with hunger. Her pruned gash was ready. Just being inside the room of her ultimate obsession made her heart pump, and the feeling of the rod reconnecting with her hole left her knees weak.

In the room, she was blind to the typical surroundings that saddened her. The dark reality that she was doomed to remain alone. Within the hall of mirrors, she was able to lose herself in her anatomy, and also immerse herself enough to reminisce about the origin of those feelings.

The sound of her moist meat conforming and stretching to accommodate the object filled her eardrums. Geraldine firmed her body and pressed her lined palms against the glass in front of her. She rode the rubber like an eager porn star as saliva seeped from her mouth.

She looked at her own leathery leer, relishing in her reflection. But it still wasn't enough.

Geraldine closed her eyes.

She traveled back to a time when there was still hope, when the outlook wasn't so dreary. When she was focused on finding satisfaction, and not robbing others of it.

The intense images played like a secret movie in her skull.

Seven-year-old Geraldine sat in the closet. The slivers of blinds in front of her nose offered an obscure but satisfactory view. She spied her mother's smooth, bare ass on the bed. It was the first time she'd gotten to see it, but far from the first time she'd thought about it. She had no idea where the feelings had come from, but, as far back as she could remember, Mildred Borden's backside was a daily thought.

It had become an obsession.

Seeing her mother's ass sitting atop another man's face stirred a strange, warm, yet welcome feeling inside Geraldine, but along with the elation came anger. Geraldine wasn't upset her mother wasn't riding her father's face. She was upset she wasn't riding hers.

Geraldine rarely got an opportunity to play-wrestle with her mom, but whenever she did, she always let her mother get on top. Each time she tried to worm her way closer to her hips, closer to having that thick, voluptuous backside suffocating her.

Geraldine's mother always realized the awkwardness when it arose. Like any logical parent, Mildred pulled away from the inappropriate positions. She wasn't quite sure if her daughter was aware of the inappropriateness of such horseplay, but as time went on, the sparkle of suspicion in Mildred's eye only widened.

Now, as Geraldine thought about her mother, she feverishly gnashed her purple, slimy gums. Her racing heart told her she'd found the closest thing to love she could manufacture.

Memories.

From that closet in her mind, more important moments in Geraldine's deranged timeline triggered.

As a teenager, she'd happened upon the panties in the trash. They were there for the taking, bonded to the pad by a patch of congealed blood. Mildred's flow had gotten a little too heavy. Geraldine had stared down at them, biting her bottom lip. The red cloth had been so close to her mother's beautiful ass, as close as she wanted to be. Geraldine couldn't just let them go to waste, so she'd plucked the ghastly underwear from the can and lifted them to her face. Burying her nose inside them, the irony, Filet-O-Fish scent made Geraldine quiver with exhilaration. She was so enthralled after her sniff that she forgot to clean the blood away from her face. After that groundbreaking day, Mildred always believed Geraldine got random bloody noses because of the spontaneous excuse she had to give.

While the penetration deep inside Geraldine's pussy continued, she continued to reminisce. She took a slobber of drool and slapped it between her legs. With the saliva on her clit, she rubbed it, attempting to escalate her erotic trip down memory lane.

"I miss you, Momma," she hissed, her tone bordering on demonic.

The obscene imagery in her head transitioned from the trash to the toilet.

In her mind, she stood inside the spacious bathroom connected directly to her mother's bedroom. In a mansion as grand as Geraldine's childhood home, the luxury alone would've been enough to distract most. But bottomless money and elegant accommodations had done little to entertain her. Snooping through her mother's belongings, however…

On that particularly twisted morning, Mildred had left in a hurry. There'd been some kind of emergency. While Geraldine couldn't remember exactly what the commotion was, it was of little relevance. The floating mass that lay in the mustardy water in front of Geraldine was all she needed to remember.

Her mother had left in such a flash she'd forgotten to flush. The log of excrement wasn't particularly large; it appeared that her mother had been interrupted and unable to finish her business.

Geraldine's eyes had been glued to the modest movement drifting in the tainted liquid.

It beckoned her.

Even though it was shit, it had slid out from between the two heavenly hams that made up Mom's posterior.

It couldn't be overlooked.

At the time, it might've been the closest Geraldine would ever get to tasting her infatuation, so she'd plucked the putrid purge from the bowl and laid her body down on the floor. As Geraldine slipped off her pants and underwear, she stared at the lurid lump with an irresistible inner lust.

Geraldine had only nibbled on it in the beginning, cherishing each experimental gnaw along with the pungent stench that clung to it. But her enthusiasm rapidly escalated. Geraldine's hot lady parts shuddered as her perverse inner spirit took a crushing hold over her. Her teeth soon parted, and she inserted the soggy mass into her mouth, all but for half an inch on the tail end.

Imagining her mother perched over her face, Geraldine chewed into the slimy secretion. She visualized that it might taste the same as her mother if only Geraldine had been able to pounce on her unwashed backside that morning.

Geraldine hadn't swallowed it—she'd savored it.

She had taken the remaining wad of waste between her fingers and positioned it upon her pleading clit, smearing the shit in a circular fashion. She'd never cum so hard as the day she'd happened upon that bowel movement—not until the last time, she saw her mother.

The gush of liquid that had left Geraldine that morning on the Spanish-tiled floor of her mother's bathroom, pulled her closer to a current climax. She held her eyes shut, reliving the rancid memory down to the finest details, knowing the best was yet to come.

The twisted slideshow moved forward in Geraldine's mind. A mid-forties version of Geraldine stood over her sick mother's bedside. For such a grim situation, the wide grin frozen on Geraldine's face certainly seemed out of place.

The oxygen mask fixed upon Mildred's mouth spelled doom. She was scrawny and hardly able to move. Speaking was no longer an option. In her bedridden state, it looked like death was looming over her, and in a way, he was. But the vehicle he'd assumed to collect the aristocrat was one Mildred would've never predicted.

When Geraldine's pants and panties had come off, so had Mildred's oxygen mask. She'd struggled to breathe without the assistance of the device, but her fight had become far more extreme when Geraldine plopped down on top of her face with her sagging snatch.

Emulating her mother's actions from years past, Geraldine muscled her malicious meat over Mildred's mouth and nostrils. An oily trail of clear and off-white fluids blanketed Mildred's horrified face. As Geraldine's legs quaked with a pleasure she'd never imagined, the sniffles and gasps her mother emitted vibrated against her lips and hood.

Mildred's perverse struggle continued to tickle Geraldine until a newfound elation championed her to the pinnacle before finally dying out altogether.

The flashback of her mother sucking at her clit for dear

life always brought Geraldine to The Promised Land. As she smashed her ass vigorously against the mirror, her arousal peaked. The scream of pleasure that roared from her throat was accompanied by an expulsion of creamy leakage.

The force of her thrusts rattled the mirror, but she wasn't worried about it breaking. When the hall of mirrors was constructed, she'd used extra thick panes. It would take a *tremendous* amount of force for these to buckle.

She grinned with glee as she ramped up her revolutions, thrashing wildly against the wall like a woman who'd been caged for years. The vision didn't fixate upon any particular detail. Geraldine consumed the scene as a whole. As she slithered closer to climax, she opened her eyes and gawked at the woman in the glass.

She wasn't sure if her mother's murder was the reason she'd become attracted to her own physique, but it seemed like the only logical deduction.

The two of them looked so much alike. During her twenties, Geraldine and Mildred had often been mistaken for sisters. But just as Geraldine slid her cunt off the stiff plastic, another recollection wormed its way into her brain. One she'd rather not ponder, but always seemed to be confronted by.

Geraldine had no one left to chase.

She looked into the mirror, wiping the drool from her mouth, a wrinkle of disgust overtaking her expression.

The shift in her psychosexual philosophy was a difficult one. Geraldine's self-lust was enjoyable at first, but it wasn't the same as the other mountains she'd climbed. The summary of sensations wasn't even a blip on the erotic radar compared to the incestual instances with her mother. It was like going from caviar to catfish.

Her fatal flaw was obvious: she hadn't thought ahead.

Even when the solution came to her, it was too late. She remembered the thought quite vividly, but it was a concept she'd rather have forgotten.

As far back as Geraldine could remember, she'd always

hated people. But a short time after Mildred's funeral, when she'd been depressed as ever, she'd decided she couldn't be alone. She hadn't been seeking to communicate with anyone, but just to quell her lonesomeness.

The playground was a random choice—a place her mother had taken her before their wealth had ballooned, a place Geraldine remembered dallying around in with a nostalgic fondness.

That day when Geraldine took her place on the park bench, she saw a mother and daughter playing together. She couldn't help but realize just how similar they looked. It was nearly the same level of replication Geraldine had seen between her and Mildred. Then suddenly, it struck her.

A child! She'd thought.

Her playground epiphany had the potential to replace the darkness she yearned for. In theory, it made sense, but an unnoticed truth confronted her.

Geraldine had over-ripened.

During the decades of blindness, where her incestuous craze had all but consumed her, Geraldine's reproductive pieces had grown stagnant. She'd slowly dried away into irreversible infertility. It was as if God knew the infernal escapades that might ensue and had given his stamp of approval.

Geraldine stared at herself in the mirror and reflected on the past. In thinking about what brought her to this moment, her expression held a measure of anger. But beyond the hatred, she was making room for another emotion. Her pupils flared, a twinkle of joy eclipsing the rotten recollections.

"You're somethin' else," she whispered.

Since finding out children weren't in her future, Geraldine had returned to the playground countless times. Ideas on how to best placate her demons had progressed, as had how she perceived the more fortunate families playing in the space.

Geraldine's gummy grin now stared back at her in the

mirror. What had begun as a simple idea was finally ready to be revealed. The structures the peasants deserved would finally be given to them, structures only an era of vindictiveness could've conjured.

The charity she'd built; the millions of dollars that she'd spent; the countless test runs she'd orchestrated; the precious years that had passed her by. It all had been building towards this moment, the impending climax of a wretched lifetime.

The privileged peasants would soon understand what peril truly was. She would bring balance back into the world around her and show them all she'd been robbed of.

Exiting the hall of mirrors, Geraldine looked at the grandfather clock near the fireplace.

"I'd better hurry."

IMPATIENTLY WAITING

The drive had gone by quicker than anticipated. Greg stood beside Lacey, his arms folded at the front doors of the castle. His initial amazement at the majestic architecture had worn off. Greg wasn't the patient type.

Thankfully, their collection of kids was occupied. He'd instructed them to play a game of tag while waiting for the owners. He always wanted his kids active and contending. He knew their futures, and he most certainly depended on the competitive spirit.

"The fuck is taking so long?" Greg asked.

"I wish I knew," Lacey replied.

His wife shook her head, her pink hoop earrings swaying. Her puffy blonde hair glistened in the sunshine as she reached for the zebra slap bracelet on her wrist.

"I'm getting pretty damn tired of waiting," he grumbled. "They said eleven, no?"

"They did," Lacey agreed.

She unrolled her gift into its alternate stiff and flat form.

Greg grimaced. "Well, he's got about five more minutes before—"

SLAP!

The sound of the bracelet connecting with Lacey's

51

dainty wrist caught Greg off guard.

"Jesus!" he said. "Do you have to do that? I heard one of those things malfunctioned and poked someone right in the damn vein. Bled out right on the spot, the way I heard it."

Lacey continued anyway. She wanted to do it again but saw Greg was getting annoyed, so she decided to refrain.

"Relax, baby bear," she said. "That story is just an urban legend. Everybody has these things. And who cares if we hang around here a little while? They're paying us to be here, remember?"

"I don't give a shit if they're planning on putting the kids through college. Nobody leaves the Matthews waiting."

Despite the tough talk, Greg wouldn't be budging anytime soon. Doing so went against his philosophy. The boys were supposed to generate income—perhaps Tanya too. They weren't *just* family; they were an investment, one that should be lucrative so long as he instilled them with the proper ethic and nudged them along. The kids reeling in three grand just to test out a stupid playground was too easy, but Greg was confident this was only the beginning.

He watched his oldest son, thirteen-year-old Bobby, get chased down by Greg's pride and joy, CJ. He was certain CJ was going to be special from the moment he got his legs under him. The boy's uncanny speed, muscularity, and intangible prowess were easy for the former athlete to see dollar signs behind.

Son-of-a-bitch is faster than a Ferrari. Little shit might even be faster than me, Greg thought.

Greg watched Bobby as he tried to close in on his tag target. He was mere inches away when CJ juked him. CJ's natural gifts frustrated his oldest, causing Bobby to give up and focus on the youngest of the litter, Kip.

It ain't even fair to the rest of them, Greg chuckled to himself gleefully. *That's money in the bank.*

Greg saw himself in his son. CJ held the same set of attributes he had before tearing both ACLs in his third college football game. While his body had failed him, he knew that CJ wouldn't be hindered by the same gremlin.

As he watched CJ's long slicing strides, Greg knew he'd have made one hell of a wide receiver. The kid had hands like Cris Carter and cut as sharp as Barry Sanders. But all that was too risky. He didn't want his golden ticket to suffer the same injury that sullied Greg's scholarship.

Although the ligament tears that ended Greg's career had the potential to happen in any sport, he wanted CJ to do something with minimal contact. The gridiron was too violent. It wasn't so much that Greg cared for his well-being; he just wanted to see his show horse run in as many races as possible.

When Greg pushed him into baseball, he took to it like a duck to water. With CJ at shortstop, sensational catches and double-plays were always the norm. And when he stepped up to the plate, there was always the chance that he might blast one out of the park. The natural, sporty talent that he harbored left him leaps and bounds ahead of his age group. And just as Greg had told himself, CJ was the king of whatever diamond he graced.

Bobby, on the other hand, was a painfully crushing disappointment. Greg had high expectations for his firstborn. He definitely didn't expect a stinker. But it wasn't like he could just return him or go back in time and have an abortion. Greg still pushed Bobby the same as all the others, but he knew there was no light at the end of his tunnel. He liked that Bobby could still beat the shit out of most kids, but he was still too fat for a pair of gloves and headgear. Toughness alone was useless to Greg in the fiscal scheme of things.

At least he ain't a faggot, Greg thought. It was all his warped, bigoted brain could find to be proud of.

Bobby's stride stretched far further than his seven-year-old brother could. In less than a minute, Bobby, red-cheeks and all, was able to close in on him. He slapped his back with a thunderous tag and Kip fell onto the grass.

"You're it, dumbass," Bobby hollered.

He ran away unleashing a hyena-like laugh.

"Hey! Language!" Lacey yelled.

It was a request she'd made to Bobby more times than she could count.

Greg watched Kip like a scout before draft day. His brother had given him a decent shot in the lungs, and he'd taken a tough tumble. Despite being disappointed with his boy getting caught, the blow and fall didn't faze Kip. The jury was still out on his overall potential—he was too young for Greg to figure—but at least he could take some pride in his son's toughness.

Welp, he ain't no pussy, that's for damn sure.

Kip lifted himself off the ground and looked to his sister Tanya, pegging her as the easiest catch.

Upon seeing Kip key in on her, Tanya readied herself. The nine-year-old coyly positioned her body beside an extravagant cement birdbath at the center of the lawn.

Fuckin' birds got a better shower here than I do at home, Greg thought.

When Kip charged in, Tanya tactfully sidestepped the boy and made her way around the fixture.

"Why is she playing with them again?" Lacey asked.

"I dunno, 'cause they're kids?" Greg reasoned.

"I just… I don't want her thinking she's going to be something she's not."

"Seriously? She's just messing around."

As shallow as Greg could be, even he was a bit shocked that his wife was irked by Tanya mixing it up. His buzz was also wearing off, making him just more argumentative than he normally was.

"We've been letting her mess around with them too much," Lacey whined "Now she's talking about swimming lessons."

Lacey and her daughter locked eyes momentarily. Tanya's shoulder's tightened and her eyes drifted as she grew distracted by her mother's scowl of disapproval. The dirty looks were nothing new. She'd seen them many times before and even grown somewhat accustomed to absorbing her glares of displeasure.

Routine didn't make them hurt any less though.

Tanya's mother had a vision for her, but the *last* thing Tanya wanted to do was stand on the sidelines of a sport she didn't care about. She wasn't looking for an eventual suitor; she wanted to compete. The idea of cheerleading felt low and idiotic. It disheartened her that it was the only thing her mother believed her to be capable of.

What Lacey surmised was best mattered little to Tanya. She might've been young, but she was already old enough to understand that no one, not even the woman she came out of, was going to control her.

Tanya didn't need her mother's belief; she had her own.

She envisioned herself swimming with the best of them, or maybe competing in gymnastics which she'd taken an interest in recently. Tanya hoped that her mom might be asking her father about the lessons they'd discussed at the table that morning.

Tanya wasn't sure what more evidence they needed from her. At the YMCA she was the fastest in the water, but her parents were never there. How could they even know? They used the club more as a babysitter for Tanya than a means to support her passion. It allowed her father to focus more on training her brothers, and left her mother to do whatever it was she did in her free time. It worked like a charm when the investment pricing was low. But now Lacey's babysitter had become more expensive than it was worth.

She'd show them.

She'd show them *right now*.

Tanya only relinquished a meager amount of her attention toward her mother's cancerous attitude. She yearned to watch her failures bloom, but today, she would have to wait.

As Kip closed in on her, Tanya let him get close enough to think he had her dead to rights. But as Kip blasted full-speed ahead, Tanya pivoted her body and went tumbling sideways. Planting her palm on the ground, her cartwheel successfully evaded the tag. As she landed on her feet in perfect form, Kip found himself sliding belly-first past the birdbath, over the impeccable front lawn.

"Whoa, did you see that?" Greg asked. "Maybe there's something to it. It's only normal for her to have a hobby. All the boys do. Hell, she might even be a little better than you think. Maybe she deserves those lessons after all."

"You're going overboard now," Lacey replied.

"Am I?"

Lacey gritted her teeth.

The move Tanya had shown off was impressive, a trick she might've even been able to use in cheer if Lacey could somehow break her daughter's will. But it didn't help convince Greg that the costly lessons might not be worth it. If anything, it was an argument in favor of the investment.

Greg and Lacey were alike in how they viewed the children that matched their gender. All Lacey wanted was a daughter that would follow in her footsteps. But she never expected Tanya to have her own ideas or have a stronger mind than the rest of her siblings. She couldn't be molded to simply worship those within her familial circumference just because they shared the same bloodline.

"She got lucky," Lacey grumbled. "The sooner she realizes that, the easier it'll be. She's not like the boys. She's thinking Olympics, but she *should be* thinking pom-poms."

Greg chewed on the thought for a moment before a jock grin graced his face.

"I remember you in those tight-ass outfits. Fuck, you were something else, baby doll."

A beam of joy crept up on Lacey's face, matching her love.

"Is that right?"

"That's right."

The intimate memory was abruptly disturbed by the sound of tires slowly churning through the gravel.

Greg and Lacey turned their attention to the vehicle heading in their direction.

"Hey! Timeout!" Greg yelled. "Watch out for the car! I can't afford to have any of you getting hurt!"

MEET AND GREET

Tom slowed the car as soon as the family in front of the castle came into view. The many members of the clan took notice of the wagon as he steered toward the van parked on the gravel.

"I guess we can park here?" Tom reasoned.

The wagon rolled to a stop beside the Matthews' big Dodge Caravan.

"I didn't know there were gonna be other people here," Molly admitted.

"Well, the more the merrier, I suppose. In a way, it actually kind of makes me feel a little more comfortable," Tom replied.

"Why would it make you feel *more* comfortable?" Isaac asked, always intuitive.

"Ah—I guess it's just nice not to do stuff by yourself sometimes is all I meant."

Isaac knew his dad was lying. Whenever Tom spoke, he didn't mince words, but Isaac had come to understand if his father stuttered, the pause itself was the tell. It was a lie but he wasn't sure why his father would fib about something so seemingly pointless.

"Alright then! Is everybody ready for some fun?!" Molly

asked.

She turned back toward her three children.

Isaac remained in a state of wonder while his sisters yelped with delight, and just as the doors of the station wagon opened, so did the two at the entrance of the manor.

As the Grimleys filed out enthusiastically, the Matthews family turned their attention to the royal, sable slabs of metal that opened at the front of The Borden Estate.

The families joined together, taking in the odd sight of their welcomers. The trio looked like a version of the Addams Family from a parallel dimension, the freshly scrambled brigade each a unique shade of strange.

Rock stood to the right of Geraldine. The big man looked every bit as dapper as he had when he'd approached the families at their respective playgrounds. His gray suit was pressed and fit flawlessly over his bulging frame. He'd even been given a matching flat cap. Rock's five o'clock shadow remained but didn't detract from his overall presentation.

Adolpho Fuchs flanked Geraldine's other side, also dressed to the nines. It was a common occasion for him, this was more the standard. The espresso ensemble he'd fitted into required no adjustments. He puffed upon a matching wooden pipe, smoke seeping out of his mouth like an old dragon.

At the center of the odd trio stood the lady of the manor. Geraldine's face was glowing for more reasons than the ones that transpired in the bedroom. Her cheeks were painted with blush, with mascara applied to her fading lashes. Her teeth had been pasted back onto her gums and sat surrounded by licorice lipstick. The makeup smoothed some wrinkles but could only do so much to cloud her age. The long, dark dress was elegant without being overzealous.

"Good afternoon, everyone," Geraldine said.

She discreetly rubbed her wrinkly hands together.

Most of the children replied politely in unison before Greg's voice overshadowed the group.

"Finally. We were wondering if you were gonna show."

"Yes, apologies for being a bit tardy. But I can assure you all, this experience shall be more than worth the wait."

Geraldine's habitually despicable persona somehow seemed absent. She was in the rarest of forms, wearing her most brilliant mask, a game face for the ages.

She stared back at Greg Matthews and grinned.

"Sorry, looks like we must be a little late too, then," Tom said.

The leader of the Grimleys guided his family up to the front of the estate, beside the Matthews.

"Not to worry, dear. Now, I take it, based on the information your wife provided, that you must be the Grimleys?"

"That's correct—"

"Let's cut to the chase, how does all this work?" Greg interjected, overstepping Tom.

"Well, that must make *you* Mr. Matthews then?" Geraldine asked.

Greg nodded his head, offering her that much.

"Excellent," she replied. Geraldine's eyes darted about, calculating the number of people that littered her exquisite lawn. She turned to Fuchs. "It seems we may be one short still."

"It appears we are," the German confirmed.

Isaac squinted at Fuchs. He hadn't expected the old man to be foreign. Isaac was curious about Fuchs, but not curious enough to interrupt the meeting.

"That's okay, I'm sure she'll be here shortly," Geraldine replied.

While the absence was a disappointment, Geraldine did her best to conceal her disdain.

"Forget about them, we're here now. The least you can do is answer my question," Greg demanded.

Geraldine whispered to Rock. "Leave the gate open for her. But when she arrives, see to it that it's shut, locked, and activated."

She rotated back to Greg.

"Absolutely, forgive me. I'm just a tad frazzled. First, please allow me to formally introduce myself. My name is Geraldine Borden. I'm the owner of this estate, and this is my associate, Adolpho Fuchs, and my butler, Rock Stanley."

Rock wanted to display his contempt openly but decided he wouldn't give her the satisfaction. After all the years he'd spent appeasing her, the dark deeds he'd done at her behest, the absolute loyalty, and still, she didn't acknowledge him as family, and even worse, only offered him the lowliest title imaginable.

"As you likely learned from the pamphlets, I'm head of a charitable organization called Helping Hearts. We deal in many things, such as donations for the deprived, shelters for the homeless, and food bank collections. But what we're here for today is a project that, up until we approached you, has been kept secret from the public. All funding is in place, but we're here today to ensure we understand what the optimal childhood experience would be prior to selecting a location to invest in. Your children shall have a hand in both of these outcomes."

Tom leaned into Molly. "That's where I heard the name. Some lady got snagged dumpster-diving in one of her donation bins."

"What?" Molly asked.

"Is there a question, Mr. Grimley?" Geraldine asked, picking up on his sidebar.

"Ah—no, I just was mentioning that I've heard of your charity before."

"Oh, excellent! Then it seems we're doing our job."

The phony grin found Geraldine's face.

"So, where the hell's the playground?" Bobby asked with impatience threading each word.

Greg turned around, shooting laser beams through the most disappointing sperm he'd ever unleashed.

"Boy, keep quiet. Don't interrupt when adults are talking," Greg reminded before turning back to Geraldine.

"Now, where the hell's the playground?"

The man's juvenile rudeness was unamusing to Geraldine, but she lofted a courteous chuckle.

"Before we can get started," Geraldine said, "we have a small matter of business to attend to. Please present Rock with the tickets embedded in the brochures you were given. As specified, you must possess the entire document wholly and intact to participate."

Rock marched down the stone steps until he was close to the families. Greg looked up at his incredible stature. Despite Greg being a former athlete, Rock still dwarfed him.

"Here you go, big fella," Greg said, thrusting the pamphlet into Rock's sternum. The tough guy antics were always alive and well when Greg was in the picture. Rock didn't play into it. He just took hold of the paper and half-nodded.

Molly made her way to the giant and thanked him with a smile, then offered the brochure. He offered her two nods in response.

"Everything looking proper?" Geraldine asked Rock.

Rock nodded.

"Wonderful."

"Right, can we get to it now?" Greg persisted.

Molly narrowed her eyes, already disliking the man.

"Of course, Mr. Matthews—"

"Greg," Lacey interrupted Geraldine.

"I'm sorry?"

"He likes to be called Greg."

Geraldine didn't normally display such grace. Had there been nothing to look forward to that day, she would've engaged Greg and Lacey with a far more volatile attitude. Instead, she diverted her emotions and reeled in the prize.

"Right. I promise, I'm getting to it in a moment. But before we can divulge any further details, I need each of you to confirm, as promised when given your retainer fee, that you haven't spoken a word of this to anyone. Without the anonymity of this event firmly in place, your participation is useless to us. If your presence here today has been discussed with anyone outside of those present, then the integrity of this event has been compromised and we cannot proceed. I need a verbal confirmation that none of you have discussed this with anyone."

"No, we haven't," Molly offered.

"I didn't," Tom cosigned.

"Nope," Greg added.

"Of course not," Lacey said, rolling her eyes.

Geraldine studied them all scrupulously, her mind pivoting like a seesaw, unsure whom she believed. All she truly believed was she wanted this to proceed, regardless of the risk and potential repercussions that could surface as a result. The idea of the spoils was too tantalizing to turn her back on.

It was *her* day.

"Good," Geraldine said. "That gag order will also apply after you leave until we instruct you otherwise."

"Gag-order? For what?" Tom asked.

He didn't particularly like secrets. It seemed harmless enough, but, like Greg, he just wanted to understand the scope of what they were participating in.

"For anything that happens inside. For any designs or structures you should have the advanced opportunity of viewing once we all walk into the property," she explained, gesturing behind her.

"Why's that? What's it gonna matter if we mention it?" Lacey asked.

"With all due respect, it matters to me. Mr. Fuchs and I have been working on these designs for years. It's only fair that they should find daylight when we see fit. In the same way that you have children and control who gets access to them, it's the same with our creations. It may seem silly, but to us, it's important."

The long-winded response was mere showmanship. None of them would ever leave the premises.

"Zon't spoil zhe surprise, please," Fuchs reaffirmed.

"Do we have your word?" Geraldine asked.

A chorus of yeses and nods pushed forth.

"Okay, then. I want to assure you that all of the playground equipment has been tested countless times over by multiple CPSIs. It's essentially—"

"CPSIs?" Tom asked.

"Certified Playground Safety Inspectors. Additionally, I've taken the liberty of furnishing the documentation in advance. And should any of you feel inclined to examine it, upon review, I'm sure it will galvanize your confidence in both our agreement and the overall security of the structures on the premises."

Geraldine held out her spotty hand to the left.

Fuchs extracted a long white envelope from his inside pocket and pulled the documentation from within it. He placed watermarked papers in Geraldine's hand, and she descended the steps, brandishing the documents toward each parent.

"Rest assured, everything is completely safe as evidenced by the dozen signatures I hold in my hand. The best in the fields of adolescent precaution and child security have all agreed. So, when you're brought into the spy room to watch your children have the time of their lives, you can appreciate their joy anxiety free."

"Wait, we're being separated?" Molly asked.

"No need to worry, they won't be far. You'll be able to see them at all times and even communicate via a PA speaker, should you feel it necessary. However, we do ask to keep that to a minimum, if possible. We're aiming to harness the true playground experience, and we can't get that if the children aren't left to their own devices, as they normally would be. It's critical we observe them with freedom and free range to understand their relationship with the revolutionary equipment we've created. And, furthermore, we understand this may create a slight discomfort, and with that in mind, we've decided to up your payments to an additional four thousand dollars each."

"Shit, as long as I can see 'em, that's fine by me," Greg said.

"Holy freakin' crap, we're getting paid for this?!" Bobby exclaimed.

"No, *we're* getting paid for this. Your payment is you havin' a nice day and that roof over your head back home," Greg corrected.

Tom and Molly looked at each other.

"Everything she said makes sense to me," Molly offered.

A look of uncertainty overtook Tom's face, just as it had on the ride to pick up the kids. Something didn't feel right to him, but four thousand dollars for a few hours of play was a life-changing sum of money.

"Can I see the papers?" Tom asked.

"Of course," Geraldine replied.

She promptly handed over the documents.

Tom fished through the sheets. They looked authentic enough. There were signatures and stamps and fine print. What the fuck did he know about the authenticity of playground safety documents though?

"It should only be a few hours of your time. Feel free to ask any questions you see fit," Geraldine said.

Tom looked back at his kids. They were all using their best beggar faces, pleading for him to say yes. Even Isaac showed rare excitement.

Geraldine's veiled description of their 'revolutionary equipment' had Isaac beyond intrigued. The potential prospects within the castle were endless.

Tom looked back to Molly. Her big brown eyes glowed with anticipation.

The immediate increase in cash would surely change their simple lives. Not only would it help amend some of their financial woes, but the experience would surely be otherworldly for the kids, a grand time like nothing they could afford to offer them currently.

Tom turned back to Geraldine and handed her the documents, subtly nodding.

"Alright. We're in."

LET'S PLAY

The group followed Geraldine through the glamorous, regal heart of The Borden Estate. A chorus of oohs and aahs trailed behind her. The shiny marble, aristocratic furnishings, stunning décor, and posh artwork were a sensory overload to a pair of families accustomed to spinning their tires, entrenched in modest lifestyles.

After passing through the dual-staircase at the entrance of the property, they made their way through an enormous parlor, then entered the ballroom. Once they passed over the polished floorboards of the dance hall, Geraldine opened a set of French doors that led to the rear patio, which brought them back outside, into the beautiful summer air.

The well-watered lawn at the rear of the estate was just as micromanaged as the one at the front; each blade of grass aligned perfectly with the others. Articulately trimmed hedges lined the grounds, and exotic flowers were in bloom. Beauty was theirs to behold.

The garden and edge of the cliff could be seen off in the distance, but it seemed so far away that it could've been on a different planet. Additionally, the variety of breathtaking trees within the space left an aura of peacefulness in the air.

However, standing closest to the castle, the focus of the backyard was the playground.

The slab was littered with truckloads of inviting soft sand and measured about the size of a football field, encompassed by black, protective fencing. Amid the calming piles of russet mulch that lined the play space was the true spectacle.

It wasn't *exactly* what the families had imagined.

Isaac had lofty expectations based on the way Geraldine had hyped her creations.

All the equipment appeared brand new. It was freshly painted, colorfully designed, and stretched around the mini-arena. It had everything one might expect when going to a playground, but as Isaac adjusted his glasses and cycled through his mental checklist, he couldn't help but be slightly disappointed as he counted the fixtures.

Belt swing, flat swing, bucket swing, straight slide, curved slide, spiral slide, seesaw, monkey bars, merry-go-round, spring riders, mega trampoline, rope climber, dome climber, sandbox, hopscotch, teeter totter, steel rings.

Granted, there were some variations in the magnitude and scale of each piece on the playground, but the fact that Isaac was able to identify each structure he saw proved they were all classic designs. It was probably the nicest playground he'd ever seen, but his excitement was no longer next-level.

She said she was working on these designs for years. Isaac looked over at the weathered old bat. *Creations my butt. You're freakin' full of it, lady.*

Still, there was one structure much different from any he'd seen before. A mountain of a slide sat in the back of the giant sandbox. The structure rose to a height that looked like it might cause a nosebleed.

Isaac hadn't noticed it initially, for the leaves and branches camouflaged it, the hunter-green chute and tan pillars sharing the color scheme with the surrounding plant life. The huge slide tucked away in the corner of the playground was nearly as tall as the towering trees in the backdrop, yet it had no steps, so Isaac wasn't sure how anyone could use the darned thing.

The extreme elevation wasn't the only aspect of the slide that was a bit odd. Additionally, the transportation tube curled side to side many times over, stretching nearly a third of the way across the playground. But maybe the strangest detail was that there didn't seem to be an end to the ride. With no bottom in sight, the tube went directly into the ground.

Notwithstanding Isaac's gripes, the rest of the children were foaming at the mouth. The spectacular fortress of fun standing before them was legendary. Sadie and Sam had already run to the locked gate, with Kip, CJ, and Tanya all in tow. Bobby hung back and studied Isaac's reaction. The snobby snarl of pretentiousness he saw on Isaac's face disgusted him. He hadn't known the boy long, but knew he was the type of person that pissed him off.

A sense of dread and discomfort found Isaac. He knew from experience that, like many of his elementary antagonists, Bobby smelled blood in the water. Isaac knew he was a snack so pathetic and easy that Bobby was ready to chew him up. But like a wild animal, Bobby enjoyed maiming and toying with his prey a bit before consuming it.

The boys were far enough away from their parents that Bobby felt comfortable taking a shot at Isaac.

"What? Not good enough for you?" Bobby asked.

"No, I just thought it would have—"

The question was rhetorical; Bobby didn't need the answer to drop his jab at Isaac.

"If it's not good enough for you, why don't you just flap those huge, fucked-up ears of yours and fly away, Dumbo."

Bobby slammed his shoulder into Isaac en route to join the rest of the children.

"Hey," Isaac moused.

"What're you gonna do about it?" Bobby asked.

Isaac remained mum.

"That's what I thought."

Bobby cracked his knuckles as a big grin found his face. He turned his back on Isaac and headed to the rest of the kids.

Isaac rubbed his arm but kept his mouth shut. He was a shy kid, one who didn't want to be the focal point of a spectacle. He also would prefer to not look like a tattle-tail in front of all the kids he was going to share the playground with. Massaging the pain in his bicep, Isaac crept closer to the group.

The parents naturally migrated together and stood in a small cluster on the other side.

"C'mon, open up!" Sadie shrieked.

"Yeah, let's play!" Sam added.

"Heck, yeah!" Kip concurred.

"Okay, ha-ha, I understand," Geraldine said. "But we have to get the okay from your parents first. What do you say, does everything look kosher?"

"It looks incredible," Lacey said.

"So, that brochure, it said that you might be choosing a less fortunate city to build something like this in. How are you deciding that exactly?" Molly asked.

"*I* won't be deciding at all."

"You won't?"

Geraldine shook her head.

"Then who will?"

"Why, the children will, of course."

Geraldine signaled to the children.

"How so?" Molly asked.

"The children who offer the best data and feedback will be the ones to decide. We want you to really let loose! Play with more enthusiasm and rambunctiousness than you've ever played with before!"

Geraldine grinned.

The feeling of delight swam laps inside Molly. She glanced at her husband, who still looked to be erring more on the side of concern.

"Like a contest, you mean?" Greg asked.

"In a way, yes."

Greg glanced at CJ and gave him a wink accompanied by a thumbs-up. If there would be a winner crowned, it damned well better be someone in the Matthews clan.

"You know what to do, killer. I don't wanna catch you running out of gas out there. I'll be watching," Greg said.

CJ nodded solemnly at Greg.

He wasn't as enthusiastic as his father, but nonetheless, he was ready to do his best to please him. He was already overly familiar with the uncomfortable pressure his father applied on him with consistency. Every day was a new brass ring to reach for, a new achievement to collect.

"What's that big slide in the back?" Tom asked, pointing out the green monster in the trees.

"Oh, that's just for aesthetic purposes," Geraldine said.

"Why doesn't it work? Is there a problem with it?"

"No, it's still operational, but we don't typically use it, and as of right now, the ascension shaft is locked."

"Good, 'cause that worries me. Might get a nosebleed just climbing the thing," Tom added.

"But with your permission, I'd like to open this gate. After which, we will head to the spy room and watch from afar. But we need everyone's consent to move forward; it's all or nothing."

"Let's do it!" Greg yelled.

He wrapped his arm around Lacey.

"Woo baby!" Lacey hollered.

"I'm not sure if I'm comfortable with the kids being out here alone," Tom said.

"Jesus Christ, talk about overprotective. Buddy, just let the fucking kids be kids," Greg scoffed.

"I'd appreciate it if you mind your own goddamn business. How about you make the decisions for *your* kids and I'll make the decisions for *mine*."

"I think that might be the problem. You're a softie. It's obvious. That's probably why your boy looks about as delicate as a dandelion. And my boys, well, let's just say he wouldn't put much fear in 'em."

"Don't talk about my son that way!" Tom yelled.

He took a step toward Greg.

The uber-competitive dad smirked in Tom's face.

Despite having the shell of a sweetheart, Tom had grown up in the slums. Getting jumped over nothing was an ordinary event. Being hassled on the streets had hardened him. He'd learned to leave all that behind and smooth himself out, but just because he'd grown tender didn't mean those rough edges couldn't rise out of him at the drop of a hat. If someone pushed it too far, occasionally the old-school Tom came out of hibernation.

Isaac couldn't believe his father's reaction. His old man looked ready to throw down. He'd always seen his father as kind and even-keeled, but another adult had never verbally attacked them before either.

Isaac was proud of his dad's badassery until he looked at Bobby, who was staring a fucking hole through him.

"You're fucking dead, dandelion-boy," he whispered.

Isaac turned his attention back to the argument, hoping that if he didn't acknowledge Bobby, the issue would just go away. Despite the tactic never seeming to work on any previous occasion, that was always his strategy.

Rock finally broke free from his ironically statuesque pose and stepped between the seething men, his colossal frame creating a healthy chasm between their puffed chests. He said nothing. Didn't even look at either of them.

He knew for certain that if the two men came to blows they could spoil the entire day. A day that Geraldine had been waiting on for years. A day that she'd invested in not only financially, but psychologically. Money had never been an object to her. It was the latter that frightened Rock. If things fell through, Geraldine would be livid. The resulting displeasure would likely fuel Rock's future torment.

Geraldine pointed to her burly servant and addressed her guests.

"Gentlemen, please, relax!" she begged. "I think this is all just a simple misunderstanding. Rock will remain outside, watching from the gate. If, by some bizarre stroke of misfortune, any child is injured, he'll be just a stone's throw away."

Tom turned his attention to Greg and thought about Geraldine's statement. But he still wasn't quite ready to end the discussion.

"I just don't understand why we can't be out here too."

His anal approach and constant scrutiny of the most minor details were really beginning to test Geraldine's patience. Still, she kept calm and collected.

"Maybe I can sum it up for you in a simple question. When you were a child, did you have more fun playing with your parents or friends?"

Molly grabbed his hand tight, understanding his concern. But she also felt like his stance was beginning to border on overprotection.

"I think they'll be alright, hun," Molly said. "We'll be watching. I mean, they're fenced in, and you know the kids. They just wanna play."

She caressed Tom's knuckles with her thumb.

Tom looked away from his wife and back to the head of the castle.

"How long will it be?" he asked Geraldine.

"Enough with the twenty fucking questions already!" Greg sniped. "Even your wife is onboard. Can you just grow a pair already so everyone else can have fun? For Christ's sake, I never seen anything like it."

Tom kept his cool, ignoring him this time. He simply wanted an answer.

"We'll need them four hours in total," Geraldine said. "If you care to do the math, with the increase we've offered you, that's one thousand dollars an hour. And again, I'd like to remind you, every inch of the playground is outfitted with state-of-the-art recording equipment. You'll be able to see and communicate with them at all times."

Even with her spelling it out for him, Tom still wasn't completely comfortable. But, with everyone else onboard, who was he to break up the party?

"Fine. Let them in," Tom mumbled.

The children cheered. The roar of excitement was followed by their adolescent arms clawing at the fencing as Geraldine twisted the key inside the lock. They filed in and bolted toward the stations.

"Seesaw, Sam! C'mon!" Sadie exclaimed.

The sisters darted toward the yellow, elongated metal with extra-cushy, cherry seating.

CJ looked at Tanya, his face was crinkled and displayed a frown of annoyance.

It was just his luck—Sadie and Sam had to go and hog the one thing that CJ had been looking forward to playing with his sister.

"Dang," he mumbled.

Tanya noticed her brother's reaction.

She felt a similar sense of disappointment but was still hopeful they'd get a chance to play. There was a lot of other fun stuff to explore in the interim.

"It's okay. I'm sure they won't be on there the entire time," Tanya explained with a sweet smile. "It'll be fun to explore a little anyhow!"

"Yeah, this will be so cool!" CJ replied.

He looked around the playground.

The entire Matthews family spread out. They were more concerned with discovering the many bells and whistles of the fancy facility before they settled on what to play with.

As usual with any group he was a part of, Isaac headed up the rear. Approaching Geraldine at the gate, he felt a strange sensation in his gut. While the haggish woman ushered him in politely, there was something about her that rubbed him the wrong way. When he passed through the entrance, the creepy woman's artificially white dentures found daylight.

"Have fun," she said.

As Geraldine gestured for Isaac to enter the playground, a sinister cackle escaped her. The old woman's laugh was the last thing Isaac heard as the black, steel gate locked behind him.

THE SPY ROOM

With the parents inside, the elevator glided to a close. Geraldine stood beside Fuchs and selected the third-floor button.

"Never seen an elevator inside a residential," Greg said, impressed by the sight.

Geraldine squinted her eyes at him and smirked. "You can do *anything* if you have enough money."

Something about the way she said this bothered Tom. In his mind, it was probably nothing, but he still couldn't shake the strange uneasiness.

"Well, if you got any extra laying around, we'd be happy to take it off your hands," Lacey said.

She was joking, but inside, she was stone-cold serious.

"Seriously though, if you have any—ah, any other gigs like this, we're happy to help," Greg said, laying the sincerity on as thick as Texas toast.

"You're already helping me more than you can imagine," Geraldine said. "But I'll certainly keep you in mind for any future opportunities."

The elevator dinged.

"And here we are," Fuchs said, first to step through the doors.

As they exited the elevator, the parents were presented with a long, dimly lit but spacious hallway. Okina black wallpaper encompassed the walls and several doors could be seen.

Fuchs casually waved the parents down the corridor. "Right zhis way."

They trickled down and followed him toward the end of the hall where a door was already open as if the room had been expecting them.

Upon entering what Geraldine referred to as the 'spy room,' the lavish nature of her lifestyle became even more apparent.

"You got a fuckin' movie theater in your house too? God damn, is there anything you *don't* have?" Greg whined, the constant reminders of their monetary variance beginning to irritate him.

"At this moment, I have everything I've ever wanted," Geraldine told him. "Well almost, everything…" She briefly thought of Rock. "Please, do take your seats. We won't be using the projector today. We'll be using a video feed."

Geraldine stood patiently as they filed in, eyeing the two circular buttons fixed to the wall. The buttons were the same in size—one black and one red. As her fingers pushed against the black knob, the crimson curtains on the wall in front of the seats gradually drifted apart.

Fuchs approached the screening area and tugged on the massive projection mat and it curled and drew itself upward like a window shade. Behind it revealed a dozen big screen TVs implanted in the wall. They were all turned off, but the display still looked like it belonged in an electronics store.

"This is so cool," Molly said, excited by the overload of cutting-edge technology.

"It's definitely somethin' else," Tom concurred.

There were three rows, each with six seats. Greg and Lacey plopped down in the center seats of the front row. In an attempt to avoid interacting with Greg again, Tom guided Molly to the back row on the far left, securing the seats furthest away from their peers.

The chair bottoms were cushy but the framework of the seats was far more rigid than one might expect for a theater. Unlike theater seats, these didn't share an armrest, but had their own.

"I feel like I'm at the dentist," Tom said.

He pressed his back into the cushion and attempted to get comfortable.

Fuchs made his way to each of the parents, adjusting their headrests ensuring they lined up comfortably with their heads.

"Thank you," Molly whispered.

Fuchs smiled. "It tiz my pleasure."

Like a carnie checking rollercoaster seatbelts, the German adjusted each chair—with each sizing, Fuchs was careful and accommodating. He finished with Lacey's and returned her smile of approval. After she leaned back and settled in, her mind drifted. Her short attention span had already burned up its fuse. Lacey couldn't help but look down at the zebra print encircling her wrist. The fidget toy Tanya gifted her was calling to her.

"Alright, in just a moment, Mr. Fuchs will activate the video feed, and your children shall be right here in the theater with you," Geraldine explained.

Lacey pulled off the slap bracelet again, but before she was able to straighten it out, Geraldine's voice interrupted.

"But, before we begin, I'd like to ask you all to be still for a moment. As guests in my home, I want you to be as comfortable as possible. It may sound silly, but meditation has been a great key to my success, so I hope you don't mind playing along with me."

"It's your money, lady," Greg said.

"Thank you, Greg. This brief exercise will provide you comfort during your time away from your children. If you could each please just take a moment and lean your heads back against your chairs. I'd like you all to relax and take a deep breath."

Tom looked at Molly and discreetly rolled his eyes.

Molly smirked at him but slapped his hand, her way of saying 'just suck it up and play along.'

Geraldine watched everyone carefully. Her bony, dotted hand slid back up over the circular, blood-red button fixed to the wall.

"Excellent. Now close your eyes and press your heads firmly against the padding behind you. When you feel that gentle pressure at the back of your skull, take another deep breath," Geraldine whispered.

Geraldine heard the air hissing out of their lungs as she made eye contact with Fuchs.

The German stood facing the four parents head-on, studying them with the same detail which Geraldine studied *him*.

Lacey listened and followed the instructions but couldn't subdue her obsession. The toy was too much fun to ignore for long. How something as simple as a silly slap bracelet brought her so much joy remained a mystery. In just a short time, it felt like the gift had become almost an extension of her body.

As she subtly twisted the material between her fingers, the gift suddenly slipped. While the bracelet fell out of her grasp, Fuchs nodded at Geraldine.

As her pruned finger pushed against the remaining red button, Lacey simultaneously jerked forward, attempting to save her bracelet from the fall.

The other parents had implemented Geraldine's commands to a tee. Unbeknownst to them, their obedience would act as their saving grace. When the unforgiving, curved steel rocketed out the sides of the occupied chairs, they arched around Tom, Molly, and Greg's neck without harm.

As the terrified trio opened their eyes, they were equally alarmed by the manifestation of the dangerous collars. Their eyes bugged out and their jaws slacked—a new dreadful reality ushered them into a series of cries and shrieks.

They grasped at the slick material as it slowly adjusted, automatically sizing up their throats. The retracting steel closed in until it reached a snugness that eliminated the slightest wiggle room.

The transition happened in the blink of an eye, but the grim surroundings they faced were irrefutable. The heads of the parents were instantly pinned in place, making them slaves to their seating. All of the parents were trapped— except Lacey.

Unlike the rest of her peers, Lacey had far graver problems than fear itself. In a comedy of errors, her flinch forward had resulted in the steel collar thrusting cleanly through the right side of her neck. The tissue had been pierced with a soulless mechanical power.

The ferocity of her injury triggered the red to gush from her jugular vein and carotid artery. Her throat became a sprinkler. There was no safety mechanism to soften the blow. The submissive device clearly hadn't been designed with care in mind.

The metal punched through everything in front of it— neck, muscle, meat, and vessels. The blood didn't just leak, it *exploded*. Like a bomb at a bus station, the bystanders felt the splatter. As the blood fountained upward and coated Lacey's entire face, Greg was splashed with his share. The warm fluid erupted with such projection that it went up his nostrils, and into his mouth and eyeballs.

While his wife gurgled and gagged, Greg screamed in horrific harmony with the Grimleys.

"What the fuck! What the fuck did you do?! You're killing her!" he squealed.

Geraldine moseyed around to the front of the theater beside Fuchs. The German had been left speechless by the ghastly turn of events until a smirk of perversion overtook his blankness. He was highly amused.

Geraldine watched the crimson flood in warm waves from the side of Lacey's neck, leaving the ripped skin and tissue flapping. The gruesome sight fostered a somberness inside her. Not because Lacey was like a cow on the path to the slaughterhouse, but because Geraldine knew that she wasn't going to get to see her children have 'fun' in her playground.

The cries of the parents were ignored. Geraldine focused on Lacey's wound and watched her fade.

Lacey's tremors and gurgles grew fainter and fainter. The blood that once oozed out of her neck so generously slowed. Her previously dry and frizzy blonde locks were now flattened and wet—a sickening brownish-red transition within the morbid mane atop her scalp. Her eyes rolled in her skull as Greg's threatening screams became the soundtrack for her final farewell.

"You sick old bitch! What—What is this?!" Greg cried.

"The stupid whore killed herself! She should've listened! I gave you very simple instructions. In fact, we know they were simple if *you're* still here!" Geraldine barked.

She'd been waiting all afternoon to get a dig in on him. While losing a parent so early in the game wasn't ideal, Greg's anguish almost made it worth it for her.

"Fuck you!" Greg screamed.

"Considering the uncomfortable position you've found yourself in, *Mr. Matthews*, I'd choose my words very carefully," she said, accenting his name in the direction of his dead wife.

She remembered the little things. Lacey correcting her when she spoke to Greg was still fresh on her mind. She didn't like being corrected.

Geraldine looked down at the zebra bracelet sitting on the floor. It had been touched with a spattering of blood.

Tom and Molly watched on helplessly—the shock was on par with sitting in the electric chair. Molly's lips quivered and her insides twisted. Tom was every bit as stupefied, his own dread leaving him speechless.

Geraldine picked up the slap bracelet. She shook some of the blood off and flattened it out.

SLAP!

Geraldine smacked the silly device back around Lacey's wrist, then leaned into her corpse and whispered, "You dropped this, dear."

UNLEASHED

Rock watched as the children found their way. Some took their time, slowly gliding through the cool ocean air on the swings, while others whipped around at breakneck speed on the merry-go-round. Some were even exploratory, making their way through the collection of various tubes that wormed their way around the entire playground.

They all had one thing in common: they played.

The rides and giant toys at their disposal were what being a kid was all about. The controlled freedom to find joy in whatever they should choose. The carefree, thoughtless nature of just letting the spirit of adolescence possess them and allowing their innocence and curiosity to flourish.

The joy was difficult to watch.

They were all things and concepts Rock wished he'd been able to enjoy at their age. But agonizingly, that wasn't to be the preordained path for him. Rock never knew the luxury of stretching his legs as a boy, nor as a young man, and certainly not as a perpetually policed adult.

It wasn't the first time he'd felt that way.

Whenever Geraldine tasked him with snatching up a new child for her playground, he was reminded of these harsh, unwanted truths.

The cycle had been going on for far too long, never failing to garner the same unpleasant emotions. The juvenile jealousy and adolescent anger mated, giving birth to his depression. The twisted feelings never waned they only amplified—occupying more space in his brawny chest and his bitter brain. There wasn't a morning that Rock awoke without being reminded that he'd been slighted.

His breathing grew heavier.

Rock had been bringing the occasional child to The Borden Estate for some time now, plucking them away from the peacefulness of their families and dragging them into Geraldine's warped imagination.

He'd watched them play, these tiny bodies that had yet to find their way. The kids were always grateful at first until their undeveloped minds realized the playground out back was just the beginning.

Those same auspicious preteens with a vivacious lust for life always ended up looking nothing like they once had, and Rock was the one tasked with gathering their remains. Disposing of their stunted bodies was a strange duty. Being confronted by their destroyed, vacant husks—purged of the promise he'd seen them previously brimming with—made him feel evil.

As he watched the pack of children in the playground having the time of their lives, it was difficult for Rock to dissect how he felt about it.

The situation was complex.

His unsovereign assimilation into a family of maniacs didn't help, a family that wasn't even a family. The sick circumstances had indefinitely distorted his logic. But despite his cruel upbringing and the cantankerous queen of the castle, at that moment, he felt different.

As Rock watched the kids frolic about, he couldn't put his finger on why. But the absence of a reason didn't stop the horrible sensation in his gut or quell the ghastly, predictive imagery he painted in his mind.

What'll they look like tomorrow? Rock wondered.

Maybe it was because he'd never seen so many children having fun all at once on the playground. When Rock was a boy, he would've cut his own pinky off just to get a chance to play by himself for a few hours. Geraldine never saw fit to reward him with the simple opportunity.

Rock had pictured it in his head before, but that was the closest he'd gotten. It wasn't the same. His imagination alone could only take him so far. And most of the time he was too preoccupied with Geraldine's bidding to truly immerse himself.

Rage swelled inside his chest.

How many friends did he miss out on making?

How many parties was he deterred from attending?

How many smiles had been stolen from him?

As each question piled onto his thoughts, he couldn't help but feel uncomfortable. Rock despised what he'd become. The pathetic slave in the mirror that stared back at him each morning. How had he allowed his fears to control him for so long?

DING-DONG!

The doorbell rang. Rock looked back through the French doors that had been left propped open, then back to the children. He had no choice but to go get the door, but the fury that lurked inside him still smarted.

Rock clenched his fists. He turned toward the patio, digging his wide fingernails into his palms. The pain felt good, but not good enough.

DING-DONG! DING-DONG! DING-DONG! DING-DONG! DING-DONG!

The doorbell echoed repeatedly like an impatient child was standing in front of it. In some ways, that wasn't necessarily untrue.

When Rock opened the door, his heart was already racing. He didn't deal well with people. But Geraldine was counting on him to keep things organized.

Geraldine always somehow found a way to bring out the best and worst in him.

The tall duty she'd saddled him with was one of Rock's greatest challenges. While approaching and coaxing disadvantaged families at the inner-city playgrounds to participate in Geraldine's experiment was an evil act, Rock surprised himself in his execution. He was astounded he was able to convince a single family, let alone three.

Fear was his ultimate motivator.

The wicked fury that fluttered through his torso intersected with a newly-emerging dread. A grim dread he was already aware of, but a dread that had been lying dormant the entire morning. Rock's instincts told him things were only set to get more tumultuous.

Caroline Clarke didn't understand just how distressed her presence made Rock. A flash of Caroline yanking her son's leash on the playground flickered in Rock's head. When he'd approached her, uncommon thoughts of violence had crept into his mind. Even after their initial meeting, the fantasies hadn't fully dissolved.

As she stood on the doorstep with six-year-old Donnie Clarke once again tethered to her, a loathsome leer lingered on Rock's face and the memories resurfaced in full force.

When he'd watched her from a distance that evening, he noticed the parallels he could draw to his own life. Just like Geraldine, Caroline was overbearing to the point of suffocation. She kept him inches away at all times. The leash that was attached to his back wasn't merely a measure of safety—it was a symbol.

A lack of trust.

A sense of ownership.

A craving for control.

A symbol of dominance.

Rock knew where Donnie's path of darkness eventually snaked, and it wasn't a good place. It was a massive black hole of perpetual terror and despair, of self-doubt and gratuitous dependence. A synthetic, pre-packaged mindset manufactured by Donnie's disturbed overseer to keep him under her grubby thumb.

Caroline Clarke knew *exactly* what *she* was doing.

Geraldine Borden knew *exactly* what *she* was doing.

It was like Rock was looking at two parallel dimensions where identical atmospheres were being cultivated. Tightly wound worlds of suffocation that used fear, compliance, and reliance as fuel.

When Rock had watched Caroline and Donnie in the park that evening, he'd felt like he'd been placed back into his own childhood under a different set of nuances. It didn't matter that he'd grown up in a prettier house or around more money than little Donnie. They were both emotionally poor.

When Rock heard Caroline scream orders at the boy, he knew Donnie wasn't enjoying the ride. The swing he sat upon meant nothing to him. With his smooth face drained dry of enjoyment, it was clear—Donnie was merely dancing for the puppet master.

As Rock watched Caroline pull and position Donnie by the literal string sticking out of his back, the metaphor in his mind was demonstrated before his eyes. The leash attached to Donnie kept Caroline physically connected, as if the umbilical cord had never been severed.

Why? he wondered.

Rock's world had always been a place of disappointment, but he was realizing he'd underestimated the scale.

Now that he'd ripened some, things had become clearer. His thirty-four horrifying years on the planet felt more like a hundred. Could little Donnie really handle that? He was just a boy, a moldable wad of putty set to be stuffed into a box, confined in a way only a corpse in a coffin should. Everyone else was oblivious, but Rock and Donnie knew they were already dead.

Dead inside, dead alive, and dead tired.

An ungodly sneer dominated Caroline's face when they locked eyes. Her mouth was moving, but he hadn't heard a word she said. As her repulsive aura pulsated, the audio finally came back to Rock, but Caroline was no longer talking to him.

"I said don't move," Caroline demanded, teeth clenched with rage.

Her demeanor gnawed at Rock's guts. He watched as she lifted the hand opposite the leash and took a massive drag of her cigarette. She exhaled, sliding her bifocal glasses up from the edge of her pointy nose, and looked back at Rock.

Fuck, he hated her.

"What's the matter with you? You don't remember me?" she asked.

Before Rock could answer, her head snapped back toward Donnie, who stood just a few feet away from her on the steps. Innocence hung in his eyes above a red tee shirt and his white and blue striped shorts. His sneakers were also white, one of which had been left untied.

"Donnie! If I feel this fucking leash move again, there's gonna be trouble!" Caroline barked.

Rock hadn't seen it move. The false claim only infuriated him further. He was also accustomed to being accused of things he hadn't done.

"Donnie, stay close!"

Caroline took another monster puff off her dwindling Parliament and the thick streams of smoke flowed from her nostrils. Her frizzled hair bobbed when she jerked the toddler tether unnecessarily hard.

Donnie stumbled over the step ahead, dragging his bare knee over the hard stone. The tumble caused a scrape, leaving his kneecap skinned mightily. The slimy patch of drippy red revealed would've surely caused any child his age both hurt and worry. But as his mother heartlessly dragged him up, Rock noticed something strange.

The boy wasn't crying.

That level of numbness was far more telling than if Donnie would've sat there screaming hysterically.

Suddenly, Rock's brain felt like it might explode. It was far from the worst thing he'd ever seen, but it was certainly traumatic.

He was at a tipping point.

"Ugh! You cut yourself *again*!" Caroline shouted. "Watch where you walk! You *never* wander away from me, are we clear?! When you grow up, you can run around and hurt yourself all you want, but until then, you're *mine*!"

Rock's angry eyes widened with horror as he heard the word that ruined him.

Flashes of Geraldine's heinous scowl and the glowing branding iron went off like fireworks in his skull. The old hag's hideous body parts. The reflections of his humiliation in the hall of mirrors. The venomous verbal lashings. The deformed husks of lifeless children.

Something inside him snapped.

Rock's arms rushed forward, moving without warning. Seeing all that he'd been robbed of just minutes prior at the playground, and now this. He couldn't take it any longer. It wasn't even a choice, it just happened.

While Rock had relinquished control of his actions to the deep-rooted hatred that infected him, his mind was also being overrun with thoughts—a forced reasoning of sorts.

They both gotta die anyhow. What's it matter if she goes early?

Geraldine wouldn't be happy with him, but it wasn't as if he could control it anymore.

Rock stole the leash from Caroline's grasp and used his meaty fingers to unclip it from the boy's back.

As he wrapped the length of leather around Caroline's neck, in his heart, Rock wished it was more wrinkled. He wished it was the flappy, weathered, loose skin stretched over Geraldine's throat. He wished it was her evil eyes that looked about to pop out of her head.

Caroline struggled, but her arms weren't long enough to reach Rock's face. In an act of desperation, she used the lit cigarette in her hand and pressed the hot ember against the side of Rock's suit.

Donnie stood frozen in place watching the assault unfold. The aggression and violence didn't break the blankness on his face.

The cigarette ate its way through the clothing until it was singeing his arm hair and skin. The pain of the scald was nothing to Rock; it was like amateur hour compared to Geraldine's track record of torture.

Burning the burly man was an unforeseeable misstep. The stinging sensation took Rock back to the time of his own helpless suffering. But he wasn't tied up or afraid any more—he was unleashed.

Rock utilized his soaring stature and leveraged the leash like a noose. He elevated Caroline off the ground, allowing the force of gravity to create a crushing pressure around her larynx. But as her face transitioned in color, Rock realized he didn't want it to end quite yet. Seeing purple or blue wasn't enough; not while he was seeing red.

He turned her over in mid-air and slammed her skull-first onto the stone steps. The same as she'd done to Donnie. It was only fair.

Caroline's face connected hard. The sickening sound of her head smashing and surging pain was more than enough to stun her. The force of the collision cracked the right lens of her glasses and buried the metal frame deep in her eyebrow. Caroline's nose let off an expulsion of blood before her awkwardly arched body turned over itself.

Rock looked at the gruesome mask of torment that Caroline's broken face projected. He'd never unleashed such violence upon anyone. Surely it would've left her an invalid, or at the very least, altered for life. But neither of them would get the opportunity to find out. Rock was too possessed to pause.

It wasn't enough; *nothing* would be enough for her.

Rock flipped Caroline's quaking body over. As he mounted her, he couldn't help but notice her messy face as a wave of blood seeped out of her babbling mouth. The fractured enamel left some of her teeth looking unnaturally sharp and demonic, a fitting new characteristic. Rock could see Caroline was unable to speak, but inside, he knew she was begging.

You got nothing to say now? he thought.

He cocked back his gargantuan mitt and launched his scallop-sized knuckles into Caroline's chin. A cringe-worthy crack erupted from her mouth as the jawbone shattered in two places.

Caroline was on autopilot.

She flailed about and lifted her head off the stone as the next punch landed on her brow. The thud of her skull smacking back against the concrete sounded like a bag of potatoes being dropped. Along with her head, the stiff shot also pushed the glasses further into the massive laceration on her face.

The size and speed of Rock's hands were a fatal blend. It was a notion he'd never comprehended before. While the violence wasn't new, the active participation aspect was. It was finally his time; the whipping boy was long overdue to exorcise his demons.

Rock never imagined he might feel relief in hearing another person's bones break and crumble, but he did. The hits he continued to dish out on Caroline became more targeted. Rock pounded into the deep gash over her eyebrow with brute force, unleashing decades of frustration.

As the devastating blows piled up, Caroline's face was pulverized. The destruction was so severe that the audio accompanying the thrashing sounded like Rock was punching a puddle.

He was too enamored with the act to notice Caroline's face collapsing in on itself. The pile of pink, mushy tissue, broken enamel, and splintered bones had been thoroughly tenderized. The once modest tear that appeared on Caroline's face had grown to disturbing lengths. She now looked like an ad for gape porn.

Still, Rock didn't stop.

The parts of her shattered lens slashed and stabbed into Rock's hand with each additional strike, but the cuts were of little deterrence. He was finally in a safe place, spellbound by the bloodshed.

Rock heard his own voice echo inside his cranium, but there were no words, only screaming.

Adrenaline flushed through his system as he went further. The mush that remained was now unidentifiable. The way Rock saw it, the distorted mini-mounds of meat and swelling tissue in front of him could've been anyone's. He used the slop to play out what he now realized to be his ultimate fantasy.

On the brink of exhaustion, Rock pushed out a final series of strikes with a subtle difference from the blows that preceded them. Each time he hit the ugly goop was harder than before. Because now the drippy gore Rock felt mush against his mitts was no longer Caroline Clarke's—it was Geraldine Borden's.

When the blackout ended, he sat atop Caroline's lifeless body. The cuts and blood that covered Rock's hands bled downward onto her pancaked head. The splatter collected by his suit made him feel like he was in a dream. But when he looked up at the ghost of his past, six-year-old Donnie Clarke, he knew he wasn't.

The little boy stood steady as ever, unflinching as he awaited whatever came next.

PLAYING FOR PRIDE

Fuchs activated the first large-screen television embedded in the wall of the theater. The screen depicted the children of the imprisoned parents releasing their childish energy like they never had before. The angles being recorded rotated. Some were far-off shots, some from a bird's eye, and others were intimate close-ups.

The parents were too frightened to register what was happening on the tube. Lacey's motionless corpse and the mass of bloodshed that painted the room were the more pressing distraction.

Tom looked over at his wife. She hadn't stopped crying and shaking since the unexpected violence. He did his best to comfort Molly. Every so often, he squeezed her hand and whispered promises he wasn't sure he could keep.

"Don't worry, it's gonna be alright," Tom said.

They'd been together long enough for Molly to know that the tremor molesting his cadence indicated otherwise. Tom's words were a sweet and loving gesture, but a flimsy one, nonetheless.

Greg was still sporadically shrieking at the top of his lungs. He would calm down for a moment and then start up again. The panic left him like a lost child.

Every so often they grabbed at their collars as if they couldn't believe it was real. The action was futile, but desperation had equally clouded each parent's judgment.

Fuchs just stared at Greg as he weaved in and out of his mental breakdown. He'd said nothing to any of them since Geraldine had left the room.

They all wondered where she had gone.

The mystery was about to be solved as the sound of footsteps in the hall grew closer and closer.

"The command center is ready," Geraldine announced.

"Wonderful," Fuchs said.

The chaotic panting and slobbering that was Greg's only form of expression irked Geraldine. He'd vomited shortly after Lacey's neck came undone. Chunks of off-white and yellow liquid ran down his neck and clung to the front of his shirt.

"Silence! I don't want another word out of any of you! I'm only going to tell you what's about to happen to you and your children once, so I suggest you listen carefully," Geraldine warned.

The audible horror Greg and Molly were expelling fell in volume drastically. It wasn't nonexistent, but low enough that Geraldine felt comfortable continuing.

"I regret to inform you, but all of you have chosen to enter my estate today under a false pretense. There will be very few winners today, if any. The sooner you choose to accept that, the easier it will be for you. The playground that you viewed outside is not the one your children will be playing in. They may be right now, of course, but soon that will change. Then where shall they play, you ask? Well, you're just going to have to watch and find out."

Geraldine gestured to the many screens inside the wall behind her before reengaging.

The horror seeping to the surface was otherworldly.

Tom and Molly were controlled enough to remain quiet, but their facial expressions screamed. Their gaping eyes and sudden shift to a pasty pigment said it all.

"To be frank, most of the details you absorbed in the brochures my associate gave you were lies. I do represent a charity, but this has little to do with that. However, amid the many falsehoods, there was one truth. As promised, your children will be afforded the opportunity to test out a playground like no other. A particularly vast playground with much diversity within each respective area. It's a linear journey, which makes it sound simple, but rest assured the various entertainments within each should be… unique, to say the least. But the hope is to have them try everything. And who knows, with your help, you may be able to see them play just a bit longer."

"What—What do you mean, with our help? Why should they need help?" Molly stammered.

"*Why* isn't for me to say. It would spoil the mystique of it all. But I can tell you that the reason they'll require help will quickly become *very* obvious to you. But on a more positive note, let's talk about one way you can keep your children alive longer—"

"Alive?! Why would you—"

"If I were you, Mr. Grimley, I wouldn't interrupt! Now that you're aware of the stakes, I wouldn't want you to miss something."

Tom quieted down.

"Smart man. Now, on each of the collars around your necks, you'll find a small circular button. Those buttons will all be activated shortly after we leave this room. When pushed, a microphone will then project your voice over a PA system where your children are playing. You'll have just a few critical seconds to relay a message of your choosing, but a few seconds is better than nothing, I suppose."

A hideous smile blanketed Geraldine's face. She was so proud of herself.

"Additionally, each button will only work *once* for each of you. So, pick your spots and choose your words wisely. They'll undoubtedly be your last."

"You're—You're fucking insane!" Greg yelled.

"Wait a minute, please! Why are you doing this? What did we ever do to you?" Tom asked.

"The reason isn't important," Geraldine replied.

"If it's not important, then why not tell us?"

Tom was trying to do anything to access the human side of her. If she offered him something, he might be able to dispel whatever notion she'd become fixated on.

"I appreciate your interest, Mr. Grimley, but I'm afraid it's all very complicated. It may not even be germane to you as an individual, but let's just say you have something I want. A privilege of sorts. And since I can't have a child of my own, then why should you?"

Geraldine brandished her dentures proudly.

The wheels were turning in all their heads, but the one with the dead hamster inside spoke first.

"Jesus fuckin' Christ, lady! You can adopt! You killed my fuckin' wife because of *that*?!" Greg bellowed.

Molly broke down, pleading with Geraldine through her tears. "Please, you can do whatever you want to us, but just let the children be! I'm begging you! I'll do anything! *Anything*!"

Geraldine's shrewd wrinkles flattened out as she considered Molly's wish. She looked back at the screen displaying the children playing merrily. Suddenly, an idea popped into her head. Geraldine lit up with a big, toothy smile as a genuine surge of excitement hit her.

"Remind me, dear, which of these girls are yours again?!" Geraldine inquired.

"What?" Molly asked.

"What do they look like?"

"They're the two small blonde girls, they—they look like twins almost."

"Mr. Fuchs, go to the control room and give me a close-up, quickly!"

"At once, my lady," he replied, disappearing through the doorway seconds later.

Geraldine began racking her brain. She couldn't be sure

of their appearances until she saw them with her own eyes, but she did her best to render an image of two young girls hovering around Molly outside of her estate.

She lingered in front of the screen anxiously, arms folded at her sides.

"There we are!" Geraldine said.

She pointed at the image of Sam and Sadie seesawing on the screen.

"These two?" Geraldine asked.

"Y—Yes," Molly replied.

Molly's face maintained a grimace—she was unsure if the answer she'd given was what Geraldine was looking for.

"Why they look nothing like you!" She switched her stare and fixed it on Tom. "They don't look like either of you for that matter!"

"No, I suppose they don't…"

Geraldine looked back at the screen in disbelief.

"And the two of you made them together?"

"Yes…"

Tom nodded after Molly spoke but remained silent.

"But how can that be? They—They don't even have your hair color."

"Variations can be passed down from prior generations. My dad was blond. It's rare, but not unheard of."

Molly didn't even know what she was trying to convince her of anymore. Geraldine's behavior seemed even more bizarre than before.

"I have one last question then," Geraldine said. An odd, hopeful inflection hung on each of her words.

Molly was afraid to ask.

"Okay…"

"How do you know they're yours?"

"I don't understand—"

"How do you know?!"

"They—they came out of me? I watched them take their first breaths."

"But imagine you hadn't seen that. How could you

possibly be sure?"

Molly was beginning to sweat. The conversation spawned a suffocating sense of paranoia in her chest.

"I—I don't know."

"Think, damn it!"

Geraldine's impatience was on the brink of exploding.

"We act the same?"

As Molly made the statement, she watched a disturbing grin replace Geraldine's scowl.

"Thank you! I thought you might say that!"

Geraldine rejoiced, throwing her arms in the air. It was as if she'd been playing a verbal game of charades, unbeknownst to Molly.

Looking back at the screen, Geraldine glared at the two young girls. Between the close-up of Sam and Sadie, she watched Tanya step into the background. Tanya eyed the girls with envy as the seesaw rocked back and forth.

Geraldine started to think deeply about her sexual fixation. For the first time, the prior conversation triggered a question she'd never thought to ask.

Did her attraction lie solely in the flesh?

She wasn't sure, but there was no reason not to find out. A newfound opportunity suddenly dangled before her. The mere possibility of expanding outside her carnal desires was provocative. Could her lust be contorted to conform to behavioral tendencies rather than physical features? If she was able to identify someone that acted enough like her, could she relish in those old feelings of sinful succulence?

Rock had been such a massive disappointment. There had never been an inkling of curiosity around the topic since he'd been brought into the fold. But with so many new faces, the odds had suddenly increased.

"My beauties," Geraldine mumbled.

Her wrinkled hand glided over the bodies of the three girls in frame on the tube.

"She's lost her fucking mind," Tom whispered.

"We have to try still," Molly said.

She shifted her focus back to Geraldine.

"Please, just don't hurt our children."

Geraldine spun back around, with a new pep in her step. "I'll tell you what. I can promise you I'm going to be watching all of these children very closely. Examining their attributes, and how they think and act. Maybe, if they make it out of the playground, and I see enough potential in one of them, just maybe, I'll take them under my wing."

Geraldine's nefarious leer upset Molly deeply. From what she knew of the woman, that might be a harsher sentence than death itself.

"And just to make things interesting," Geraldine said, "there's one other final stipulation I had already planned on offering. But again, this reward is also contingent upon the children making it through my entire playground. Should any of them make it to the other side, I'll afford you the opportunity to see each other one last time before… before we do what we must."

"This is really happening," Tom said to himself.

The shock and disbelief were beyond anything he'd felt.

"Although, we may want to keep them away from Mom here," Geraldine said, pointing her thumb toward Lacey's blood-soaked body. "That could be… traumatic."

The comment lifted Greg back out of his trauma trance. Like Tom, he had to pinch himself to believe it.

"Evil fucking bitch! I—I promise you're gonna pay for this!" Greg screamed.

Geraldine giggled.

"What do you mean? I already have! And just wait until you see what I've invested in."

THE HIDDEN HURT

Donnie wasn't terribly impacted as his mother's warm blood dribbled down his wrist. He felt Rock's hefty hand delicately clenched around his and found a peculiar comfort as he entered the bathroom.

Rock sat the boy on the closed toilet seat and looked down at the nasty scrape that painted most of his kneecap. A few uneven, flapping lines of the boy's once smooth surface dangled off the side. The red was still coming out of the wound quite generously.

"We'll get you patched up," Rock said.

The boy offered no words in response.

Rock's big bloody paws shook from the adrenaline rush, the outpouring still rumbled inside him. Steadying himself, he twisted the hot water faucet on the sink. Rock dampened a cloth and used the bar of soap to create a lather.

The emotions he was holding in check were dangerous.

Rock didn't know how to feel about what he'd done to Donnie's mother. Just managing to think enough to clean the boy up felt like a victory. He was just doing what he thought was right, but inside, nothing was right.

He felt himself coming undone. He felt high, and that overload of pure panic and pandemonium was like a drug.

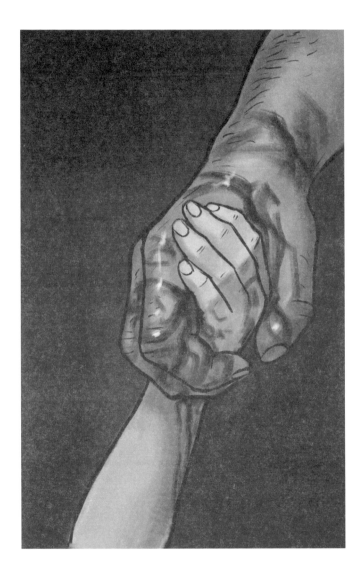

Hold it together. You killed her, but everything else is fine. It's all fixable. More fertilizer… she's just more fertilizer is all. I can tell Geraldine she tried to leave. She'll understand. I had to do it. I didn't have a choice, Rock thought.

The scarred tissue underneath his suit and shirt pulsated. The flesh that had been inflamed long ago via the glowing irons still ached somehow.

She'll understand, he lied to himself.

Once Rock washed the blood off his hands, he removed cotton swabs and a brown bottle of hydrogen peroxide from behind the mirror. His relationship with Geraldine had forced him to become intimately familiar with the items.

Rock kneeled in front of the boy and tried to make eye contact. While their pupils had connected, Rock still didn't feel like the boy actually saw him. It was like he was looking past his gruff face and the crimson stains that were splattered all over his chest and collar.

Donnie's glazed-over gaze was one Rock was all too familiar with, one that concentrated on living inside his own head instead of dealing with the grim certainty of the wicked troubles that plagued him.

"It'll be alright," Rock grumbled.

As he doused the cotton with antiseptic, Rock knew that his words were hollow. The cut might be alright, but would anything else be?

What the hell am I doing? Fixin' him up just to send him out there? What sense does that make?

He saw so much of himself in the boy. When he lied to him, he felt like he was lying to himself.

"This might sting a little, but I'm sure it's nothing that you can't handle."

Finally, he'd told the kid something that was concrete. Donnie didn't say a word back, but he nodded a touch. While it wasn't much to Rock, it felt like they were starting to communicate. Even if Donnie's gesture was minor, it meant a lot to him. It was the first time he'd been able to talk to someone he related to.

Rock applied a big bandage to the raw area on Donnie's knee. He was careful to ensure the sticky parts didn't touch any spots with torn skin. Once the dressing was in place, Rock gathered the soiled swabs and disposed of them in the trashcan. Then he turned the hot water on again and slipped the washcloth back under the spout.

"Just gonna get that blood off your hands, little fella," he explained as if it were somehow an ordinary chore.

Ironically, to a pair of broken souls like them, it was.

Rock noticed the blood had drizzled down further than his wrist. It must've traveled in toward Donnie's armpit while he was holding his hand. As Rock cleaned Donnie with the damp cloth, he moved from his palm, over his wrist, up his arm, and then finally into the pit.

Up until the moment that the rag entered Donnie's armpit, he was fine. But upon contact, the boy jerked his arm from Rock's tender grip.

"I—I'm sorry," Rock stammered.

He wasn't sure how to respond next. Donnie's reaction was something that he hadn't expected based on the boy's overall numbness.

Donnie remained static.

"I'm not gonna hurt you. I'll be more careful this time, I promise."

Rock slowly lifted the boy's arm up again, testing his trust. Donnie allowed him to do it without resistance. Rock leaned over and peered under the shirt into his armpit. At first, he couldn't tell what he was looking at, but after a moment, it struck him.

The circular, flaring nature within the speckling of wounds in Donnie's pit was a texture that Rock was quite familiar with. The spherical bumps were burns. Burns that were consistent with the tip of Caroline's Parliament. In Rock's mind, it was the only logical conclusion. The tobacco embers had been present on each occasion he'd crossed paths with Caroline. They were a weaponized extension of her evil.

Cigarette burns.

Poor Donnie's armpit looked like it had a case of concentrated mumps. The gathering of puffy dots could've been mistaken for a cluster of warts. Rock didn't have to imagine how much blistered skin on such a sensitive area would hurt. He had experience.

Rock and Donnie were bound by their suffering.

While Rock couldn't undo the damages inflicted upon the boy, the revelation made him feel better about killing Caroline. The doubt that had crept into his mind started to settle. The savagery he'd allowed to assume him no longer seemed so overzealous.

While there was still a level of shock attached to the dream-like assault, he considered that the most shocking aspect might've been in how long he'd held himself back.

Why hadn't he found a way to harness his rage and unload it on Geraldine? After all, *she* was the person responsible for his tortures. Or what about Fuchs, who stood by idly and watched it happen?

The questions baffled him.

Maybe I deserved it?

Rock couldn't be sure if he did or not. There wasn't a single day where the guilt of his unfailing worthlessness hadn't been beaten into him. But he still couldn't help but wonder about *that* day. It was different from any other. Sure, he'd brought children back before, but it was always single children, never entire families.

Seeing how the 'normal' families, Donnie's aside, treated each other, widened Rock's eyes. Their loving nature and adoration for each other were so equally reciprocated. Their kindness and innocence left him to wonder if society was far different from the stone walls he'd been regulated to roam.

How can this be right?

Rock considered what came next for Donnie as his eyes twinkled with tears. He didn't want to see Donnie's life end that day, but if his childhood was any indication of his future, then the boy would be better off heading outside with the rest of the children. If Caroline was granted full custody of the boy, as it appeared she'd been, then how much worse was the alternative?

He had no idea about the boy's father, but he didn't imagine him to be a saint. He hadn't even cared enough about Donnie to keep him from falling into Caroline's wicked clutches.

Maybe he's dead?

What future could that offer? Would Donnie be exiled into the same broken system that had landed Rock at The Borden Estate?

Sizing it up from every angle, it all looked crooked to Rock.

The thoughts saddened him, but he knew what lay ahead for young Donnie. The misery he'd already grown accustomed to was unavoidable. Things weren't going to get any rosier than the pool of blood he'd just watched drain out of his mother's skull.

As much as Rock had no desire to watch him venture into the playground, he understood it was probably for the best.

THE BIG SLIDE

Isaac climbed higher, setting in his footing on the giant rope structure. His initial idea was to stay as far away from Bobby as possible, but the sense of impending doom that continued to loom was finally prepared to blossom.

CJ and Tanya rushed around, cycling through the many parts of the playground. Sam and Sadie continued to seesaw. The constant chorus of laughter kept them occupied and every bit as fulfilled.

Bobby had already had his fill. He'd tasted enough of the entertainment to know he needed another form of it. He craved a different variety than the silly structures could offer. An enjoyment that he'd been thinking about from the moment Isaac's father had squared up with his.

Isaac knew the results could potentially be disastrous for him. He'd survived in schoolyards long enough to sense when the crosshairs were on his back. When he saw Bobby, and the malleable minion he'd enlisted, Kip, flank each side of the rope tower, he knew he was about to have a terrible experience.

Shit, shit, shit, Isaac thought.

He discreetly shifted his body to stay in between Bobby and his little brother.

107

"You're fuckin' dead now, dandelion-boy," Bobby snarled from below.

He took hold of the cherry-colored rope and pulled himself closer to Isaac.

"Yeah! Dead!" Kip affirmed.

The brothers climbed up the structure like spider monkeys closing in on succulent vine fruit.

As they moved in on Isaac, he looked down behind him; the fall was at least fifteen feet above the soft sand. Unsure of the best way to avoid them, he raced straight down. If he could get below Bobby and Kip before they got close, he'd still have a chance to make a run for it.

"Where you goin', nerd-boy?!" Bobby yelled.

With fright fueling the swiftness of his strides, Isaac carefully knifed his way between the many ropes. He paused his descent about halfway from where he was originally positioned to look up.

Kip was only a short distance away.

When Isaac twisted his head in the opposite direction, Bobby was already within arm's reach.

"Come 'ere!" Bobby yelled.

The surprise made Isaac twitch. As he tried to evade Bobby's swipe, the foot Isaac was using for leverage slipped off the rope. The sudden shock of his full body weight instantly fell upon his hands. Isaac's grip wasn't strong enough to hold him in place. The skin over and above his palms ripped down on the coarse twine as the instantaneous rope burn tore into him.

Isaac tumbled back-first and bounced off the ropes, hitting their harsh textures, causing his body to twist. The rope scraped against his face, then his arms as his body slid through them. Isaac's glasses rocketed off his face and down to the dirt below. His fall finally finished a few feet down when a rope landed square between his scrawny legs.

"Ahhhh!" Isaac cried out.

He immediately clasped at his balls as a stinging hurt spread through both of his testicles.

Bobby and his brother laughed hysterically.

"Ha-ha, right in his privates!" Kip yelled.

"That's alright, this dork ain't gonna need his balls for anything anyway!" Bobby said. Then to Isaac, "Aww, what happened? Did you lose your glasses, four eyes?"

"Why don't you guys leave him alone?" CJ interjected.

He stood at the bottom of the structure with a look of disappointment. He'd seen this idiocy from his older brother many times before. Kip wasn't usually that mean, but CJ noticed, for better or worse, his youngest brother tended to be easily influenced.

"Why don't you mind your own business? We didn't even do anything to him. He just slipped," Bobby lied.

"Just knock it off," CJ said.

"Or what?"

CJ didn't answer Bobby back. He knew arguing wasn't going to change anything. Instead, he scanned the ground underneath Isaac. He saw the glasses half-buried in the sand below the rope tower and decided to focus on something productive.

"All children, please move towards zhe big slide at zhe back of the playground," Fuchs' voice instructed, via the loudspeaker mounted on the top of the black fencing.

"Huh? I—I thought they said we couldn't use the big slide," Sam said.

She stared across the seesaw at Sadie, who mirrored the same confusion.

"Me too," Sadie replied.

A few yards behind them, they heard the fence closing shut. When they looked in the direction of the noise, they saw a young boy that was new to the group.

Donnie Clarke stood with a fresh bandage on his knee and a lost look in his eyes.

Behind the boy, through the fencing, Sam and Sadie saw Rock's massive backside as he walked away from the gate.

"Who's that?" Sam asked.

Sadie shrugged.

Sam wasn't sure why, but something about Donnie was interesting to her. The feeling wasn't new. Like her mother, she was a people person. The urge to interact crept up inside Sam. But the crackle of the loudspeaker interrupted her thoughts.

"Once again, please, everyone must move to zhe back of zhe playground. Your parents are watching and zhey want you to go zhere now," Fuchs continued.

The confused children began to slowly migrate away from the fun that they'd been having.

Tanya dropped off the monkey bars into the sand not far from Sam and Sadie. She mirrored the confusion they were feeling. Both sisters followed Tanya, moving further away from the play area.

Sam looked back at Donnie, who still stood dumbfounded near the gate.

"Hold on a sec," she whispered to Sadie.

Sam jogged over to the little boy.

"Hey, what's your name?" she asked.

The boy gave no response.

"Are you okay?"

Donnie continued to look at her with kindness in his gaze but said nothing.

Sam wasn't upset, she just didn't understand. The lack of reply only made her more curious about him.

"I—I think we're supposed to go to the back now. Do you wanna come with us?" she asked.

Donnie took a moment and looked toward the massive slide that Tanya and Sadie were heading towards, then back to Sam. He slowly nodded his head.

"Okay, cool! Follow me," she said.

A girlish smile displaying many of Sam's freshly grown adult teeth appeared on her face. She grabbed Donnie's tiny hand and tugged him along.

Back at the rope climber, Bobby and Kip watched the others migrating toward the rear of the playground.

"Should we go too?" Kip asked.

As usual, he looked to his big brother for guidance.

"I guess so. Everyone else is," Bobby replied.

The duo dismounted the web-like structure and followed Tanya.

CJ watched them pass, then looked back at Isaac. "Sorry, man. Sometimes they can really be jerks."

He cleaned the dirt off Isaac's specs with his tee shirt.

Isaac continued to lower himself down until his feet finally touched the ground. The jarring landing sent aching reverberations through his testicles. Isaac weaved his way through the remaining ropes until he finally found freedom outside of the tower.

"Here you go. I tried my best to clean them off," CJ said.

He handed him the glasses.

"Thanks. And I guess it's okay. I'm pretty used to jerks," Isaac replied.

"Yeah, but try living with them."

Isaac put on his glasses just in time to see CJ's silly smirk.

The frames sat crooked on Isaac's head. They were a little looser than before, but he was still more than grateful to be able to see again.

"I'd rather not. I'll just take your word for it," Isaac snorted.

"I'm CJ, by the way. I promise I'm not a total butthole like my brothers can be."

CJ extended his hand.

"I can see that," Isaac said, accepting the handshake. "I'm Isaac."

A genuine sense of both shock and appreciation echoed in his tone. CJ looked like the kids in class that were always ready to dump on him, but he didn't act like them.

"Everyone, move now! Quickly!" Fuchs blurted out, his voice seeming angrier than the previous announcements.

The two boys looked up near the side of the big slide where everyone else was gathered.

"Why the heck do they want us over there?" Isaac asked.

"I don't know, but it seems kinda weird," CJ answered.

The sound of barking dogs suddenly cut through the refreshing sea breeze. The boys could see through the grid fencing in the distance as Rock's enormous frame stepped closer to the gate.

In front of the big man were a pair of over-agitated Doberman pinchers. They each frothed at the mouth, clawing their way forward with rage and chaos in their piercing eyes.

Rock's grip on the dog leashes remained firm as he unlocked the gate.

"What's he doing?!" Isaac cried.

"I—I dunno! They didn't say any stuff about dogs, did they?" CJ asked.

"No!"

"Maybe we should get to the back like they told us to. C'mon, let's go!"

CJ bolted toward the rest of the kids that were already gathered at the back of the playground.

Isaac hesitated for a moment, looking back at Rock as he reached for the fencing.

"He can't be…"

What was happening didn't seem possible; it stretched beyond Isaac's logic and reasoning.

The sudsy slobber flew from their muzzles as their rage boiled. Their snapping jaws unhinged while their spiky teeth glistened in the sunlight. The thunderous barks roared, providing bone-chilling motivation.

Isaac had seen it enough. He took off toward the rest of the kids.

The other kids at the back of the playground were now also aware of the dogs.

"What's going on?!" Tanya cried.

"I hate dogs," Sadie whined.

She looked at Sam and Donnie for comfort, but neither had anything to say. Donnie's dark overall emptiness dominated his expression while Sam's mouth was slacked in terror.

"What the hell's wrong with that dude? He's—He's not gonna let those loose, is he?!" Bobby asked.

"Why would he do that?!" Kip asked.

Suddenly, the rectangular shaft beside them attached to the monstrous slide opened. The forest green walls lifted like a garage door and a steel, cube-like room appeared before them.

"Enter zhe big slide now!" Fuchs commanded.

As the gainy screech of the German's voice bellowed out, Rock let go of the leashes. The pair of ravenous dogs shot forward and the shrieking children all rushed into the belly of the slide.

"How do we close this thing?!" Kip cried.

The children chattered in fear, but there was little they could do. The room didn't offer any buttons, knobs, or doors. Only the opening they'd entered through and three metallic walls.

"CJ, hurry!" Kip cried.

The all-star athlete had already turned it on, CJ closing in on the slide. But when he cranked his head back to check Isaac's progress, it wasn't what he'd hoped.

Isaac was mid-stumble, heading face-first toward the ground. The boxy, wireframe spectacles flung off his head again and landed in the sand.

CJ peered past Isaac. The dogs were already en route.

"Don't do it, don't do it… ugh!" CJ mumbled to himself.

He turned back toward Isaac, feeling dread and regret instantly swell inside his chest.

"CJ, what the fuck are you doing?!" Bobby yelled.

He ignored his brother and focused on the task at hand. CJ ran past Isaac as he searched for his glasses in the dirt, attempting to create a distraction to divert the dogs away from him.

"You better find 'em fast!" CJ yelled.

The tactic worked—somewhat. The dogs split. One pup veered in CJ's direction while the second made a beeline for Isaac.

Isaac's fingers finally found the spectacles, but as he slipped them back on, pointed canine teeth penetrated his triceps. The dog clamped down hard, drool secreting from its jaws as it jerked its head side to side. The ferociousness made it clear the dog had been trained to inflict agony.

Isaac cried out as the meat on the back of his arm broke open. The heavy pressure of the canine jaws caused a stinging terror to surge, pushing and amplifying the internal tsunami of anguish inside him.

CJ jumped up the wide steps, past the monkey bars, and towards a smaller tube slide he'd played on just a short time ago. There was a series of four additional stairs he needed to ascend to reach the pinnacle. While the structure was designed for children, the athletic Doberman had no issues following CJ up each of the rubbery platforms. The dog was every bit as athletic as the boy.

In hearing the scratching of the Doberman's overgrown nails right behind him, CJ knew he needed to think fast. As he reached the summit, he quickly slipped off his tee shirt. Bare-chested, the boy snapped around to face the direction of the dog in chase. The hound was nearly in his face when CJ opened his shirt as wide as he could stretch it.

As the Doberman pounced with its fangs brandished, CJ knew he only had one shot at the patchwork plan he'd invented on the fly.

When the dog lunged for his hand, he yanked it upward, slipping the shirt over the relentless head of the beast. He was able to get the dog's snout through one arm of the tee. The hole that the Doberman was stuck in was tight enough that the rest of his head couldn't squeeze through.

Blinded, the Doberman whimpered.

Isaac's screams found CJ's ears again. He had to act fast. He pinned the distracted dog against the structure. The Doberman flailed wildly as CJ peered toward the tall perimeter fencing that surrounded the playground. The steel divider was only a few feet away.

CJ knew what he had to do but had no idea if it would

work. He leveraged every ounce of his athleticism to wrap his arms around the dog's belly and hoisted it up.

He'd done a German suplex wrestling with friends but never a dog. CJ channeled his inner Bret Hart and tightened his arms around the dog's underbelly. In a stream of steady momentum, he yanked upward with everything he could muster and tossed the chaotic canine.

The shirt-draped Doberman almost made it clear over the perimeter fencing. The hind of the dog came down on the pointed steel atop the fence, scratching several streaks of deep lacerations into its fur. The impact caused the dog to land neck-first on the ground.

Upon the Doberman's stiff landing, a thunderous *crack* erupted from its skeletal structure. The pup's fuzzy jaws offered a single, heart-wrenching whimper as the animal's drive was snuffed out.

The sight of the motionless dog sickened CJ. To know he was the force behind such violence was jarring. But, as Isaac's screams rip through the air, CJ knew he had no choice.

CJ saw himself at a disadvantage being shirtless. But he dashed back down from the slide, nonetheless. His body and mind raced. When he saw the other Doberman gnawing on Isaac's arm, his brain nearly went blank. The shirt idea was lucky enough, how on Earth would he deal with another one?

Isaac wailed. "Get it off me! Ahh! Get it off of me!"

As the hound clamped down ever harder, blood oozed from Isaac's arm. CJ took in his surroundings. There were no weapons to get the dog off the kid.

Suddenly, it hit him. He was standing on a potential solution that there was nearly an endless supply of.

Without thinking, he scooped up two big handfuls of sand. He crept up from behind the occupied Doberman and thrust the clumps directly into its eyeballs.

The dog mewled and CJ landed a stiff kick into its throat. The Doberman relinquished its grip on Isaac's arm and rubbed its face into the ground. The dog howled as it attempted to use its paws to clear the dirt from its eyes.

"Get up!" CJ screamed.

He slapped Isaac's back and lifted the wounded boy by his shirt.

The dog continued to moan, scratching at its face. The boys took advantage of the distraction, running off toward the rest of the other kids.

Isaac tripped again, but this time, CJ was there to keep him moving forward.

When the boys stumbled into the cube, Isaac dropped to the ground, blood squirting from the back of his arm.

"Everybody, get back!" CJ yelled.

His nerves were on fire, but he found a tiny ration of relief as he watched the retractable door descend. CJ stared at the blinded dog in the distance, hoping it wouldn't recover anytime soon. His limbs trembled uncontrollably as the last traces of daylight between the door and the ground disappeared.

BATTERED AND BADGERED

Geraldine's liver-spotted backhand slapped against Rock's wiry cheek. The roughness of his face hurt her thin skin, but it wasn't enough to deter her from cocking back and pelting him again.

"You fool! You worthless fucking excuse for a man! Now she won't be able to watch!" Geraldine barked.

"But she was going to—"

Another smack stunted Rock's statement.

Tom and Molly watched fearfully through their peripherals. Slouched against his wife's corpse, Greg remained in a daze.

"Look at you!" Geraldine barked at Rock. "You're a giant, you idiot! You could've easily corralled her! Christ almighty, must I think of *everything* for you?!"

The rage remained at a low rumble inside Rock but as he tried to swallow the lump in his throat, dread dominated him.

Geraldine kept him constantly shaken. Her toxic conduct was all he knew. Breaking ages of obedience was a difficult task. As much as Rock would've enjoyed giving Geraldine the same treatment as Caroline, there was a firm, submissive muscle memory in place. The conditioning that resulted from an endless cycle of abuse was a profound manipulator.

"I'm sorry," Rock said.

"I've heard it all before. The biggest problem with your sorrys is they always come in bunches and at my expense. And they're always at the most inopportune times. You're well aware of how much planning has gone into this, how special and dear this day is to me. I know your tiny mind isn't even of a mediocre standard, but I know you can understand this much. You've come up short twice now. Don't let there be a third time, or else…"

Rock nodded his head as the hot embarrassment and humiliation danced off his reddened face.

"Make sure nothing outside of our plans happens in here. Make sure they watch very closely, because you damn-well know I will," she threatened.

Geraldine pointed her bony finger up to the cameras fixed to the front corners of the spy room.

"I will," Rock replied.

Geraldine discreetly ground her dentures as she turned away from him and paused.

"I should be able to assume these basic things, but due to your recent performance, clearly my assumptions have been too generous. Have you disposed of the dogs already?"

"I disposed of the dead one and the other is back in the kennel."

"Get rid of them both! Neither lived up to expectations. Despite *your* presence, we don't shelter losers here. See to it this evening. Tell me you at least activated the electricity on the front gates?"

Rock nodded.

Geraldine exited the room, leaving Rock to wallow in his shame. He was suddenly alone with nothing but the quiet sobs of the restrained parents.

Tom and Molly were overrun with anxiety. They'd been forced to sit helplessly and witness their oldest child, Isaac, get mauled by a dog.

Pleading with Geraldine fell on deaf ears. She was wholly drawn to bloodshed. Tom and Molly had observed the wicked woman as she savored the video violence. She was a fattened parasite gorging on horror. Like a cigarette after sex, Geraldine had fallen in love. And now, that love was all she knew.

Tom understood he would have to be the one who pushed things along. Molly's spirit was too broken to accept such a burden. While Tom was also affected by the savage visuals, he forced himself to live in his head. As he analyzed their situation for potential avenues of escape, one thing had become overly clear to him: the pickings were slim.

Escape wasn't going to be possible outside of an act of God or mechanical malfunction. They were both essentially one and the same. The metal clamp around each of their necks wasn't going anywhere.

The only minuscule crack of hope that Tom believed could be a potentially viable option stood just a few yards away. The massive, chiseled specimen seemed different to him. Rock didn't seem passionate about what he was doing. He didn't seem filled with hate and bloodlust. He wasn't like the old witch. Tom could only pray to find the means to reason with him.

He looked over to Molly and was confronted by her hysterical sobbing. His wife's watery gaze begged for an answer. Tom didn't know what to say, but had to say something.

"Sir… those dogs hurt my son. He needs to see a doctor. Please, just let us go and… and we won't say anything. It'll be like we were never here. We just want our family back in one piece. I'm begging you," Tom pleaded.

Rock just stared at the gamut of TV screens.

"I don't understand. Whatever we did, we're sorry. Can't you just forgive us?"

Tom studied Rock's body language looking for any clues that might help. There were none. The uncomfortable silence soon became too much for Tom.

"What the fuck is even going on?!" Tom yelled.

Rock's jaded eyes found the concerned parent. "You'll find out soon enough."

PLAYGROUND RULES

The children had been sitting in the metallic cell for some time. The air had grown stale, and the mounting tension was thick enough to cut with a knife. Tears, terror, and frenzy were the only company they had.

CJ found a way to push his fears aside and focus on Isaac's wounds. He squatted down, arms wrapped around his shirtless torso, addressing him as gently as possible.

"I just need to take a look at it, dude. I know you don't want me to, but we need to see how bad it is," he explained.

Isaac sat slumped against the far wall of the cell. He was still in tears, trying to deal with the throbbing pain.

"I—I don't wanna look," Isaac cried.

"You don't have to. It's on the back of your arm anyhow, so you won't even see it. I'll be extra careful, okay?"

"O—Okay."

CJ lifted the back of Isaac's tee shirt sleeve up and examined the damage.

There were several deep indentations from the canine teeth that left a sizable tear in Isaac's skin. CJ was no doctor, but he figured having a look at it might give him an idea of how to best assist Isaac. As the blood continued to flow out of the rip, he knew he needed to find a way to stall it.

"Holy shit," Bobby said.

"Is it bad?!" Isaac screeched.

CJ turned around, glaring at his older brother.

"No, it's fine, Isaac. We just need to make some kind of bandage is all."

Rising up from the ground, CJ approached Bobby.

"I know what you're trying to do," CJ whispered.

"What?" Bobby asked.

"Do you not get how serious this is? Just stop messing with him. We have other stuff to worry about."

"Fuck him. I'm your brother, not that piece of shit."

CJ sighed. "Sometimes, I wish that wasn't the case."

"Get bent."

"Ahh, ugh! It hurts so bad!" Isaac cried.

Isaac continued to groan, holding his arm, and staring at his sisters. He could see their profound terror as they stood sobbing in each other's arms on the other side of the cell.

CJ was done squabbling with his brother. He refocused and moved on to the more pressing issue. Getting through to Bobby was a lost cause; he'd known that much since the day he was born.

He turned to his youngest brother.

Kip stood by idly after watching Bobby and CJ bicker with each other. He seemed on the fence over whom he should side with in the argument.

CJ examined Kip's clothing and noticed the unbuttoned, casual collared shirt and particularly the white tee that was underneath.

"Kip, I need your undershirt," CJ said.

"What? Why?" Kip asked.

Bobby rolled his eyes and huffed.

"Isaac is still bleeding. We need to tie something around his wound. Like they showed us in that first aid class. You remember?"

"Can't you just use *his* shirt?"

CJ took a step closer to him until their noses almost touched.

"Look, this is how it's gonna go," CJ said, "and this goes for both of you. From here on out, I'm calling the shots. If either of you got a problem with that, we can figure it out right now."

Kip looked at Bobby, who would not hold his tongue.

"I'm the oldest! I should get to make the decisions!"

"Yeah!" Kip said.

"Yeah, tough shit, that's two out of three!" Bobby yelled.

"No, it's not," Tanya interjected.

She'd been following the conversation closely. Tanya wasn't about to let her nerves control her. Like everyone else, she had no idea what was going on but understood a level-headed approach was critical.

While Tanya was young, she was still mature enough to realize that Bobby and Kip were clones of her father. Even if they weren't the clones that her dad would've hoped for, their personalities had been set in stone.

They weren't bad to the bone, but she'd seen all her old man's worst traits in them at one time or another. Sure, her father had some nice specs within his pushy personality, but he was shackled to his own selfishness and operated in a narrow-minded fashion. She would not be comfortable with anyone but CJ leading them.

"I vote CJ. He's the fairest," Tanya said.

"He's Dad's little fucking pet," Bobby snarled.

"Exactly, and that's the tiebreaker. You know yourself that Dad would pick him for this, not you, and definitely not Kip."

"We want CJ too," Sadie announced, still holding her sister Sam in her trembling arms.

Donnie stood beside the girls but kept his silence. No one was certain if he even understood the conversation. His blankness was all-encompassing.

"I guess that settles that," CJ said.

The red rose to the surface of Bobby's entire face.

"Like hell it does!" Bobby barked.

CJ stepped up as close to Bobby as he could get.

"I don't think you get it. I'm not asking you. I was never asking you. I'm *telling* you. We can fight for it if we have to, but you know how that always ends. I'll whip both your asses if I have to."

CJ's hand pressed against his knuckles and let out a sickening crack. He never bullied either of his brothers before, but they'd had their share of sibling rivalries. Their current situation called for the callous and uncomfortable measures braising in his brain.

CJ hated bullies.

He hated how Bobby acted and the pieces of his persona he saw rubbing off on Kip. It was like an infection of idiocy that was spreading out of control. But he didn't have time to pull out the Crayola and explain to them why they were wrong. He knew asserting his physical dominance and threatening them into compliance would be the only timely method.

Neither Bobby nor Kip found the gall to challenge him.

"Okay," CJ said, turning back to Kip. "We don't have any more time to waste. So, you're gonna either give me your fucking shirt right now," CJ rammed his finger into his sternum, "or, I'm gonna take it."

Bobby's face was seething with anger, a mega-load he had no way of exorcising.

Kip obeyed. Peeling off his shirts, he handed his brother the white tee, then slipped the collared shirt back over his shoulders.

"Thank you," CJ said.

He stretched the tee shirt, knelt beside Isaac, and reexamined the wound.

"This might just hurt for a second, but we've gotta cover up the wound, okay?"

"It already hurts," Isaac said.

He cringed in pain but nodded, giving CJ the go-ahead.

CJ looped the white shirt around the gash and carefully increased the tension. Isaac emitted an exhale of agony as the knot CJ fashioned applied additional pressure.

"Almost there—"

"It's gonna be okay, Isaac," Sadie said.

Just as CJ finished tying off the wound, the metal box elevated. Uncomfortable cries and howls of terror erupted from the nervous children.

No one was itching to find out what came next.

Isaac's chest thrashed with increasing intensity for each increment the steel cube climbed. He recalled that the big slide was all the way up in the trees, so it didn't surprise him when the cell continued to ascend higher.

And higher.

And higher.

When it finally screeched to a halt, the doors at the front of the box retracted, revealing a small lip before the tube slide began. The face of the slide and tube chute was constructed from ominous ebony plastic. The thick piping took a steep decline into the darkness that none of the sunlight outside was powerful enough to penetrate.

Isaac held his arm. The compression around the afflicted area felt comforting but panic still stirred inside him. All things considered, CJ had done a damn good job with the bandage. But fresh distress dawned in his mind. He remembered where the slide went.

The unnerving image of the enormous human hose dropping below the beach sand was strange enough to stick in his head.

"What the heck is this?" CJ asked.

He moved closer to the lone sign posted on the wall beside the entrance to the slide.

The heading read: PLAYGROUND RULES.

"What do you think it means?" Sadie asked.

Tanya stepped up beside her brother and squinted at the font below the heading. She read the small paragraph aloud.

"After your ride don't stand too tall, don't look too hard, don't look at all. If you want to move on after you fall, just use your ears and have a ball."

The words made little sense to Tanya.

"Any ideas?" CJ asked.

Tanya shook her head.

"It sounds like some kind of riddle," she said.

"*When you fall…* I don't like the sound of that," Isaac interjected. "I don't know if anyone else saw, but this slide, it goes into the ground."

Out of the blue, the wall behind them rumbled. The shrill hiss of steam released flooding the cell, making it much harder for the children to hear each other. The cold, metal wall crept forward, nudging them all toward the slide's black hole.

Inch by inch their claustrophobia increased; time was running out.

"Noooo!" Sam cried.

"What are we gonna do?!" Tanya screamed.

The room was changing rapidly; it was three-quarters of the size it had been when they entered it.

"I guess we have to go!" CJ replied.

He pointed at the unsettling hole ahead.

"But we—we don't know what's down there!" Kip cried.

"We know what's up here though! We're dead if we stay!" CJ said.

"So, who's first?!" Sam asked.

Warm tears trickled down her cheeks.

"It doesn't matter, we've all gotta go!"

The room was now reduced to half its initial size.

"Go! Go! Go!" CJ yelled.

CJ ushered the kids into the slide.

As the first five pushed off into the unknown abyss, the same horrifying grimace found each of their faces. Sam was brave enough to go first, and Sadie shadowed behind her. Tanya was the next to take the plunge, followed by Bobby and Kip.

CJ looked at Donnie. His emotionless face left everything to the imagination.

"C'mon, buddy! It'll be alright!" he yelled, guiding him up to the slide.

After Donnie disappeared into the cylinder of darkness, Isaac forced his way to his feet and set himself up. He looked back toward CJ.

"Thanks for saving me from the dog!" he yelled.

The sound of the steam was almost deafening.

"Don't thank me yet! You can thank me if we get out of here!" CJ replied.

"*When* we get out of here, you mean *when*—"

CJ pushed him forward. The wall had gotten a little closer than he was comfortable with. While he appreciated Isaac's gesture of gratitude, it would have to wait.

With little breathing room remaining, CJ kicked his feet forward and slid away from the pursuing doom.

Or so he thought.

CONTROL ROOM

"Wonderful, the design worked just as you predicted," Geraldine said, beaming.

"Zhe blueprints were drawn with only success in mind," Fuchs replied.

"I knew you wouldn't fail me again, not after all I've invested." Her vocal inflection grew more serious, and the euphoria waned.

A flurry of memories trickled into her head. She thought of the winding path that had brought their twisted minds together. It was in 1977, when she was forty-eight-years-old. An aging woman with little time left to figure out how to craft her legacy.

The idea had manifested shortly after her mother's demise. She was to find a man—any man—to plant a seed inside her. Once she secured the seed, she no longer required the donor. She craved a child in her likeness, just like she'd seen frolicking in the playground that beautiful day from the bench. The child would allow her purpose again. The flesh of her creation would mirror her image and not only continue to control the Borden fortune and legacy, but more importantly, serve as an endless outlet of elation for her perverse narcissism.

While Geraldine's unhealthy infatuation controlled her, the limitations had left her sexual demons salivating for more. Having another glowing replica to stare back at her, mimicking each expression, would surely eliminate the stagnancy that clung to her.

For the longest time, masturbation had been the only answer she could find, but her mindless self-indulgence could only take her so far. Her initial plan wasn't ideal, but it was viable and simple. The chore of being with men she had zero attraction wasn't enjoyable but was a necessary discomfort.

She targeted young men with strong intellects whom she suspected to possess vivacious sperm. Even the most brilliant minds in her social circumference bowed to her when enough money and prestige were at play. But as the weeks of perversion turned into months, and the count piled up, Geraldine grew concerned. Maybe a handful of the men she'd run through could've been duds, but *all* of them?

She had no choice but to consider the problem might lie within. A visit to her clinician would eventually confirm her suspicions. The harsh truth gave birth to Geraldine's new nightmare; she was infertile.

Unable to create a potential partner to exile her sexual burden, the weight of her lust became unignorable.

"Zhere seems to be some issues with zhe camera in Room 1."

Fuchs' update shattered her remembrances.

"Just get it working," Geraldine demanded.

"Of course, my lady," Fuchs replied.

He tapped at the various keys on the control panel and computer keyboard in front of him.

When Geraldine's glare fell back upon the disturbed engineer's haggard face, she recalled the connection.

After escaping Hamburg, Germany in April of 1945, just a week before Allied forces bombed the state into oblivion, Adolpho Fuchs found himself on the run. His struggle to evade and survive was no novice pilgrimage.

As a Nazi scientist, they had molded him into an asset for an evil that knew no bounds. Dabbling in taboo and inhumane experiments was his forte. Fuchs was a man of macabre brilliance, but for all his varying attributes, it was his range that might've been the most impressive.

His trials involved a wide variety of fields, ranging from mechanical engineering, to programming, and the initial reason that Geraldine had gravitated toward him— medicine. His expertise in his homeland's sinister affairs had made him something of a known commodity. A man with knowledge that, in the eyes of the Americans, was priceless. His war crimes, while not known by name to the larger public, were the stuff of legend within the espionage and government intelligence circles.

Fuchs' unique understanding of biology led to the farm-raising of soulless tissues within the walls of his lab of horrors. The fetuses were of a Frankenstein nature, but the results were perfect for what he'd envisioned: a race of pureblood, obedient super soldiers.

He artificially magnified their muscles, numbed their pain, and bonded their flesh with robotics. He fathered a glorious and frightening new hybrid species. The prototypes hadn't turned out perfect, but they were promising. In his blackened heart he still believed that if his funding had been increased, the additional finances would've seen his spawns find the battlefield in mass and thus propelled the Nazis toward a more favorable, alternate outcome in history.

Fuchs also contributed to the construction and renovation of several concentration camps in the early 40s. Using his mechanical and engineering background, his heinous blueprints came to light, and countless souls perished due to his atrocious ingenuity.

Along with the several camp proposals Fuchs had seen accepted, were many others that didn't see the light of day. The feedback from officials highlighted that his designs weren't focused enough on making the exterminations quick or easy to apply to a mass population.

Some were considered too involved.

Some were considered too messy.

Others were considered too extreme, even for the Nazi regime.

The insidious inventor remained at large for years before the Americans eventually caught up with him. Once the war concluded, Fuchs, along with approximately sixteen hundred other German scientists, was finally captured. His murderous track record should've punched his ticket to the beyond, but United States leadership thought otherwise. They decided, despite the nefarious nature of the knowledge Fuchs and his counterparts collected, it was too valuable to be lost. Such a gleaming advantage couldn't be squandered. After the indecent proposal, a hushed private pardon was granted to hundreds of war criminals.

As a result, Fuchs became part of a black project that remained in the dark for decades. Instead of being put to death, or left to rot in a cell, Operation Paperclip was born. The program harvested criminal intellect and positioned the scientists to use their past data to advance American technology and many other fields.

As Geraldine continued to study the marvel of malice that pecked at the keyboard beside her, she felt fortunate. Only in the exclusive community of personalities that had procured such bottomless wealth could she have learned of Fuchs. She'd grown exhausted and defeated during her search for a solution, but it seemed society had destined to connect their paths.

The dinner party where Geraldine first encountered Fuchs was like any in her circle, full of aristocrat chatter and braggadocios grandstanding. It was a chance meeting. If not but for the grace of alcohol, humanity's purest social lubrication, the pieces might not have fallen into place.

Martin Pearl was a wealthy, talkative, and overly jittery acquaintance of Geraldine's. But it wasn't until Mr. Pearl pulled her to the side for an exchange of gossip that she realized the potential that stood inside the room with her.

A brash blow-hard, Martin was an attention whore, and always on the lookout for his next fix. A politically inclined man of many words for many reasons. Reasons that were always self-serving to his overstated ego.

Geraldine liked to listen to the man not because of his unpolished personality, but talking with Mr. Pearl was like watching a train wreck. Seeing as he'd already dumped a few cocktails into his tank, she was excited for the fireworks.

He often enjoyed sharing things he shouldn't and defending controversial positions. Mr. Pearl offered Geraldine a few nuggets about the old German that, among ears with a more patriotic perking, would've surely ruffled some feathers. He not only expounded upon the long list of horrors Fuchs had been associated with, but also justified them. He rattled on about Fuchs' success with the space program on American soil, and how it was really the Nazis that landed on the moon.

Geraldine looked at Fuchs' wrinkly face. The German had certainly accumulated a few more lines of definition since the evening they met. It had been some time, but still, as Geraldine recalled the gathering, it all felt like just yesterday.

Mr. Pearl continued with their conversation, drink in hand, flaunting his vast knowledge of the inner workings of war and politics. But after his revelations about Fuchs, nothing else he said seemed to hold the same punch. Even as Mr. Pearl shared dangerous claims that could've seen him suicided in a shitty motel room, Geraldine couldn't peel her eyes away from the Nazi.

Despite the sensitive and salacious nature of the claims Mr. Pearl spewed without filter, the squeaky wheels in Geraldine's brain turned in a different direction. On any other night, she would've been over the moon with the direction of their conversation, but this wasn't any other night any longer. Geraldine had reached a tipping point; her mind had been blown wide open. She wouldn't be able to think again until she addressed her prospect.

While Geraldine couldn't have cared less about the man's opinions, acquiring the knowledge of Fuchs' vast array of capabilities did more than intrigue her. The stories of his groundbreaking work with flesh in his experiments served to push a breath of life back into a potential endgame that Geraldine believed to be dead.

By the time their gathering ended, she knew that an assembly of a more private nature, just her and Fuchs, was immediately in order.

The meeting was short and simple; she bought him out.

When Fuchs took the deal, he disappeared from the government's radar entirely. It would've been a dangerous move had Geraldine not been so privatized and wealthy. She gifted Fuchs anything he desired within the walls of her castle. The option of living like a king in solace was too tempting for the Nazi to turn down.

She'd given him a once-in-a-lifetime opportunity. One that allowed him to disappear and lead a simple, anonymous life in private housing, with luxurious accommodations. One that offered a delicious diet, infinite resources, and freedom as far as the eye could see.

The only problem was, Fuchs couldn't deliver on the miracle Geraldine bargained on. Even with the countless years of unethical research, coupled with Fuchs' foreign experimental techniques, Geraldine's weathered, brittle body remained barren.

Geraldine continued to stare a hole through the sweaty SS descendent working feverishly to correct the camera issue. The memories were still infuriating.

While her biology remained a puzzle that Fuchs had never been able to put together, Geraldine didn't allow the resulting rage to control her. The draining disappointment fostered gloom, but as years of failure flashed forward, the bitter taste in Geraldine's mouth transitioned.

Fuchs continued to experiment with her fertility, but she wasn't betting on a breakthrough. Instead, she was thinking about the other attributes that Fuchs had to offer. Geraldine would need to reap something from her investment, even if it wasn't what she'd initially planned.

It wasn't until Geraldine found herself back at her childhood playground watching the children frolic with their parents that it finally dawned on her—the peasants that arrived and left with their futures in control and in hand, didn't even deserve the standard option of genetic replication that Geraldine had been stripped of. There was a gross misbalance in society, and it needed to be corrected. The time had arrived for her to put Fuchs' other talents to use. To create equality that was long overdue. The children shouldn't find joy in the playground; they should find their destruction.

In shifting the old man's focus, the obscene relationship they had didn't seem like such a waste anymore. Geraldine's investment would no longer be without fruits.

Even once Rock was added to their evil equation, and Geraldine was greeted with an even deeper, permanent disappointment, she could take comfort in knowing that Fuchs was driving her toward an epic release of wrath.

Geraldine recalled the evil epiphany with a grin.

She felt the same calm wash over her as it had initially. The tantalizing thought of the parents confined to the spy room. The idea they'd soon be forced to watch their precious spawns find the violent finality that they deserved internally tickled her.

"Ah! Zhere we go! Got it!" Fuchs bellowed out.

The camera feed on the screen activated.

"Marvelous! And that means that the video is visible to the parents as well, correct?"

Fuchs smiled and removed his hand from the knob in front of him. He used his overgrown fingernail to tap against the glass on the other monitor beside the one he'd debugged. On the screen, they could see the faces of the seated parents contort with horror and agony.

He looked away from the ghastly expressions of the guardians on the monitor, then back to Geraldine.

Her smile stretched just as far as his.

HAVE A BALL

As CJ made his way down the slide, it didn't take long for him to realize that something was wrong. What should've been a trail of smooth plastic underneath began to feel warm and wet. As the drop continued, hot lines of stinging pain periodically found CJ's legs and backside.

"Ow!" he cried.

The pain only intensified when the slide's trajectory morphed, curling his body down a steeper slope. The harsh cutting sensation stretching from his calves to his lower back grew deeper and deeper as the angle became more exaggerated.

"Ahhhhhhhhh!"

The slide seemed endless. CJ couldn't be certain that his brain was calculating the seconds correctly. There was a strong possibility the trauma had decelerated his capacity to perceive how time was passing.

Of equal concern was the mental mystery. He wasn't sure of the origin of his pain. It wasn't until he caught a hint of glimmering steel whizzing by that it became clear. The occasional twinkles of metal flying by coincided with the rhythm of his hurt because the slide had razor blades embedded in the plastic.

Just as he figured out the source of his anguish, he saw the horseshoe of barbwire. Draped across the top of the tube, the cruel, prickly curve drew closer. Fear meddled inside his torso as CJ calculated the best means of avoiding the fast-approaching horror.

The slide's curve decreased in steepness as he drew closer to the barbwire and the light beyond it. CJ stiffened his body against the plastic and dodged the barbs by mere inches as he made his way into the brightness.

When CJ spilled out onto the floor, he was serenaded with the familiar blend of screams from both his immediate family and the other children.

The landing was painful. Before CJ could even register his surroundings, he felt them.

The pain pushed through his skin and deep into his bones. It wasn't so much the hardwood floor that hurt, as it was whatever it was covered with. He heard what sounded like countless balls rolling on the ground and turned to take in the sight.

The room looked about the size of a gymnasium. The countless aching points that crashed into his body upon landing became obvious.

The entire floor was covered with marbles.

Under a laxer set of circumstances, CJ might've considered the sight beautiful. There were more colors and sizes than he could count. As the scattering swirls of vibrance and variety rolled around on the floor, their beauty overloaded his optics.

The room had several stone pillars ahead and a sizable ball pit. A pink neon sign reading 'EXIT' hung at the other end of the space.

CJ looked left to right at his surroundings. A thick steel fencing contained them and ran all the way up to the roof. Behind it was weathered stone walls that looked similar to those comprising the exterior of The Borden Estate. The space was essentially an oblong cage confined to an even larger stone coffin.

Cries compelled CJ to focus. No one's flesh had been spared on the ride down. Everyone's clothing was sliced through and blood secreted from the lengthy lacerations carved beneath. The columns of unforgiving cuts varied in size and placement, but the violence was consistent across the board.

The children looked like a platoon of grizzled veterans fresh out of battle.

Bobby was probably in the worst shape. The flesh on his forearms had been carved up considerably. There were a few sheet-like flaps of skin that dangled from each of his mangled limbs.

Being that Bobby was the oldest and far larger than everyone else, he couldn't dodge the barbwire cluster at the end of the tube. The other children were all compact enough to avoid the brunt of it.

Suddenly, CJ shifted his focus away from his big brother. The chorus of panic-stricken cries from the group was overwhelming him. Everyone was frightened, and even CJ had much anxiety of his own.

He'd volunteered himself to somehow lead the children through the horizon of hell, but now, such a task seemed impossible. That didn't deter him from the duty, but his confidence secretly plummeted.

CJ forced his racing mind to slow. If he was going to be any help, he had to keep his shit together. But with everyone crying, it seemed like it would be a lot easier just to break down along with them.

Then, CJ noticed something that he hadn't initially: not *everyone* was crying.

He didn't even know Donnie's name, but that didn't stop him from being astonished. To see the child who appeared to be the youngest of them all, somehow strong enough to hold in his pain gave CJ hope.

If CJ had hope, then they all had hope.

Gotta get it together. Gotta get up, CJ thought.

He groaned as he returned to his feet.

"Hey, you guys, stop screaming!" CJ yelled.

He tried to avoid the countless marbles. At the same time, he heard a cluster of loud, popping noises erupt from the opposite end of the room.

By the time CJ got his head around, he nearly got drilled. The white dot coming at him was a blur. It closed in, zooming right by his ear.

"Holy crap! Everybody, stay down!" he said.

CJ immediately ducked just fast enough to avoid the next pop that followed up behind the first.

The objects being launched crashed into the chain-link fencing behind them. The circular white balls dropped to the ground and rolled into various bunches of multicolored marbles.

"What—What is that?" Sadie asked.

CJ examined the projectiles. It was fairly obvious what they were. The objects were a big part of his life. The bone white cowhide held together by the red stitching was unmistakable.

"It's a baseball," CJ replied.

The balls kept shooting, flying overhead, it wasn't just one at a time either. The onslaughts were coming five at a time in mini waves that covered the width of the room. Standing wouldn't be a smart move if they planned on avoiding more agony or advancing forward.

CJ turned away from the barrage of balls and back to where they'd piled up. Even the chaos attempting to suffocate him became background fodder. Something else was clouding his mind. When CJ fixed his eyes on the heap, he didn't just see a bunch of baseballs—he saw his life.

His life according to Greg, anyway.

It was a life that felt more alien to him with each day he awoke. A life that he was beginning to realize wasn't really his at all. He knew his father was a die-hard competitor, but he wasn't. To CJ, every moment of his existence was not some play school pissing contest.

Sure, he was good at baseball and harnessed raw talent,

but playing didn't make him feel fulfilled or excited in the same way it did for his father. There was still an empty void aching inside him for something *he* wanted. He might not have known what that passion was, but he certainly knew what it wasn't.

Furthermore, CJ was okay with not knowing yet. But putting in the tedious work to accomplish someone else's dream was running him ragged. His father's vicarious living and voyeuristic tendencies had drained him. He was tired of being a project instead of just being a son.

This extraordinary turn of events fostered an undeniable evolution within CJ; baseball was dead. If he found a means to make it past the unknown trials that awaited him, CJ was going to live for himself. No more pressure, no more lies, no more judgment, no matter what the cost.

The game was over.

Playing out the liberating fantasy in his head helped CJ cope with the crude reality facing them. He snapped back into survival mode—thoughts were once again racing along a mile a minute.

Everyone else, save for Donnie, was sobbing hysterically and examining their injuries. The horror was deafening. The environment made it difficult for CJ to settle on an idea, but finally, something came to him.

CJ scanned the damaged group until he spotted Tanya. He quickly dragged himself over to his sister's side.

"Tanya! Before we went down the slide, what did the sign say again? Something about *don't stand too tall*, wasn't it?" CJ asked.

"I've—I've got cuts all over," she cried.

"I know, I know," CJ said, cautiously sliding his arm around his sister. "Just turn a little bit, but stay low."

CJ examined his sister's legs and thighs. The cuts were nasty, but not life-threatening. It was as if the razors were implanted to do just enough to create panic.

He looked up from the slices at Tanya's gawk of terror. CJ grabbed her gently by the shoulders and looked into her eyes. He hoped his cool and collected vibe might rub off.

"I know that you're scared. I'm scared too. But I promise you the cuts aren't that bad."

"But—But there's so much blood."

"Yes, but that's *everyone's* blood, it's not all yours. You're gonna be okay. I've gotta try to get us out of here, but I can't do it without you. I need you, Sis."

Tanya let his words resonate inside. He always had a knack for making her feel better.

"You trust me, right?" CJ asked.

She nodded her head, wiping the tears out of her eyes.

"Good. I think that sign—those rules might've been some kind of hint. It had to mean something."

"I—I don't remember them though," she sniffled.

CJ could see his sister was still panicked. There was an uncommon frustration in her tone.

"Just try to relax. Now think for a second. Just try to picture the letters on the sign," he whispered softly.

"I think I might remember the end."

"That's good! I knew you could do it!"

"To find and exit when you fall, just use your ears and have a ball."

"Ears?" CJ paused for a moment. "I don't hear anything over here, do you? Except for those baseball machines."

Tanya looked around and listened. "Me either, but they're pretty loud. Maybe we'd hear something different down that way?"

CJ looked at the neon pink exit sign that glowed eerily in the direction his sister was pointing. He nodded his head and turned to the rest of the crying kids beside them.

"I guess there's only one way to find out."

THE MENTAL WAR

"Please! They're bleeding so much. They need help. How can you just stand by and watch!" Tom cried.

The large screen on the wall portrayed both Tom and Molly's worst nightmare: all three of their kids in anguish. The pool of blood surrounding the children grew as the red continued to drizzle down the tube slide in the background.

Rock remained stoic, staring at the dark drama as it unfolded. There was no answer forming inside his oversized head, but his eyes sat fixed on Donnie.

He was all stained up again. This time with a far greater amount of his own blood than before. Still, the boy remained every bit as stone-faced as the massive man studying him.

Rock reached into the pocket of his jacket and played with the submissive instrument he'd detached from Donnie earlier. It calmed him when he felt the touch of the gore-caked leash. He didn't understand what compelled him to keep it. He just couldn't bear to part with it.

Molly couldn't hold her tongue for another minute. She remained at the mercy of the television, but amid the anguish, she'd noticed exactly what Tom had—a gap between the twisted people that had orchestrated this event.

143

"You don't wanna do this! I can see it in your eyes! You know she's wrong!" Molly yelled.

Rock glared at Molly in the screen's reflection.

"You know she's sick! For Christ's sake, she treats you like a dog! You don't have to be like her—"

"Quiet!" Rock roared.

The same fingers that had just been toying with Donnie's leash so gingerly, suddenly applied a death grip.

She'd struck a nerve. The big fella, to that point, had been calm and collected. Enough so that they'd been able to communicate with him several times. When the talk wasn't about him specifically, no one had garnered a reaction. But with Molly mentioning him directly, there was a sudden, radical shift in his demeanor.

"I'm sorry—"

Tom elbowed his wife. The massive man seemed angry. He figured it was best for Molly to obey Rock's command and keep quiet, at least until the tension eased up.

Rock grunted, perturbed by her apology.

"You don't know what sorry is."

PUSHING FORWARD

"Hey, what's your name, buddy?" CJ asked.

Donnie still looked like his consciousness was in limbo.

"I don't think he talks," Sam yelled over the roar of the pitching machines.

"Do you know if he can understand us?"

"I'm not sure. I—I think so."

CJ faced Donnie with a deathly serious demeanor.

"When we go that way," CJ motioned toward the baseball machines, "you've gotta stay down, okay?"

Donnie gave no indicator that he understood.

"I'll stay with him," Isaac interjected.

He grunted, still trying to manage the pain.

"Besides," Isaac continued, "I think he might be short enough that the balls would miss him even if he was standing up."

Isaac grimaced holding tight onto the makeshift bandage that CJ had applied to him. He used his free hand to grab hold of Donnie.

CJ couldn't help but notice the extreme discomfort that Isaac was enduring.

"Okay. Are you good, dude?" he asked.

"Yeah, I think I'm okay. Just hurts like heck."

CJ glanced away from the collective toward the steady and swift hail of baseballs. The fear he'd seen in their eyes rattled him to the core, but he couldn't show any cracks. If he broke, then they'd all fall apart.

"Alright, go slow and try to stay as low as you can," CJ instructed.

"But my—my fucking arms are all torn up," Bobby cried.

CJ looked at the wounds. The bright red was flowing generously from the thick gashes. His younger brother Kip was crouched down beside him as white as a ghost. They both looked so lost. Their horrified behavior begged for CJ's guidance.

"We've gotta get out of dodge first. Then we'll get those cuts covered up, like we did for Isaac's, okay?"

Bobby nodded, snot bubbling out from his nose. The fighting spirit had left him. Following orders seemed much easier than giving them.

"Let's go!" CJ yelled.

The group of torn-up tweens and teens left a long and slick trail of hot crimson as the collective bloodstain migrated through the marbles.

As CJ dragged his leaky limbs over the hardwood flooring, the glass balls rolled forward. Midway through he looked back to check on the others.

Isaac kept young Donnie low and guided him along close to Sam and Sadie. Tanya and his brothers crawled along carefully behind them.

"We're almost there!" CJ reassured them.

Upon inching closer to the final pillar, CJ could see the space that would allow them to get around the corner and clear of the endless assault of line drives.

As they approached the neon exit sign beside the ball pit, the long trail of blood that was their ghastly imprint of progress finally diverted around the last pillar.

"What's that noise?" Isaac asked, still holding tight to Donnie's hand.

The struggling gasps of what sounded like a man gagging and choking were more than noticeable. The audio wasn't excessively loud, but it was enough for them to hear the consistent struggle over the ball machines.

The children all looked in the direction that the macabre wheezing was coming from—the ball pit.

Upon closer inspection, the depraved elements of the area were made evident. The pit wasn't massive but maybe half the size of an average McDonald's Play Place. The simple, square space was filled with a variety of balls inside. Much like the marbles, they accounted for every color their eyes could register.

A pedestal stood in the center of the pit with a set of narrow, circular platforms, barely offering enough room to hold two feet inside them. The act of ascending these intentionally tricky steps would require a nimble poise.

In the center of the pedestal above, a 'man' hung from a fraying rope. The dummy looked to be comprised of a stuffed animal type of material, his limp feet dangling just above the center platform.

The orange sphere representing the figure's head was made of soft rubber. The old dodgeball showed signs of deterioration in addition to a jigsaw line of stitching that ran down the side. An unsettling grimace was painted below two large X markings that represented the creepy figure's dead eyes. Continuing the cartoonish depiction, a big floppy tongue leaked out of the mouth slit.

A pointy, birthday party hat sat affixed to the tilted head. The tip of the hat was angled up at a boxy speaker in the corner, revealing the source of the gruesomely realistic sounds of strangulation. In the figure's stuffing-filled hand sat an eight-inch retractable hunting knife and twine that had been spun around the blade to hold it in place.

"What the heck is this?" CJ asked.

"It's hangman," Tanya replied, looking beyond the floppy figure that hung in the center.

"She's right," Isaac concurred.

Covering the entire back wall of the ball pit, behind the creepy hanging man, hung a giant schoolhouse chalkboard. The green material had the etchings of a game many of the children had played in the past: hangman.

The depiction of the hanging man on the chalkboard displayed a full-body outline, just like the real-life version in front of them. There were several words beside the man that only had certain letters revealed.

Since there was no curator to ask how to play, it could only be assumed that the game was already over. Whatever letters had been revealed would be all that they had to work with. The puzzle read:

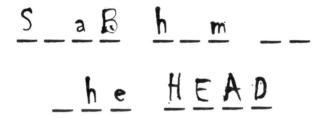

"Use your ears…" CJ mumbled, turning toward his sister. "These choking noises, they must be what that riddle was talking about, right?"

"I—I don't like him. He's really scary," Sam said.

The frightened girl's eyes started to water again. The events had become too much. Sam felt stress that was foreign. She just wanted to get away from everything. Something about the creepy, hanging man was too much for her to handle. She couldn't look at him, talk about him, or think about him.

"We should just get away from him," she cried.

Sam shut her eyes as Sadie wrapped her arm around her.

"It's gonna be okay, Sam. We'll figure it out," Isaac said, with a tremble in his tone.

"Just try to stay calm. We're only gonna figure out what to do if we work together," CJ replied.

"I don't wanna help! I can't!" Sam cried.

"But the puzzle might have something to do with—"

Before Isaac could finish his sentence, Sam broke free from her sister's loving hug.

"Sam, wait!" Sadie yelled.

"Don't go!" Isaac screamed.

Sam didn't respond, her glossy eyes were already fixed on the exit sign above the wide corridor. She could see a door at the far end of it. The path seemed much more attractive than the one being debated amongst the children. Anything was better to Sam than facing the hanging man for another second.

"I wanna see Mom and Dad," Sam wailed.

In her head, the entire playground was just a sick joke. Mom and Dad would both be standing behind the door at the end of the tunnel, waiting with open arms.

"You shouldn't go alone!" Sadie yelled.

She wanted to follow her sister, but Sadie's own fear of well-being paralyzed her.

"The door's this way!" Sam said.

She trotted under the hot pink exit sign and entered the dark tunnel. Suddenly, a dimmer, traditional exit sign triggered at the far end of the passageway. The faint flicker of the red lettering illuminated, further pronouncing the metal door she had in her sights.

"There's a way out down here," Sam said.

Sam had never been afraid of the dark, on the contrary, she always found comfort during the evening. Within the shadowy space, her dread of the hangman powered her.

CJ looked to Isaac and Sadie for council.

Sadie wasn't eager to retrieve her sister, but she knew she might be the only one capable of calming her down. Against her instincts, she decided to volunteer herself.

"I'll get her," she said.

Breaking through her initial reluctance, Sadie bravely tailed her sister down the dark corridor of uncertainty.

"Sam, slow down! I'm coming!" Sadie pleaded.

Sam looked back at her sister, who was quickly closing the gap between them. She ignored Sadie's request and continued on.

Sadie was several yards away from her sister when the odd noise occurred. She watched Sam step into the dirt as the sharp clicking sound echoed. The fiery explosion that ensued rattled the entire tunnel.

The blast was powerful enough to send Sadie tumbling to the floor. The shock of the detonation left her wrapped in a cloud of disorientation. She did her best to shake off the cobwebs and squinted through the thick smoke in the direction she'd last seen Sam.

Panic suffocated Sam. The drippy crimson residue caked on her blood-splattered cheeks crudely complimented the horror of the situation.

Nasty burns dotted her once smooth flesh, scorching through various layers of her skin. One of her legs had been blown off just below the knee. The detached limb was morbidly garnished with a pointy bone that splintered out of the slick nub. The muddle of shredded meat still clinging to the mangled calf lay forlorn on the ground.

Cries ripped out of Sadie's throat, and the echoes of agony reverberated. She stared into her sister's stunned pupils then at her own hands and legs, trying to ensure that she remained with her factory settings intact.

"Sam!" she yelled.

"What happened?" Isaac bellowed.

Sam remained silent, stupefied by the horror.

Despite her screams, Sadie picked up on another clicking noise, growing louder by the second. It sounded different from the one that led to the explosion. With the smoke still fuming in her face, she couldn't quite figure out what it was.

All the children outside of the corridor gathered at the far end of it. To their dismay, the outside perspective gave them the information that Sadie currently lacked.

Isaac yelled. "You guys have to get out of there—now! The ceiling's coming down! Ruuuuuuuun!"

The dread soaked into his skull as he watched the structure slowly descend on his sisters.

Wails echoed, steadily bouncing off the walls within the smoke and darkness.

Isaac turned to CJ. "I've gotta get them!"

CJ shook his head, but as Isaac's feet pedaled forward, he realized he was more compelled to listen to his heart than his head.

"Oh, God!" Isaac screamed.

As he penetrated the smoke, Isaac couldn't help but feel like he'd made a mistake.

Tears bled over Sadie's eyelids as she tugged Sam's mangled body along. She was grateful to see Isaac arrive since each attempt only accounted for inches.

Upon seeing his sister's mutilated leg leaking copious amounts of blood, Isaac froze.

"Hey! Snap out of it! We gotta go!" cried a voice beyond the smoke.

CJ cut through the fog with urgency.

He still felt dizzy and nauseous from the gruesome sight, but as Isaac felt the vomit crawling up the back of his throat, he battled it.

CJ took the lead and approached Sadie.

"We'll get her outta here, you've gotta get moving!"

Taking control of Sam's limp wrist, CJ pulled.

"Isaac, grab her other arm!"

Isaac's cheeks puffed out like he was about to lose his lunch. Struggling with the partially processed food, he swallowed hard. He knew there wasn't enough time to be sick *and* survive; it was one or the other.

The two boys tugged Isaac's dazed sister down the increasingly claustrophobic path. But just as they hit their stride, the pace of the plunging ceiling quickened. As they closed in on the clearing, the boys hunched down. While neither Isaac nor CJ would've openly admitted it, the selfish thought of dropping Sam and running crossed their minds.

"I don't know if we're gonna make it!" CJ said.

Isaac tried to focus despite each step becoming more difficult than the last. Every second was of paramount importance and held a grave responsibility.

But as they came to the last few paces, Isaac's worst fears came to fruition. He'd taken the awkward step he'd been trying to avoid.

His foot rolled sideways and sent him tumbling to the ground. His scrambling body landed in the dirt just a few yards from safety.

"Isaac!" Sadie screamed.

She wondered if it might be the last time she saw her big brother. The countless instances of her picking on him and calling him mean names all slapped her in the face at once. Sadie was too young to realize that life was so short, but the hard lesson arrived early.

CJ's eyes shifted to Isaac mid-stumble.

He was in the midst of a spontaneous decision. It was a choice he didn't want to make, but under pressure, was forced into. He dropped Sam's hand just over the end of the dark corridor and pivoted to Isaac. Grabbing ahold of his shirt, he yanked.

"Get her! Quick!" CJ yelled.

The direction was intended for the rest of the children, but as CJ dragged Isaac out of the path of the descending ceiling, he realized it might be too late.

Sadie and Kip rushed to pull Sam through the opening while the ceiling closed in. As they got hold of her arms, the heavy stone pinned Sam to the ground. They tried to jerk her forward, but she was stuck.

The sound of her bones shattering paired horrifically with Sam's screams—wails that no longer sounded human. The shrill pitch of Sam's voice and the bodily destruction bequeathed legendary trauma.

"Help me! Help me!" she frantically begged.

A massive expulsion of blood flooded from her cracking jaw. As Sam's chin buckled into her face, it became clear those pleas would be her last.

Sadie clenched Sam's hand tight and jerked back in desperation. The upsetting popping noise coming from her sister's collapsing framework gave way to an even more disturbing soundtrack. Sam's tissues continued to condense until the burden of the ceiling moved onto her squishy organs. The sequence of internal explosions sounded like a string of cheap fireworks. As Sam's bodily cogs compressed into mush, an even grosser racket commenced. It resembled a wet boot struggling to un-stick from a pile of muck.

Kip stepped away from the unforgiving roof and froze. It was obvious there was no saving Sam, and the carnage had become too much for him to swallow.

The children watched on in revulsion as the ceiling cut into the back half of Sam's head. Her cranium opened wide, releasing an inner violence the likes of which their juvenile minds would never forget. Each child watched on, bound by the identical tear streaks of terror.

Except for Donnie.

He stood within the chorus of disturbed moans, dry-eyed. Donnie's outlet for emotional expression had been clogged long ago.

As the ghastly outbursts vomited out of the small spaces between the ruby floor and ceiling, the tension Sadie applied to her sister's arm finally snapped. Sadie tipped backward and landed on her rump, yet somehow her little fingers remained interlocked with Sam's.

The long strip of razor-metal lining the edge of the ceiling could've been easily overlooked, but as it dropped to the floor, and the fractured bone dislodged from the standard anatomical positioning, the glimmering horror became painfully obvious.

Sadie wailed uncontrollably, still holding onto the arm resting on her lap. While the mangled body part gushed all over her shorts, she couldn't allow herself to relinquish it.

The metaphor wasn't even intentional. She wasn't ready to let go.

"Noooooo!" Isaac screamed.

The section of Sam's sloppy head that hadn't been squashed was now the lone identifier of Isaac's sister. The mash of pulp, teeth, skeletal fragments, and morbid juices that comprised the pile was a version of Sam her brother wished he'd never seen.

THE FIRST OF MANY

"Zoom in on it! I want them to see *everything*," Geraldine instructed.

Fuchs tapped a few keys on the control panel in front of him and then twisted a black knob clockwise. The camera angle displayed on the massive primary monitor encased in the wall crept into the gory details of Sam's face. The stomach-churning specifics within the massive pile of human puke blasting from the edge of the drop ceiling were pure nightmare fuel.

The glistening hill of blood and bodily beef—the dead eyes, crushed jaw, and soggy crimson mane—offered a disturbing final portrait.

"Like zhis, my lady?" Fuchs asked.

Geraldine rubbed her hand together.

She reset her gaze on the champagne bottle to her right and plucked it off the counter. Aiming the cork through the open door behind her, careful not to damage any of the equipment, she popped it.

Despite the majority of the décor in the house being upper echelon, the bubbling fizz spilling over onto the Turkish rug below didn't faze Geraldine in the slightest.

It was a special day.

She tilted the bottle sideways and dumped the contents into the glasses. Once each reached capacity, Geraldine took one for herself and dispatched the second to her cackling cohort.

Fuchs looked away from the monitor he'd just finished tweaking to show the agony on Sadie's face.

She purged tears while still clinging to her sister's severed arm. It was as if she believed the cells might suddenly spring back to life.

The girl's breakdown tickled him. He hadn't seen such hellish reactions since piloting his methods in the concentration camps. It was his job to extract such extraordinary emotion, but he was happy to do what he loved. Though Fuchs rarely displayed his pleasure, the destruction of mankind was his natural calling.

But more important than his own gratification, Fuchs had simply calculated what he knew Geraldine yearned to see. He'd been around her perverse personality long enough to take hold of the reigns.

"Here," Geraldine said.

She offered a glass to Fuchs and they toasted.

The old Nazi pried his attention away from the demented imagery. Grinning, he grabbed the glass and lifted it towards Geraldine's.

"To our first," Fuchs replied.

"To the first of many," she corrected.

"Undoubtedly."

They lifted their fizzing drinks with pinkies raised. After their glasses clanged together, Geraldine and Fuchs each ingested a celebratory gulp.

"I feel so thankful. Part of me still believed, despite the increase in participation, that this would be a short venture. But not today. Not today…" Geraldine trailed off.

There was a slight tremor in Geraldine's voice. Her feelings had blindsided her. The unexpected surge of excitement left her on the verge of tears. She had done it. Her darkest dreams were coming true.

"Yes, it is a shame zhat no child has made it past zhe second playground. But today, zhe odds are in our favor," Fuchs replied.

The German took another swig of champagne, reveling in the bubbles as they popped upon his palate.

"But now, it's time for zhe real special part."

Fuchs tapped on the keys several times, triggering the gory video feed to transition back to the spy room.

Geraldine was attracted by the bluish light from the screen connecting with the tear streaks on Tom and Molly's faces. Just like Sam, they were crushed.

"If you cannot have zhem, zhen neither can zhey, my lady," Fuchs said.

His bitter tone echoed in Geraldine's mind as he turned another knob on the control panel.

The horrifying howls and soul-crushing moans from the parents bled through the dotted openings of the speakers. The anguish relayed in the evil audio would've shaken even the most heartless of humanity.

Geraldine lifted the glass to her lips again.

It was lovely to see others share in her pain. She'd been dealing with loss for some time. The loss of the simple bodily amenities that the peasant's procured naturally. The loss of climbing her mountain of desire.

The infernal cries gave her a prickly numbness inside. A diabolical sensation she'd only hoped to attain one day. The murderous structures established below The Borden Estate were finally paying dividends, bestowing her with an involuntary comradery.

Geraldine sipped her drink, taking comfort in the new truth staring back from the spy room.

She was no longer alone.

THE HANGMAN

The children were disoriented from the overdose of shock. Bordering on mania, many of their beating hearts found rhythms of excess. The next steps were uncertain. Hesitation lingered, the idea that death might lurk around any corner was now undeniable.

CJ looked on at the unglued group—it was all going to hell. The leadership role overwhelmed him. It was a position he regretted opting for.

Sadie sat covered in blood, still snug against her sister's severed limb.

Isaac stood hunched over, throwing up a short distance from his sister's pulverized body. The reserve of vomit he'd held back could no longer wait.

Kip cried, standing beside Bobby, watching him hold his shredded forearms against his tee shirt to stunt further blood loss.

Donnie remained by himself, seemingly oblivious to the atrocities unfolding around him.

As the maddening sound of the baseball machines continued, CJ wondered where Tanya was. Dragging his mind away from the distractions, he turned back around toward the ball pit.

Tanya stood in front of the pit, just a short distance from the tall but narrow steps. She was shaking uncontrollably, mumbling to herself as she gazed upon the hangman's chalkboard puzzle:

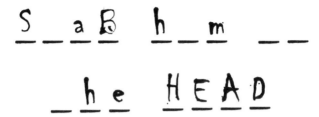

Wiping the fresh tears, Tanya didn't let her focus budge.

CJ decided detaching himself from the uncontrolled emotion of the majority was the best thing for the collective. He joined his sister at the ball pit.

"Stab him! Stab him in the head!" she yelled.

CJ looked up at the circular, kickball sphere that was the hangman's head. His eyes then dropped to the shiny blade of the hunting knife fixed to his fluffy hand.

"You think that's it?" he asked.

"What else could it be? Nothing else makes sense."

"Maybe that's why the knife is there."

Tanya bit her lip.

"But what if it's another trap?"

"It could be. But I don't know what else to do. I don't think anyone's coming to find us here."

A question dawned on Tanya that the non-stop chaos hadn't allowed her a moment to consider.

"What do you think happened to Mom and Dad?"

"I don't know."

CJ didn't feel comfortable speculating.

"You don't think they knew, do you?"

Tanya couldn't even believe she asked the question, but everything was so backward that, as sick as it sounded, the notion seemed possible.

"What? Of course not—"

"My arms are still bleeding," Bobby moaned.

Amid the commotion, CJ had forgotten to help his brother. Bobby appeared paler than ever before. CJ guessed that part of his transition had to do with stress, but the excessive blood loss wasn't without fault. From what he'd learned in school, the human body only had so much blood inside. If Bobby lost too much, it might spell his doom.

CJ rotated his perspective back to the hangman dangling on the platform. While the dummy appeared to be made out of stuffing, the clothes fixed to his puffy body looked like a normal flannel shirt and jeans.

"P—Please, I need your help," Bobby begged.

CJ approached his big brother and grabbed hold of him. He softly guided him to the ground before helping him into a seated position.

"I've got an idea that should help get you patched up. You just gotta hang tight for a minute, okay?" CJ asked.

Bobby was getting weaker. He nodded his pale face, hoping his brother would implement his idea sooner than later.

CJ looked over at Kip.

"Come and hang with Bobby for a minute."

"What are you gonna do?" Kip asked.

"I'm trying to figure it out."

CJ approached the narrow platforms that acted as a staircase to reach the hangman. He took a deep breath and looked at Tanya.

She was ensnared by the same debilitating dread that everyone else was, yet somehow, she remained operational. So much time had passed them by. The more CJ considered their relationship, the more he felt like he'd neglected it. He'd been far too focused on his hobbies and achieving his individual accomplishments. He suddenly saw the aspects of Tanya's persona he'd overlooked. The strength and heart she possessed bordered on supernatural.

He'd never been so proud to be her brother.

CJ felt his lip quiver as he spoke.

"I'll be right back," he said.

"Wait! What are you doing?!" Tanya cried.

"I'm gonna get the hangman down. We can use his clothes for Bobby's cuts. The puzzle says we have to anyhow."

"I don't want you to go."

Tanya's voice was cracking.

"Just make sure the others don't go too far," CJ said.

He made a quick arm gesture toward puke-drooling Isaac and the rest of the kids.

"Hold on! Maybe you shouldn't," Tanya cautioned.

She didn't have to say it; CJ could see it in her eyes. He knew that she wasn't prepared to see him potentially take his last steps. He wasn't prepared to die either. But for a soul of his nobility, no matter how terrified he was, the sacrifice of absorbing the risk that lay ahead wasn't even a choice.

CJ stepped toward his sister, not wanting to alert the others to what he was about to say.

"Bobby's bleeding a lot. He looks pale. I need to get those clothes," he said.

"I'll go," Tanya said.

Her bravery astounded CJ, but the excitement of avoiding the dangerous task was a fleeting one. As athletically underrated as Tanya was, CJ had the best chance at getting to the hangman without issue.

"I'll be right back, Sis," he replied.

As CJ turned away from Tanya, she looked at the long bleeding streaks running down his back. The ride down the sharp slide looked to have done a number on him. But upon closer inspection, the mass bloodshed made the damage look worse than it was.

"Be careful," Tanya said.

CJ focused on the task in front of him and blocked out all the mayhem. As the crying, chatter, and loud shooting sounds of the pitching machines died out, suddenly, he found himself alone in his head.

CJ wondered what the fall into the ball pit might entail. What could've possibly lingered below that wasn't visible to the naked eye?

"Forget about that, you're not gonna fall," he whispered to himself.

He squinted at the slim, circular platforms in front of him and held his breath.

CJ had always been relatively balanced whenever he needed to be. But this wasn't a time that he could just hope for the best. He needed to be perfect.

Trying not to overthink the challenge, CJ exhaled and extended his leg to the first platform.

The stand wasn't more than a foot or two from the ground, but its size was the tricky part. He wobbled side to side a few times before planting his other foot successfully next to the first.

Feeling stable enough, CJ shifted his focus to the next platform. It was no higher than when he hurried up the stairs at home and went two steps at a time. However, there was far less room for error.

Coming off the solid surface allowed him room to balance. But the tiny platform he was on made the next step even more difficult than the first.

CJ's leg shook and his muscles grew tense as he lifted the limb up from the circle. He dropped his heel down on the next platform, regaining his poise. With his legs parted slightly, he tested his equilibrium.

Believing his stance to be steady enough to ascend further, CJ repeated the successful method on the next four steps. He found himself several feet high in the air gazing downward. As he calculated the length of his potential fall, his knees wobbled.

Shifting his view away from the goal was a mistake. CJ's focus blurred the moment his concentration transitioned from the task at hand to the worst-case scenario. As he aimed his head at the hangman, his legs buckled. He was now faced with an all-or-nothing opportunity.

CJ reacted by taking his best shot. He vaulted forward and attempted to bounce back and forth between each of the remaining steps to reach the hangman's platform.

His first foot planted strong, causing relief to blossom in his chest. The generational athleticism he was blessed with could potentially be the deciding factor in CJ reaching the hangman.

While his agility may have been superior to his peers, it didn't matter so much when his second foot came down too close to the edge of the platform.

Panic pulsated through CJ's body as his sneaker slipped. He fell sideways with his shirtless, blood-drenched back closing in on the army of colorful balls below. As his body sailed downward, reality slowed. The fall felt much higher than it was. Flickers of CJ's brief life manifested before his starry eyes.

The first images to occupy his sights were telling—a patchy compilation exclusively made up of the many moments CJ had lived for others. The long hours he'd spent in a grassy field under the sun. The hundreds of times the baseball found his glove. The ping of the metal Easton bat launching the ball over the chain-link fencing. The countless curses and scowls that crimped his father's face.

The box Greg had created for CJ was big, but still a box, nonetheless. Within was the long, grueling path his father had carved out for him, and no finish line.

Next, CJ witnessed recollections of Tanya, Bobby, and Kip. While he didn't always get along with his brothers, a forgotten flood of good times rushed into his mind. There wasn't an abundance of memories of doing things he enjoyed, but when they all came at once, there was enough for CJ to completely reconsider their sibling dynamic.

The late-night ghost stories in the walk-in closet. The exciting games of tag and manhunt in the neighborhood. The countless trips to the video store. The cooperative games on Super Nintendo. The choreographed wrestling matches in the living room.

CJ considered that he might've spent too much time focusing on the things that perturbed him about his family. Looking back, they were much better than he'd given them credit for.

"CJ!" Tanya cried.

She instantly rushed toward the edge of the ball pit.

He had expected a somewhat cushy connection initially, followed by whatever sick trick the old witch had in store afterward. But to CJ's surprise, the balls that filled the pit weren't the standard. While the skin on them looked the same as any pit he'd ever seen, it wasn't.

As his bloody back crashed into the heap, he realized their exteriors were far thinner, almost balloon-like. The weight of his body landing full force caused them to erupt, and a white grainy substance fluttered outward.

Underneath the spheres laid the same hardwood flooring he'd just left. Except, instead of the marbles, there was more of the white substance from inside the balls.

The substance became less mysterious when the agony arrived. It spread like flames on a dry day all over CJ's back. Not only did the grainy pieces coat his backside, but the popped balls shot some of the sprinkles up into his mouth.

The taste reminded him of the ocean.

"Ahhhhhh! It burns!" CJ bellowed.

The salt crystals wormed deep into the wounds on his slimy back. The combination of blood and sweat hugged the stinging sand and acted as a bonding agent. In just seconds, the once snowy salt had become tainted by his fluids. As it sank further into the lengthy crevices, scorching burns stretched across the symphony of slashes.

"CJ! Are—Are you okay?!" Tanya asked.

He powered through the pain and crawled over to the platform. Forcing himself to his feet, CJ cried out in anguish. He tried desperately to use his arm and wipe off the crystals congealing to his back, but he was only pushing them deeper into his cuts. He just hoped that what he was experiencing was the worst of it.

"It hurts like hell, but I—I think it's just salt," he said.

CJ's back was suddenly beet-red. The flaring irritation on the surface wounds was the ultimate distraction, but his watery eyes darted around, calculating his next move. When they arrived on the backside of the hangman's platform, he noticed a small steel ladder had been affixed to the rear. It led all the way up to his destination.

"I think I found a way up," CJ said.

"Be careful," Tanya begged.

CJ pulled himself up each rung of the ladder until he reached the hangman's platform. He took hold of the blade in the dummy's hand and lifted it above his head. Sawing the knife side to side, he severed the rope after a few revolutions. When the hangman's lightweight body fell into his hands, he measured the toss.

"Everyone step back, I need to throw it down," CJ said.

The small group of children now cluttering the entrance quickly backed away, making space for the hangman.

As CJ wound his arms backward, he realized he finally was ready to throw a pitch that he actually cared about. And just like on the baseball diamond, his aim was true. The blade of the knife scraped across the floor, while the body of the hangman landed in front of Tanya.

With the salt still burning up his back, CJ made his move. Descending the steps would be far easier than climbing them, but he still had no desire to go for another swim in the salt. He bounced side to side, landing each foot rapidly in a plunge toward perfection.

But as CJ went tumbling to the floor near the hangman's limp body, he saw something unexpected. His eyes widened and a gawk of deep disturbance clung to him. A faint sparkle remained in his pupil, but it wasn't a sparkle of hope. It was the light reflecting off the twinkling blade whizzing toward his face.

GRUESOME GRIEF

"You fucking monster! How could you?! You just let her die! You let her fucking die!" Molly cried.

Her glossy eyes stared a hole through Rock.

Rock stood stoic, staring forward at the giant monitor.

He tried to ignore Molly's harsh words, but they weren't completely lost in him. If the room wasn't so dark, the other grieving parents would have seen the subtle crack forming in his expression. The growing gash of guilt on his lips. An understanding of the evils that had attached to him like a leech inside a lake.

"My baby's gone! My baby's gone!" Molly continued.

Tom sobbed uncontrollably as he reached for her hand, but he couldn't find the words to distract her. There was no way for him to compartmentalize his feelings any longer. Grief that no parent should have to digest expanded inside him. Drool poured from his mouth as an unignorable sequence of hysterical sobs rattled off his lips.

Rock tried his best to disregard Molly's words and Tom's devastation. What they were saying made too much sense. The guilt in his gut was as salty as the wounds he'd seen on CJ's back. It was a first; no one had ever loomed over his shoulder to offer such an agonizing commentary.

In past instances, while piloting the Playground, Rock was completely detached from the parental side of the trauma. He had simply watched each lone child find their way to an untimely demise. The deaths were swift, and the tension was low. Geraldine tasked him with cleaning up the remnants of violence. But the leftover limbs and ravaged carcasses had little to say. There was never a protest or philosophical insight to offer. Those elements had long left the children by the time he'd become responsible for them.

Rock likened the current situation to what it might've been like had he been forced to visit the homes of the little boys and girls he'd disposed of.

"She didn't even have a chance!" Molly yelled.

Rock retracted into his damaged mind like a turtle tucking into its shell to protect itself. Suddenly, the familial cries and groaning were no longer harassing him. Rock focused on his half of an internalized argument.

Maybe it ain't the worst thing. Not having a chance might be the best thing she ever got. I got a fuckin' chance, Rock thought.

***

Greg remained horrified, but the water in his eyes had dried over his stressed cheeks. The surreal feeling of his loss continued to weigh heavy on his mind. But now that he'd seen one child die before his eyes, it felt like someone had slapped him across the face. While the Grimleys fractured into shambles, he felt himself awaken.

He squinted at the big bastard watching over them in the darkness, then back to the TV screen. Greg had already lost his wife, but his children had survived. He was grateful for that much, especially for his prospects, CJ, and to a lesser extent, Kip.

The uber-competitive, shameless piece of shit that stood on the sidelines living vicariously through his own children had returned. Greg's warm thudding heart slowed as an icy, calculated intensity cascaded over it.

His eyes slid back to the big screen ahead. Close-ups of the Grimley kid looking like a can of crushed tomatoes didn't make him feel good. But it made him feel grateful.

Better theirs than mine, Greg thought.

FLAMING PAIN

The steel flashed by CJ's face and plunged directly into the hangman's. His fall occurred so quickly that he wasn't able to register anything prior to his crash landing.

He hadn't seen the hangman lying by his side. Nor had he seen Sadie take hold of the knife, or the look of darkness bubbling in her eyes when she stared at the fictitious man's head. CJ had zero forewarning of the hate she directed toward the hangman.

In Sadie's mind, the inanimate figure was responsible for her sister's death. And as she slammed the knife into the weathered kickball and watched the blade slice through the rubber, she could no longer control her fury.

"You killed her!" Sadie bellowed out.

After stabbing the hangman's head several times, she shifted her vengeful thrusts to the fluffy body. Poke after poke saw small streams of cotton from the dummy's interior sent streaming outward.

"Isaac, we need the clothing still," CJ reminded.

Isaac took CJ's hint and stepped up behind his sister.

"Sadie, calm down," Isaac said.

Sadie didn't hear his words. She remained lost in her inner torment, slashing away at the hangman.

As the knife cocked back for the next stab, Isaac grabbed her wrist. He even surprised himself by the way he took charge of the volatile situation. CJ had given him the shirt off his brother's back to patch his arm up, the least he could do was try to reciprocate.

It wasn't until Isaac got Sadie restrained and pulled the knife from her clutches, that Tanya started screaming.

She kicked her legs wildly, side to side.

"Ants! There's ants everywhere!" she cried.

Tanya stepped away from the hangman's hellish head. She observed a mass of flame-colored fire ants as they scrambled about feverishly with rage and hunger. The army of tiny hellions climbed up the feet and calves of the children, pinching onto flesh with malicious intent.

The bites were true to the sadistic insect's name. A sharp, stinging pain blazed around Tanya's ankles. The intense burning sensation spread as she continued to yell and kick.

"What the?!" CJ yelled.

He gawked down at the horde of agitated ants. Waves of the insects continued to pour from their previous area of confinement. All of a sudden, the stitches on the face of the hangman made more sense; the ants had been intentionally implanted inside his head.

As the rest of the kids backed away from the countless fire ants, CJ spied a plastic baggy sitting inside the deflated dodgeball. Through the transparent bag, a key and a piece of paper could be seen.

He knew the contents had to be critical.

CJ sacrificed a moment to bend over and retrieve the plastic bag and also removed the collared shirt from the dummy. The minions pounced on him, scurrying off the shirt and up from his shoes. He flung his legs and used his arms to shake as many bugs off as possible.

Thinking quickly, CJ kicked the hangman's head into the ball pit. Clusters of the pests still contained in the rubber landed on the salty floor. There were still plenty of fire ants rallying around them, but CJ had bought a little time.

"They're gonna climb out of the ball pit soon! We've gotta go now!" CJ screamed.

He continued to shake off the bugs. Once he displaced enough of the angry creatures from his body and the items, he tossed the long-sleeve flannel at Bobby.

"Hold on to that! Tanya, we need to look at this, fast!"

Tanya was still knocking off ants from her body, but tiptoed around the larger masses and arrived beside CJ.

She looked at the plastic baggy he'd just ripped open and grabbed the small note beside the skeleton key inside.

"What's it say?!" CJ yelled.

"I'm opening it as fast as I can!" Tanya replied.

Her shaking hands pulled the parchment apart. She did her best to focus on the scribbled words amid the stampede of insects.

CJ stomped out the fire ants as they continued to trickle towards them, trying to allow Tanya to focus.

"You must follow directions or all shall bleed, remember the *playground* chooses when you actually leave. If your reaction was swift, like the crack of a whip, then you'd notice the lever to the left of the pit. Pull down and in the ceiling, you'll see, the hole inside the pink is awaiting a key," Tanya said.

CJ's eyes moved to locate the red lever sitting in plain sight. When Sam freaked out, they didn't exactly get any time to think out their next steps. But the poem had spelled it out for them. Had they been able to solve the puzzle first, the path to certain death that Sam went down would've been completely avoided.

Upon Tanya's reading concluding, CJ didn't even need to say it. Each of the kids was already listening closely. They all watched on, ready to follow him. As CJ approached the sloppy pile of horror that Sam had become, he was able to overlook the nauseating sight in his haste.

He gazed upon the glowing pink exit sign that once sat above the hallway. It was now so close to the ground that he had to squat to align with it.

In the center of the hot pink sign, just like the riddle said, a small hole appeared ready to accommodate the skeleton key. Had he not known it was there, it would've simply blended in with the rest of the wall.

CJ cranked his head back toward his sister.

"Give me the key," he said.

As CJ inserted the key and twisted, the ants continued to flow up out of the ball pit. The red-spotted trail of torment was rapidly closing in on them.

He felt relief as the wall above the signage collapsed in on itself. The newly fashioned opening was made of cold metal and the dimensions of square tubing ahead were about twice the size of a standard air duct.

While a fear of the unknown still loomed over them, the agonizing jaws of the tiny terrors outweighed it. CJ, Tanya, and Isaac all helped the smallest children inside first, followed by Bobby.

As CJ crouched inside the aluminum with the rest of the group, his hands shook. He couldn't avoid pondering what the next set of horrors they'd be up against might be.

The possibilities were beyond chilling.

A GROWING DIVIDE

Molly and Tom sobbed steadily, but each worked internally to control their shock and hysteria. The atrocious feelings of ghastly imagery lingered; they wouldn't be easy to overcome.

But as Tom watched Isaac and Sadie each climb into the duct, he pushed his psyche to shift. He knew he had to concentrate on the children that were still alive for any of them to have a chance.

While the notion felt like it would require a miracle, Tom knew nothing was impossible. The more he dulled his emotions, calmed his body, and rationally analyzed the situation, the more room for opportunity he saw.

The gateway to their children and their horrors suddenly went black. The TV monitor displayed nothing.

A confused expression overcame Rock's face. He furrowed his brow up toward the camera in the corner of the room, then back to the TV monitor. Since the screens the parents watched were embedded in the wall, Rock knew the camera angles wouldn't provide the control room a look at the malfunction.

Rock looked at the three captives, his squarish face brandishing a curled grimace.

"Don't do anything stupid. I'll be right back," he said.

When Rock exited the dimly lit room, Tom and Molly immediately looked at each other.

"We—We've gotta get out of here. What are we gonna do?" Molly whispered.

"He's the key," Tom replied.

"What do you mean?"

"I mean we have no options. He's our only shot. We sure as shit aren't getting out of these chairs unless he lets us. I know you see it too. His eyes are showing his hand. He knows this is fucked. He's not like them."

"Then why the fuck are we still here, genius?!" Greg exclaimed.

"Lower your Goddamn voice! I'm not saying he's ready to crack right now. He'll need some convincing. But we all saw the way that old witch controls him. He's under her thumb. We've gotta work together and help him realize what she's done, not just to us, but to him."

"What?! For all we know this could've all been his doing!" Greg refuted.

"Now who's speculating—"

"Oh, fuck you, tough guy. That piece of shit walked in here covered in blood! You—You think that was some kind of accident?"

"I don't know, but it's not like we have a better option," Tom reasoned.

"What do you mean?! He told her right in front of you that he killed someone for trying to get away, and now you think he's just gonna let us walk?"

"Listen to me, I don't give a shit what he's done. Forget about that. I'm telling you, sure as the Superbowl's on Sunday, he's the only chance we've got."

The football reference seemed to be the dog whistle that made Greg's ears perk up. He found himself actually listening to Tom.

"I'm begging you, Greg. Just give it a chance. Work with us so we can all get the fuck out of here. Please."

Greg turned to his blood-drenched wife with confusion. It was almost as if he was looking for guidance from her. Had Lacey's body throbbed with a pulse, her husband's response might've been different. But now alone in the world, Greg could only be himself.

"No! No one's getting out of here! You're just afraid! You know your kids don't got what it takes! I know you see it! My boys are out there doing all the heavy lifting! They'll make it to the end, and when they let me see 'em again, when they let me out of this fuckin' chair, there's gonna be hell to pay."

Greg glared over at the gaping wound in Lacey's pale neck. The blood in her body had finally run dry, while the twinkle of madness in Greg's eye had only grown. Inside, he knew it with utmost certainty; she would've been proud of their children.

"Who gives a shit if they make it or not! Even if they get to the end, you think they're gonna just let us go after that?! People are dead! *Dead!* What about that doesn't register in that thick fucking skull of yours?!"

Tom lost his cool; Greg knew exactly how to get to him.

"A pussy like you wouldn't get it," Greg laughed.

"Get what?!"

"While I'd like to think I'd tear some ass if they let me out of this chair, in the grand scheme of things, it probably doesn't even matter."

"Why do you say that?"

"Because, in all likelihood, we're already fuckin' dead. The future is fried. All that's left is the competition now. It's my blood against your blood, in one last duel for old time's sake. And guess what?"

Tom didn't humor him with a response. But that didn't stop Greg, after a moment passed, he carried on.

"The Matthews clan ain't going out like losers."

Greg extended his hand over to his lifelong cheerleader. He cradled his love's dead palm with boundless sincerity.

"Ain't that right, baby doll," he whispered.

A fresh teardrop pissed out of his eye duct.

"For such a competitive asshole you sure give up easy," Molly said.

She didn't know if the comment might help to bring him closer into the fold. But Greg's response proved that her attempt at reverse psychology had fallen flat.

A manic grin formed on Greg's face.

"Oh, I haven't given up, not by a long shot. Just you watch. Let the games begin."

DISOBEDIENCE

When Rock entered the room, the remnants of celebration stung him. He wasn't confronted by just a single champagne bottle—Geraldine and Fuchs were on their third and their glasses had just been refilled.

He figured it must've been sweet to take a few moments and drink nice booze. To pause and recognize their many years of hard work coming to a head. Things had gone off *almost* without a hitch. Rock's poisoned mind instructed his heart to ache; he just yearned to be part of something, even if it was something evil.

But after years of obedience, there was still no thanks. Decades of hard labor and following Fuchs' complex instructions meant nothing. Kidnapping men and using their slave labor to help erect their sinister playground didn't deserve praise. No matter how hard he worked maintaining the grounds, a peep was never said. Regardless of how many destroyed corpses of used-up men and test children he disposed of, Rock would always be taken for granted.

The presence of the German and Geraldine caused him to cringe. He ground his teeth and clenched his fists at the sight of them. Rock's ears grew red hot and the discomfort under his skin bubbled.

179

The rotten memories of insignificance and unflinching abuse were gnawing on Rock's limbic system.

They didn't understand him.

They'd never understand him.

He'd always be shit to them.

The joyous chatter between Geraldine and Fuchs died down. It was as if the lady of The Borden Estate could sense a presence in the room. As she sluggishly craned her head backward, her suspicions were validated.

Geraldine's cold, drunken gaze cooled Rock's steaming fury. He'd seen those bloodshot, perverted eyes too many times to count. Flashes of unpleasantness bled into his brain. The many repulsive chores she demanded of him molested his mind. Rock's hammy fist slowly un-balled and his jaw slacked as he attempted to speak.

"The monitor in the—"

"What the fuck are you doing here?! How many times have I told you not to leave them alone?! There was one rule for you to follow, one rule and—ugh, I should've known it was too much!" she screamed.

With her tantrum in full swing, the filled glass of champagne Geraldine had just lifted off the counter went flying toward Rock's face.

When it slammed against his jaw of steel, the glass burst into fragments. The sharp remnants sinking into his flesh shouldn't have stunned him, but it did. The cuts weren't deep, but the trauma was and the shards were mighty enough to draw blood. Several slices of various dimensions resulted in a drizzly expulsion of blood from Rock's overly-defined cheekbone.

He lifted his big mitt and wiped the blood and bubbly off his face. Rock had grown physically immune to the abuse, but emotionally, it was another story. He didn't know what to do next, so he did nothing.

An uncomfortable silence surfaced as Geraldine, and Fuchs gawked at him. The look of irritation shriveling Geraldine's expression was wince-inducing.

"Well?! Why are you here?!" she barked.

"The monitors in the spy room went black. You may wanna fix it if you want them to see what happens," Rock replied.

The big man watched as Fuchs turned back around and quietly sipped at his champagne. Just as the Nazi bastard had always done, Fuchs had no issues watching the violence unfold without protest.

"That's because we're shifting to the second playground, you buffoon! If you'd just listened the first time you'd understand. I told you *we* would come to *you* if we saw a lack of reaction in the parents! If you could just learn to listen, then your face wouldn't have to look the way it does."

Rock raised his hand up to his cheek and wiped away the new blood. Some of the tiny glass particles remained in his skin. As his calloused fingers pulled them downward, they scratched at his cheek again. Save for the branding of his chest, most of his other scars had been subtle. Similar to Donnie, they seemed to manifest in places that most strangers weren't privy to.

He took pride in not selling the attack; he didn't want Geraldine to get the satisfaction of hurting him. The outbursts occurred frequently enough that he'd conditioned himself. He was like one giant ball of pins and needles. Tough as nails and numb as Novocain.

Whenever the darkest feelings came to Rock, Geraldine knew how to counteract them. But this time felt different from the others.

For the first time, she saw the inner rage lingering on his face. Such berating usually erased all emotion in the massive man. The emotional positioning Rock presented puzzled Geraldine.

The detestation Rock typically subdued caressed his brain. He enjoyed thinking about Geraldine and Fuchs. He was enjoying it so much that the blood creeping down his face had stained much of the yellow enamel that formed his unhinged grin.

"What the fuck are you smiling about?! What do *you* have to smile about?! Another failure?!" Geraldine yelled.

She picked up the champagne bottle at her side and took a swig directly from it.

"Just happy is all," Rock lied.

"Well, go fucking be happy in the spy room, you feeble-minded waste!"

Rock tipped his flat cap at the old hag, not allowing his wide grin to waiver. The irony taste of blood that entered his mouth would act as his champagne.

For now…

In the back of his mind, Rock wondered if he might ever have a celebration of his own someday. The possibility didn't seem out of the question, but first, he would have to find something worth celebrating.

HOPSCOTCH

As the children departed the metal duct, they landed on a rock platform. The heavy stone material was about the size of a tight bedroom, but unlike any of their bedrooms, the edges of the platform dropped off into a pit of darkness. The uncertain borders were frightful, but they were soon drawn ahead to the next path of peril.

A ruthless, mechanical hum reverberated in their ear canals. It was the first hint that what lay ahead might not be pleasant. Secondly, a flurry of shrill, bellowing cries could be heard integrated within the machine-driven noise. But the visuals were more jarring than the veiled clues.

At the end of the circular, rock platform the stone narrowed into a slim path. A straight stretch of hopscotch lay ahead. The chalk outline displayed a single column that consisted of eight steps. The setup was traditional; one that all the children had seen at one time or another.

The first three steps consisted of numbered squares marked 1, 2, and 3. Afterward came a pair of squares set side by side, numbered 4 and 5. Then, a single square with a 6, another set of double squares numbered 7, and 8, and a single square with a 9. Lastly, concluding the gauntlet of horror, was a final space labeled 'HEAVEN.'

Excluding the chalk, the Heaven platform was the same as the one they were standing on. Besides the word, there were also various disturbing depictions that were drawn with an inordinate amount of detail. The imagery took up nearly the entire space.

The colors that comprised the 'artwork' were simply white and red, but the color scheme was chosen with intent. The chalky sketches were gruesome in nature. They portrayed several angels being ripped apart. One had been stabbed and was covered in gaping wounds, while another hung lifelessly from a noose. There was even a third angel that was being strangled with its own halo by a pair of devilish hands.

Beyond the blasphemous artwork stood a cracked open door. Nothing could be seen except the ominous crimson glow that bled out from the other side. Above the framework, painted in a drippy red font, read the word 'HELL.'

While all of those details were beyond alarming, there was nothing that could compare to what had been erected on each side of the hopscotch path.

As CJ inched closer to the edge, the powerful, machine-like churning noise grew in intensity. On each side of the childish game, two enormous, rectangular meat grinders spun their sharp, steel innards without fail. The spikey metal doom he gazed upon churned mercilessly. When faced with the man-made beast, the thoughts of hope and progress sailing through CJ's skull were overshadowed.

The shrieks and cries that ripped towards them from above also could not be ignored. The foursome of full-grown cows had been divided equally; two to each side of the hopscotch trail. They stood uneasily in their barred cells, hooves chattering on the solid metal floors.

"What the hell—"

CJ's speech was interrupted by the slashes that straddled his backside. The salt hadn't let him forget just how much had been slathered across his wounds.

But CJ wouldn't allow himself to wallow in anguish, and instead, quickly recalled his brother's.

"Isaac, can I have the knife?" CJ asked.

He stretched out the collared shirt.

"Sure," Isaac replied.

The boy could barely tear his gaze away from the dreadful machinery.

"I've got you, Bobby," CJ said.

CJ approached Bobby with the knife and snatched the hangman's shirt. He cut the fabric into lengthy strips until he had multiple pieces ready. He slid the blade behind his waistband and readied the flannel sections.

"This might hurt a little," CJ said.

Bobby's eyes were wet and his face was still pale, but he seemed prepared enough to manage the pain.

CJ softly tightened several strips of fabric around his brother's forearms. As the pressure grew snug, Bobby did his best not to cry.

Kip watched on, hoping not to see his big brother wince. Each time Bobby showed weakness, it was like a dagger in his heart. The visuals made him even more nervous than before. Up until that day Kip hadn't even seen Bobby cry. Despite CJ being championed to lead them forward, seeing his eldest brother so vulnerable hurt.

Sadie remained brimming with trauma. She barely had her bearings enough to keep little Donnie by her side. But occupying her mind with keeping him safe had distracted her just enough to remain operable.

Isaac felt the same horrible sensations as his sister but had no distraction to lean on. The flashes of Sam's pulpy head and gushing body haunted him.

Isaac put his arm around Sadie.

"I love you. Don't worry, I'm—I'm gonna protect you," Isaac whispered.

He was lying through his teeth. Things would never be all right with Sam gone. Furthermore, the path that lay ahead of them oozed with danger.

But the words he chose were the type a good big brother spoke to his little sister in a time of doubt. Isaac didn't even have to think about it; it just happened. He'd put aside their petty grievances; the next few moments might very well be life-defining.

"Here's another one—ouch! Dang it!" Tanya yelled.

"What's wrong?" Isaac asked.

"Freakin' ants. Must've missed one."

Tanya scratched at her irritated ankles. The raspberry rise upon her skin gave way to an itch with no end. The dotted red blotches peppered her legs. Her semi-sharp nails clawed against the corrupted flesh, drawing a little blood and causing a modest amount of translucent liquid to leak.

Tanya pushed through the pain and returned to her prior effort. Another sign was in her sights that was eerily similar to the one she'd seen before going down the slide. It read: PLAYGROUND RULES.

CJ turned back to the commotion and saw Tanya examining the sign. He finished binding the final measure of cloth around Bobby's arm, then turned his attention to his sister. There was an added interest in the words since he now knew that understanding the riddles could potentially be the difference between life and death.

"What's it say?" he asked.

"Forget throwing stones just make it across, but losing this game is the ultimate loss. For what lies ahead is a horrible drop, one you've got to move past to see Mom and Pop. But first things first, go for a hop, but take a wrong step, and become the slop. You have no choice, you must play the game, and learn that Heaven and Hell are one and the same."

"The fuck does that even mean! What do you want?!" Bobby screamed.

He looked up toward the ceiling as if someone might somehow answer them.

"Hey, be cool," CJ said.

"Cool?! How can you fuckin' be cool right now?!"

"You know what I mean. Screaming isn't gonna change stuff, we've gotta work together."

Tanya looked back at the massive meat grinders and noticed something she hadn't before. At the end of the hopscotch outline, in front of each meat grinder, there were two clear tubes that ran upward. The squared spouts at the end of each were angled in the direction of the hopscotch path. From the darkness below she couldn't determine exactly where the tubes led.

"What are we gonna do now?" Sadie cried.

The general tension and arguments within the group had her anxiety to a pinnacle.

CJ stared down the line at the area they needed to reach. He certainly would feel like he'd reached Heaven if he made it through. At least for a moment, anyway.

He spun his head toward his brother, Kip, then Bobby, before finally locking eyes with Isaac. The seriousness of his glare spoke volumes telepathically. It transferred a message that screamed 'get ready.'

"We're gonna play hopscotch, I guess."

LICKING THE WOUNDS

"We've gotta talk to them at some point," Molly whispered.

Her fingers softly traced over the white button attached to the side of her steel collar.

"Not yet," Tom whispered back.

Tom kept a close eye on Rock. He needed to ensure they didn't attract his attention. From his vantage point, the big man seemed to be living in his own head anyhow. The fresh blood still trickling down his cheek, and the flare of madness that wavered in his eyes told him that much.

Tom used his shaking hand to pull his wife's fingers away from the button and squeeze it tight.

"We've got two chances to talk. We can't use one just for the sake of talking to them. It's too important—"

"I can't watch my babies die again," Molly cried.

Her entire face still leaked; the drool, tears, and snot splurged in a trifecta of visible torment.

"Shh," Tom begged.

He was doing his best to keep Molly quiet while juggling the task of keeping his own emotions in check.

"I know you don't, honey, but there's nothing we can tell them that's gonna change how they approach this. Just like with—"

This time Tom had to cut himself off. His emotions clogged his ability to articulate the makeshift plan.

"Just like with Sam," he finally managed.

A quiver ripped through Tom's body as he attempted to regain his composure. He was trying to think as strategically as possible for his family.

Tom's eyes bounced back from the screen containing the cluster of children. They landed on the fiendish hopscotch path, then back onto his unraveling wife. His nerves were through the roof. Any second, another child might have their final moment pass on the screen. The thought felt selfish, but he couldn't be overly concerned about anything. He needed to solidify a means to end the madness they'd been ensnared in and whisk those who remained to safety.

Tom zeroed in and turned off as much of the distracting sadness inside as possible.

"If we're gonna help them, we need to be able to offer them something besides comfort. We don't know how any of that shit works," he explained, pointing toward the meat grinders on the tube. "We need information that's—that's useful."

"It'd be so much easier if you'd just accept it," Greg interjected.

A harsh cackle escaped Greg's lips.

"Forget about him," Tom whispered.

"Forget about the Matthews? Highly unlikely. *We* leave our mark. Me, baby doll, and all my young ones'll be standing at the top of the mountain when it's all said and done. You watch. Just you watch," Greg promised.

Greg gritted his teeth and squished his grip even tighter on his dead wife's hand.

"Sir," Tom said.

Rock stared ahead at the screen mindlessly. Tom's words had yet to find him.

"Why are you doing this? Why do all of our children have to die?" he asked.

Rock tilted his head slightly toward Tom and Molly.

"They're just kids. Their lives haven't even begun yet. It doesn't seem fair to have them play a game that they don't even know how to."

"Playground rules are listed on the signs," Rock said.

He pointed to the screen at Tanya. She appeared to be reading some of the lettering to the rest of the group.

Tom thought about his daughter Sam getting crushed by the ceiling just a short time prior.

Her cranium exploding.

Her arm separating from her body.

Her corpse being juiced like a blood orange.

The painful image of Sadie clinging to the dead extremity caused him to cringe.

It took everything for Tom to keep his composure, but, in his fiery state, he couldn't help but let an f-bomb slip.

"Then why didn't my daughter know she'd be crushed by a fucking ceiling."

Rock pondered the question a moment. He looked at the young boy on the screen. As Donnie's flatline features clung to his expression without fail, Rock clenched the bloody leash in his pocket again.

"Not everything's on the signs."

"Do you think that's fair? Or, do you think these kids should all have a fair shake at making it through the playground?"

Rock remained mum, neither agreeing nor disagreeing with the logical notion that Tom laid out.

"Please, if there's *anything* that you could tell us that might help, even if it's something small—"

"Oh, woe is me. I raised a bunch of pussies so I need an advantage. Is that what I'm hearing?" Greg asked.

Tom looked back to Molly.

"Just don't listen to him," he whispered.

"Well, guess what? The Matthews don't! My boys—hell, even Tanya can take care of things on her own! Advantage or not, you ain't got a prayer in the world," Greg continued.

"Shut up, you sick son-of-a-bitch!" Molly screamed.

"It's okay, I'd be upset too if that little dandelion faggot was my last hope."

Greg grinned again; he enjoyed reminding them of the nickname he'd branded Isaac with.

Venom and disgust saturated Molly.

She'd found a way to grit her teeth with Tom. They were actually making progress. The wheels were turning with Rock, but Greg was dead set on throwing a monkey wrench into things.

"Don't play into it," Tom said.

Tom applied his own advice and returned to his conversation with Rock.

"Why are you bleeding?" Tom asked.

It was clear as day; the still-fresh dribble of crimson slid lethargically down Rock's cheek.

Rock didn't respond audibly, but Tom could tell the nuances within his body language had registered the query. He watched the gruff man thoroughly while he tightened his jaw and extended his hand upward. There was a symbolism to behold; the question had triggered Rock to wipe the blood away.

"You don't deserve to be treated like that. No one does. Not you, not us, not our children…not even Greg," Tom explained.

The latter part of his statement caused him to wince, but Tom still meant every word.

"I don't need a whiny cunt like you telling me what I need. Now, if you'll excuse me, I'm trying to watch the show," Greg replied.

The smile he brandished while watching his son CJ step up toward the hopscotch squares was nothing short of sociopathic.

"That a boy, that a boy," Greg whispered to himself.

Tom ignored Greg, continuing his attempt to break through to Rock.

"You don't have to keep taking her abuse and licking

your wounds in the shadows. Following her lead is a choice. You don't have to be like her."

When the last words hit Rock, they lit a fire inside him. The hand in his jacket that still clenched the bloody leash suddenly flew from his pocket. His mammoth fist blasted through the drywall, leaving a sizable hole. The comparison enraged him.

"Shut your goddamn mouth! I'm not like her! You hear me?!" Rock screamed.

Tom's eyes studied the ruby-soaked leash hanging from Rock's grasp. Fear flooded into his chest and confusion clouded his mind. His vision toggled from the big man in his unhinged state, over to the screen with his children who stood close to the edge of the platform.

The tension had reached a new high.

Tom nodded submissively while Molly remained mum. Even Greg seemed to pipe down accordingly.

"I'm not like her…" Rock whispered to himself.

SAVOR THE INSANITY

Geraldine set the empty bottle down beside her and let out a cackle. She turned to Fuchs who acted as a mirror, also projecting an evil grin of excitement. Their expressions clarified that things were going *exactly* as planned.

"Shall I do it now zhen?" Fuchs asked.

"Are you mad?" Geraldine asked.

Fuchs had just let his smile rest, but now his sharp teeth had once again found daylight. The facial gesture the German presented her with screamed, 'I very well might be.'

His oddball nature made Geraldine chuckle again; they mirrored each other.

Geraldine felt even tipsier than before, but she wasn't filled with her normal angry drunkenness.

Things were going so well.

The mayhem unfolding before her eyes was masterful. Even the sting of Rock's idiocy had faded for the moment. She was so enthralled at the thought of what came next.

However, Fuchs seemed a little too eager. Like a pervert that had just slipped inside a whorehouse, he was ready to blow his load immediately.

Even though they both chased the high, Geraldine reminded herself, the event they were witnessing wasn't ever going to become a common occurrence. She would not allow her investment to be foolishly squandered. They needed to take their time. They needed to savor every second the disturbing trauma offered.

Despite her drunkenness, she studied the dread on the children's faces. She had it on video, but she wanted to do her best to firmly grasp the organic memory.

"We want them to get as far as possible, maybe even all the way. Killing them all now, well," she hiccuped, "what fun would that be?"

Geraldine couldn't take her eyes off Tanya. Amid all the excitement, she hadn't given much thought to which girl might take after her enough to potentially become her protégé. It was quite possible the answer was none.

She wasn't aiming to get her hopes up just to have them dashed. The fact that one of the girls had already perished didn't help her odds any either. But as Tanya stood in front of the sign displaying the playground rules, she felt there was hope.

"Understood, my lady. Zhey have so much to see, so much to experience," Fuchs said, concurring with the more methodical approach.

Geraldine's grin grew even wider.

"As do we. As do we…" Geraldine replied.

She meant the statement in more than one way; there was a lot more slaughter to absorb, but also, a lot more to learn about Tanya.

The girl's intelligence was certainly on par with her own. Mental aptitude was the most imperative attribute she desired. Geraldine could see it clearly. While CJ might've appeared to be the leader, every time the children plotted, the attention turned to Tanya. She was the one pulling the strings and strategizing.

Tanya's strength couldn't be overlooked either. Sure, she had fallen to pieces a few times, but who hadn't? The most important thing was that she'd found a way to churn through each horrific situation and remain level-headed.

In Geraldine's eyes, it was undeniable; she was a natural-born leader.

If the girl had an Achilles heel, it was most definitely her soft, kind-hearted nature. Tanya was as sweet as pie and never held a grudge.

"We can fix that," Geraldine whispered.

"Fix what, my lady?" Fuchs asked.

"Oh nothing," she replied.

Geraldine knew for certain Tanya's tender approach wouldn't be difficult to break. If she'd been able to impose her will on Rock, the girl would be no different. And if Rock became more useless than he already was, Tanya might even be able to serve as his eventual replacement.

While the girl may have found the courage to overcome the physical obstacles in front of her, Geraldine knew the emotional roadblocks she had in mind would surely break Tanya's resolve.

Geraldine felt an intense attraction to Tanya's spirit swelling inside her bosom. She would now watch the screen differently than she had before; she had a new stake in the events that were set to transpire.

As unlikely as it seemed, Geraldine suddenly found herself rooting for Tanya.

MEAT AND BONES

"Are you fucking crazy?! We can't cross that thing!" Bobby cried, adjusting his newly affixed bandages.

CJ looked at the humming grinders, then back at his brother from the edge of the platform.

"What else are we gonna do, just wait here?" CJ asked.

"Maybe we should, maybe someone'll come here and save us."

"The last time we didn't follow the rules…" CJ hesitated, glancing over at Isaac and Sadie, "someone died."

"Well, if she wasn't dumb enough to run down a dark hallway by herself, maybe she'd still be alive."

"Don't talk about my sister!" Isaac yelled.

"What are you gonna do about it, you little dandelion dipshit?" Bobby barked.

He remained a parrot of his father's persona.

"Hey! Just stop! We're moving ahead, with or without you. Stay here if you want. But I'm gonna get to the end of this thing. I'm getting out of here," CJ said.

"Fucking traitor," Bobby muttered.

CJ ignored his words, looking away from Bobby and Kip and over toward Sadie, Isaac, Tanya, and little Donnie.

"Does everyone know how to play hopscotch?"

They all nodded except for Donnie, who looked as lost as always.

"Does everyone think they can make it across?"

"I think so," Sadie replied.

She was frightened, but CJ's courage gave her strength.

Tanya nodded. She took a deep breath, preparing herself mentally, but she was firm in her confidence.

"I'm not the best at hopscotch, but I'm not the worst either. But what about him?" Isaac asked.

His index finger was pointed at Donnie who was yet to break his silence.

Without warning, Donnie broke away from Sadie. He zipped past the entire group, heading directly for the hopscotch path.

"Wait!" CJ yelled.

But young Donnie didn't listen. He immediately stuck one foot out, and in a fearless blur, set a chain of multiple hops in motion.

The others all collectively held their breath, watching him jump past the gargantuan meat grinders as he made his way to the opposite end of the path.

But Donnie didn't stop there…

CJ watched on in awe as the boy's feet landed on the platform titled 'HEAVEN,' but what Donnie did next was the last thing he was hoping to see.

Continuing to hop in place, Donnie turned his body around, as would be expected of a player in a traditional game of hopscotch. But this was the furthest thing from a traditional game. As the boy headed back toward his point of origin, CJ released a horrified gasp in unison with the rest of the children.

"No!" CJ cried.

His natural response was the most dangerous; CJ promptly sprang into action.

CJ would have to cross the path himself, regardless. He hoped as he hopped closer towards Heaven, his presence would be enough to force Donnie to turn back.

Donnie didn't flinch. He continued on the path, his foot dropping quickly onto the 9 square.

The pressure and danger of the situation increased as CJ accelerated his pace. He aimed to beat Donnie to the midpoint of the bridge where he could set both of his heels on the ground in unison.

The star athlete's God-given assets brought him to the 4 and 5 squares before Donnie. Luckily, as Donnie entered the 6 square, CJ planted both of his feet firmly. In a single swoop, he scooped Donnie up in his arms and carried on in the other direction without hesitation.

His footing and balance were flawless as CJ propelled them past the final hazards. They both fell forward to safety, landing on top of the depictions of dying angels.

The joy the children felt after the success of CJ's death-defying stunt was quickly overshadowed. A loud clicking noise echoed out from the ceiling above where they stood.

As the ticks increased in both their pitch and pace, Isaac looked up above them. The same fate that he'd failed at stopping his sister from suffering was suddenly staring back at him again. For the first time, as he watched the large slab of stone closing in, he felt guilt. However, he didn't have enough time to simmer on Sam's final moments, or his body would end up juiced by the identical method.

"Go! Go now!" Isaac commanded, looking at Sadie.

The little girl found her gusto. She didn't cry or argue, knowing the clock was ticking. Sadie's blonde pigtails bobbed along as she methodically skipped her way towards Heaven.

Tanya and Isaac both looked at each other.

"Ladies first," Isaac said.

As Kip watched Tanya take her hops, he glanced over at his big brother. The fright in his eyes was dominant.

"We—We've gotta go now, right?" Kip asked.

"Duh!" Bobby yelped.

Isaac watched holding his breath as Tanya made her way across without fail.

The ceiling was now coming down even faster. The threat of descending death was a mega-dose of motivation for everyone to move fast.

Isaac rushed up to the edge of the chalk outline, struggling to set his worries aside.

Kip and Bobby hustled, lining up behind him.

As Isaac committed and took his first few hops, the steel bottoms of the mooing cages above came loose.

The parting screeches of agony the animals unleashed caused Isaac to nearly lose his foothold. He teetered to the left, trying to keep stable, as he peered down into the blades of chaos. The rapid spirals of malicious metal tore into the cows' overfed frames breaking the wailing animals down before his eyes.

As the cows became further entangled, the sickening snap of limbs mixed with the sound of the metal dividing the meat was unignorable. An ultra-violent stew of sinew, beef, fur, and blood painted the chrome.

Regaining his balance, Isaac ripped his eyes away from the destruction and pushed forward.

"Hurry up!" Kip cried, nipping at Isaac's heels.

Bobby watched the ceiling drop closer and closer as he waited anxiously for both Isaac and his brother to progress. He didn't have much time left. Bobby had more grace to his step than one might assume. His obsession with skateboarding offered him enough practice to believe in himself. However, he would've preferred that the lane be clear when he took his shot. As he watched on, that luxury appeared to be questionable at best.

The boys were oblivious to the pulverized porridge that had suddenly occupied the clear tubes erected in front of the Heaven space. The spouts at the end of them dribbled with hunks of gore and juices drawn out from the crushed cows.

The gushing gunk finally caught Isaac's eye. As he took another hop forward, the sickening stream grew thicker. What was about to transpire had finally become obvious.

With only a split second to react, Isaac did his best to gauge the projection of the slaughterhouse slop. He paused momentarily, hunching his shoulders to prepare himself.

He vaulted forward past the final squares, propelling himself to Heaven, just before the wave of garbled, drizzly violence reached him.

"Ahh!" Kip cried.

The hunks of horror splattered all over his face, eyes, and entire body. The wet, twitching meat hit him with force, instantly sending Kip tumbling toward a gruesome demise. He toppled over head-first and the sharp, blood-drenched blades minced through his upper body with ease. The familiar sound of bones breaking and meat being mauled found the airwaves again. The machine tore through Kip's tender tissues like Kleenex at a funeral parlor.

"Kiiiiiiiiip!" Bobby wailed.

CJ looked back, a sickness the likes of which he'd never known growing inside the pit of his stomach.

Tanya and Sadie were equally distraught, releasing high-pitch screeches that were so intense they sounded demonic.

Donnie was just there.

Bobby mustered all of his strength to keep himself from fainting. Forced to consume the short-lived cries of his kid brother, he watched as the warm fluids erupted from the pile of slop that no longer resembled Kip's body.

Amid the flood of fluid and gore-caked elements, pieces of Kip peeked out within the mess—the patches of mashed cranium and hair were scattered about, the drippy eyeballs separated from each other divided at such a distance that the possibility of survival was no longer an option.

Bobby remained slack-jawed, as the ceiling dropped lower and lower. The initial shock waned in his system. He knew it wouldn't be long until another meaty regurgitation was set to commence.

As the cold stone closed in just inches from his skull, Bobby had no choice but to step out onto the first square. He secured both feet and paused.

The glimmering instruments of horror were in his head. With his eyes steadily fixed on the sharp edges, he watched them slice and dice Kip's already divided sections. As the portions multiplied repeatedly, Bobby dug his fingernails into his palms.

The sound of his favorite sibling's shredded meat being sucked into the industrial-grade, modified meat grinder, filled his ears. He noticed one of the gunky tubes at the end of the path filling up to capacity again.

As the bloody pieces of his brother dribbled out of the spouts, Bobby had a decision to make. The cow blood and pink chunks that littered the hopscotch outline made the entire surface slick. The condition effectively eliminated the option of running to avoid Kip's regurgitated remains.

He would have to withstand it.

Bobby froze in place and squatted, still being serenaded by the cries of the other children. He lowered his shoulder and prepared himself. As the glistening mixture launched out, the idea that he'd just had a conversation with the macabre money shot headed his way entered his mind.

The vomitus mixture engulfed him, but he remained sturdy. The splatter covered his hair, face, and the entire front of his body. The smell of the fresh death crept up his nostrils while chunks of his sibling slid off him in every direction. It was like he'd just taken a long shower in Satan's bathroom.

Bobby was screaming but maintained his balance in the face of the flurry. He wiped Kip's ground remnants away from his eyes first. The flow ahead had gone dry, but a hazardous trek still remained. With the pieces of Kip now added to the already slippery track, his venture would surely be the most volatile of all the children.

"Bobby, be careful!" CJ said.

CJ's words were barely audible. He'd been shaken by Kip's grisly demise. His mouth curled up and his bottom jaw chattered. The last thing he wanted to see was both of his brothers taken from him in the same breath.

Bobby inhaled deeply, trying to concentrate on getting through as safely as possible. He carefully tight-roped his way past the first three squares, opting not to jump, relying on his balance instead of momentum. But his next step would be far more difficult.

Bobby looked at the pair of double-squares that came next. They had accumulated the thickest portion of bodily slop by a landslide. The mini-mountain of gore left a sensation of intimidation running rampant inside him.

Bobby kicked away as much of the ground flesh as he could. But his fears manifested when he planted his foot on the cleared surface. Overlooking a pinkish wad camouflaged by the carnage, as Bobby set his heel, his legs slid apart. Reacting quickly, he replanted his sole and avoided slipping into a full split.

The children let out a collective gasp, before finding relief when Bobby's equilibrium leveled out.

"There's only a few left!" CJ said.

CJ was more distraught than he'd ever been but found a way to offer his brother words of encouragement.

Bobby repositioned himself and drove forward. Despite his clumsy approach, he was able to set his feet on cleaner spots within the last series of spaces before stumbling across the finish line.

When Bobby pulled himself up from the ground, he was panting hard and teary-eyed.

CJ moved in to hug him, but Bobby shrugged his only remaining brother off. He had other ideas in mind.

Bobby cocked his meaty fist back and rushed Isaac. The pieces of his brother were still dangling from his hand as he slung it forward.

The onslaught shocked all the children.

When the heavy blow connected with Isaac's nose, it might as well have been a sucker punch. With no inkling that he should brace himself for a fight, his lanky frame collapsed backward onto the floor. Blood and snot rushed out of his face painting his lips and chin.

"Bobby!" Tanya cried.

"What are you doing?!" CJ screamed.

"Leave him alone!" Sadie demanded.

The little girl began swinging wildly. Her hands collided several times with Bobby's big gut.

Sadie's assault wasn't much of a threat, but it was more about the principle of her actions than the actual result. The conflict resembled a fly pestering a bull. Sadie's weak blows bounced off Bobby's blubber, only serving to agitate him.

Bobby stiffened his fingers and took aim at her. The backhand sent the little girl reeling until she landed butt-first on the ground beside Isaac.

"Bobby! Stop!" CJ barked.

He tangled his arm around Bobby's attempting to stunt any further violence.

"Get the fuck off me! You wanna be on their side?! I'll put you down too!" Bobby yelled.

"They didn't do anything!" Tanya interjected.

"Shut up! They don't care about you! Kip's fucking gone now! Because of them!"

"That's not true!" Sadie exclaimed.

Bobby pointed his bloody finger at Isaac.

"He—He went just slow enough to get Kip knocked off! He could've gone faster, but he didn't! He didn't want either of us to make it across!"

"Maybe if you just would've crossed when the rest of us wanted to, instead of arguing, Kip might still be here!" Tanya yelled.

She regretted her words immediately.

The hurt in Bobby's eyes somehow compounded. In his own mind, he didn't believe it, but that didn't make it any easier to accept. Especially coming from his own sister.

"Stop fighting!" CJ yelled.

He threw his hands by his side and squared back up with Bobby. Their glossy glares entangled together with an uncomfortable intensity.

"Do you wanna get out of here?" CJ asked.

He did his best to keep as cool as possible, but the situation was beyond explosive.

Bobby stared him down, the seething wrinkles of disgust frying like an egg in a pan on his pupils. They drudged up and condensed all the discomfort he felt.

"Well, do you?!"

The question was an easy enough ask, but, under the circumstances, it still required confirmation.

Bobby's head remained in a state of lockjaw. His teeth dug into the side of his mouth as he nodded.

"Then we need to move. We—We don't even know how much time we have until the next wall collapses or ceiling tries to crush us," CJ explained.

"So that's it? We're just gonna forget about Kip I guess?" Bobby asked.

The watery look resurfaced on CJ's face.

"I never said that."

"Then say it! Admit what that faggot did!" Bobby yelled, again gesturing toward Isaac.

"I love Kip just as much as you, but I don't wanna see anyone else get hurt! The only way we're getting out of this is together! Don't you get it?!"

A crooked smile crept up on Bobby's face. He took a few steps away from CJ.

"Oh, I get it. I see who you are," Bobby whispered.

CJ didn't know what else to say to him. He found a small victory in Bobby's overall demeanor seeming slightly calmer, but the situation remained complicated. The end of their exchange didn't make him feel like Bobby was on the same page as he was.

A clock remained ticking in his head, as CJ internally re-acknowledged that time wasn't on their side. Spending time translating his words into something Bobby might get behind was a poor allocation of his effort.

CJ severed the interaction with his brother and panned back to the other kids.

"We've got to get going," CJ said.

As his gaze landed on the group, he couldn't help but notice that it looked smaller than before. Kip was obviously absent now, but even so, it seemed like there was still someone missing.

"Wait—where—where's that kid?" CJ asked.

He quickly started to scan his surroundings, eventually falling in the only direction that he hadn't looked yet—directly behind him.

His eyes found the four deep red letters that lingered ominously over the doorway. The sign read: HELL.

Inside the opening, little Donnie was already making his next move. The crimson glow bleeding out from the crack covered Donnie's tiny body as he slipped inside.

HEAVEN

Fuchs retrieved the pipe from the inside of his jacket and took a few pinches of the tobacco sitting in the tin beside him. Once the wooden head was filled to capacity, he gently placed the tip between his lips and flicked his lighter.

"I must have a smoke after zhat," Fuchs explained.

"It couldn't have gone any more perfectly. We've never had a single child make it this far, let alone six," Geraldine replied.

She gazed at the monitor feed of the parents trapped in the dimly lit room. They remained in a frenzy; tears and trauma aplenty. Rock stood in the same space, continuing to quietly watch over them.

"I feel we may see zhem play on all of our toys today. Zheir comradery is commendable," Fuchs said, taking in another big pull of smoke from the glowing pipe.

She looked back at the monitor that contained the group of children. They had the audio turned down, but their mannerisms portrayed a bitter exchange.

"Overall, I suppose it is, but not entirely. Your splendid timing with the cows certainly created a few ripples in the water, and now it's painfully obvious. They're beginning to fracture. I can see it."

Fuchs nodded and exhaled a dual mass of thick smoke from his nose and lips.

Geraldine looked at the dismay and anger on Tanya's face as she yelled at Bobby. She didn't know what she was saying, but she liked how she said it. Her assertiveness was on the increase. Geraldine was also impressed that she could act with such a powerful grace despite just having watched her brother be ground to bits.

She liked the fire she saw in the girl. It excited her in such a way that she squirmed in her seat as a taboo jubilation ravaged her body.

You're even further along than I imagined, she thought.

While she was impressed with Tanya, she couldn't help but wonder how her father was feeling about the recent turn of events. Her gaze drifted past the plume of smoke to the monitor near Fuchs.

"Interesting…" Geraldine mumbled.

"What is it, my lady?" Fuchs asked.

"Mr. Matthews in the front holding his dead wife's hand. He doesn't seem terribly affected."

Fuchs leaned in toward the screen to get a better gander at Greg. The stone-faced sociopathic stare was powerful.

"It was his boy that just got minced to meatloaf, wasn't it?" Geraldine asked.

"It was," Fuchs concurred.

Geraldine leaned in and squinted, watching closely as Greg's face contorted.

"What odd behavior. I would've imagined a parent to be so much more—more emotional after such a loss."

"People handle zhings in different ways."

"But he's grinning."

Fuchs inched in closer to examine Greg's reaction for himself.

"Hmm, zhat is quite odd."

Fuchs pondered his reaction, puffing on his pipe again and blowing a copious cloud of smoke from his nostrils.

"Maybe he's a psychopath," she suggested.

They both shared a hearty laugh, as Geraldine's eyes drifted back to Tanya.

HELL

As the children filed through the door, an unsettling glow blanketed their bodies. Raining down from a series of blood red floodlights anchored around the otherwise pitch-black space, the hot bulbs beamed. The area beyond the lights was so dark that anything could've been beyond them. But it wasn't the outskirts of the room that most of them were focused on—it was the strange track set up within.

The single-file path ahead was designed with high, stone walls that sprouted up from the ground several feet. While the uncertainty of the route wasn't comforting, they had no option but to proceed.

As CJ cautiously led the children through the castle-like corridor, the bizarre sight that entered his line of vision gave him the chills.

They'd reached a fork where the space opened up. They were now presented with a choice. Their potential selections could be seen in the distance, and so could the next point of progress.

Similar to the prior room, they were again surrounded by a vast black space that offered a surefire fall into the abyss. Beyond the pit stood a final platform that contained a lone, doorless hole.

Above the rocky hole previewed what CJ assumed to be the next part of the playground. A single word painted in red lettering read: SLIDES.

As the crusty slashes in their bodies could attest, the children were yet to have a pleasant experience with slides.

While the thought of the sneak peek was concerning enough, it wasn't the targeted destination that disturbed them the most; it was the means of reaching it.

The nerve-racking, demonic glow shed light on the worrying sights that each route had to offer.

At the end of the first path, stood a two-seated swing set. Placed within a rectangle of soft sand, the series of metal bars erected to hold each of the swings up were so tall that the chains stretched close to double the span of a traditional playground. The remaining dead space between the edge of the beach sand where the swings sat and advancement to the final platform accounted for a sizable gap.

On the route opposite the swing set, was another rectangular slab filled with soft sand. This platform sat upon a steel-reinforced track. The metal rail led directly to the final platform, the caveat being there was a much larger distance to conquer in order to advance.

Atop the grainy space sat a small collection of eight different spring riders. Each of the riders had a large metal coil embedded in the sand and each represented a different design. However, these designs were not the typically gentle variety one might commonly see at a normal playground. The innocent horse, colorful car, and jolly ladybug were nowhere to be seen. The eight unique designs before them were upscale representations of a human heart, a devil, a brain, a Venus flytrap, a rat, a cockroach, a vampire, and a maggot.

Isaac brought up the rear of the group still holding his bloody nose with one hand and his sister Sadie's fingers with the other. Despite feeling too emotionally numb to cry, tears ran from the corners of his warped glasses. But his internal discomfort paled in comparison to his physical.

Sadie was silent but, like a small dog in the rain, she remained shaking.

After CJ corralled Donnie, he'd asked her to keep him close. The last thing any of them wanted was to see him run off randomly again.

The Grimleys kept their distance from Bobby. They didn't want to reheat the bad blood that had reached a boil just a short time ago. While it seemed like they were all at least trying to work together, their trust in Bobby remained tarnished.

After taking in each of the sights at the fork, Tanya took an extra two paces toward her brother who stood in front of yet another sign that read: PLAYGROUND RULES.

"Two on the swings, the rest on the springs, then you'll just have to figure some things…" Tanya said.

It was by far the vaguest and unnerving set of rules they'd encountered.

"That really doesn't tell us much," CJ said.

"Oh yes, it does. It tells us everything we need to know," Bobby interjected.

"How so?" Tanya asked.

"We're going on the springs, the three of us and that little weirdo."

Bobby pointed at Donnie.

"Because I'm not sitting next to those two freaks."

"Why—Why do *we* have to swing?!" Sadie cried.

"Because I'll fucking toss you over that wall if you don't!" Bobby threatened.

"No fighting!" CJ said.

As the argument died off, CJ looked back at the sign.

"It doesn't even tell us what to do," he grumbled.

"We know we have to get across," Tanya replied.

"Yeah, but how…"

"The swings are extra-long. They look like they reach out far. If you get enough speed, I think you should be able to jump off and make it to the other side."

"That's a long jump," Isaac said.

"Too bad!" Bobby yelled.

"Stop it! We're trying to think!" CJ said.

"I don't know about those though," Tanya said, pointing at the collection of spring riders. "Seems like that track would get us across, but I don't know how."

"Like the sign says, I guess we just have to figure it out," CJ replied.

"I don't wanna go on the swings," Sadie cried.

CJ inched closer to Sadie and dropped to one knee.

"I saw you playing on the swings before, you looked pretty good at them."

Despite his stomach twisting in knots, he offered the little girl his calmest smile.

"You were getting some good height, remember?"

"I—I don't know," Sadie said, her eyes continuing to well up. "I never been on ones that big."

"I know you can do it. I saw you jump really far today. Plus," CJ leaned into Sadie's ear, "I think the swings might be easier."

A tremor rattled CJ's words. He didn't know if they might be the last exchange he had with the little girl.

"Hey, no secrets!" Bobby yelled.

CJ ignored his brother and looked up at Isaac.

"I really think you can do it."

Isaac looked down at CJ and then at his sister.

"You can do it," Isaac whispered.

Sadie tried to stop crying but she couldn't. She looked over toward her brother, mustering all of her courage.

"You mean *we* can do it, right?"

"Yeah."

Isaac forced his words out, unsure of their actual value. He didn't enjoy lying to his sister, but he knew they needed to steal some confidence to overcome the obstacle ahead.

"Okay. I'll go on the swings with you," Sadie conceded.

CJ rose from his knee and extended his hand toward Isaac. The uncertainty in his eyes was glaring, but his words couldn't have been more genuine.

"Good luck," CJ whispered.

"You too," Isaac replied.

CJ grabbed young Donnie by the hand and led him in the other direction alongside Bobby and Tanya.

As the little boy followed along thoughtlessly, his heart remained beating at an average rate.

***

Isaac and Sadie both had the shivers upon finding their seats on the swings set. From across the way, in the red radiance of the floodlights, they could see the other children had also selected their own seats. While little thought had gone into their individual choices, each spring rider seemed oddly appropriate for the saddled children.

On the first two spring riders toward the front of the platform sat CJ. He'd selected the human heart. Beside him, his big brother Bobby rested on the devil. A row behind them sat Tanya on the brain and little Donnie on the Venus flytrap.

All the children were looking around, still not exactly sure what they should be doing.

"These chains are super long. We've just gotta swing really fast," Isaac said.

"How fast?" Sadie asked.

"When we start to swing, we'll find out."

"I'm scared, Isaac."

"I know, me too. But we've gotta do this. It's the only way we'll ever get out of here."

Across the way, they could hear the spring riders rocking back and forth. Both Isaac and Sadie turned their gaze to CJ and the others.

"It's moving forward! When we move back and forth it powers it!" CJ exclaimed.

In the distance, they watched the platform start to move at a decent pace as each of the four children bounced around on the toys.

"Why do they get the easy one!" Sadie snarled.

"Because Bobby's a fucking asshole."

Sadie's eyes widened. She'd never heard her brother use curse words before. But there were more pressing matters to think about than her brother's shift in language.

Suddenly, in the darkness behind the red flood lights on the wall, a loud unhinging noise rang out. A glimmer of metal launched forward, powered by an incredible speed. Slicing through the darkness, two pendulum axes appeared. Each of the curved blades measured roughly about the size of a motorcycle. A collision with such a mass would surely be the end of the road for the unfortunate party.

They were positioned at different junctures on their path toward progress. The first was at the early point. It was so close that it *whooshed* past both CJ and Bobby, just narrowly missing their faces.

The second pendulum was further ahead and swung with extreme momentum at about the midpoint of the track.

"Crap! Everybody stop!" CJ yelled. "We've gotta time this right!"

While CJ, Bobby, and Tanya all screeched their motions to an immediate halt, Donnie just kept bouncing away. They weren't progressing as fast as when all four of them were moving, but they were still creeping forward.

"Fucking stop! What are you retarded?!" Bobby yelled.

His words had no impact—threats meant nothing to a boy who got his beatings whether he listened or not. Donnie kept on, his motions creeping the platform toward the swinging axe. Their speed had slowed to a crawl, just slow enough to get them killed.

"We've gotta bail!" CJ said.

He dismounted his spring rider and pancaked his body against the sand. Upon landing, the knife from the hangman stashed in the back of his waistband fell into the dirt. Amid the commotion, CJ didn't even notice.

As the axe came screaming back toward the platform, Bobby followed suit and hit the deck.

The enormous axe smashed into both the heart and devil riders. The impact shattered the plastic, distorted the metal, and caused the platform to violently shake.

"Hold on!" Tanya yelled.

Her brothers each held onto the large coils at the base of the platform, doing everything in their power not to slip off the edge.

As Bobby held on for dear life, his eye caught a twinkle. The blade of the knife gleamed under the red light, calling out to him. Bobby slyly tucked the steel into the back of his waistband.

"Hey!" CJ yelled.

Bobby looked to the side.

"We gotta get on the other ones!"

"Okay!" Bobby replied.

As the axe continued its uptick, the two brothers mounted the pair of riders behind Donnie and Tanya.

"Let's go! We've gotta go as fast as we can before it comes back!" CJ commanded.

With all four of them seemingly on the same page, the rapid acceleration propelled them past the first pendulum.

Meanwhile, as Isaac and Sadie watched on in horror, their own problems began.

The sand and platform under their feet suddenly vanished. Two steel slabs that, unbeknownst to them, were hidden under the heaping pile of dirt, slid off into the black oblivion.

The only parts of the platform that remained were the outskirts that supported the swing set's framework. As the grains and metal slipped into the darkness, the mechanical purr was replaced by the sound of crackling flames manifesting below.

"Crap! Start swinging now, Sadie!" Isaac yelled.

The firepit beneath them was quickly expanding, matching the pace of the intensifying heat.

Isaac, being a few inches taller than Sadie, was the first to feel the plastic bottoms of his sneakers softening.

216

As the flickers of orange licked up toward them and continued to grow, so did their momentum. The chains stretched so high that, before long, each of their swing strides appeared to have extended out far enough to make the jump seem feasible. But with each revolution over the flames, the rubber seating of the swings below their butts only grew weaker.

As Isaac swung backward, he looked under him at the pool of ebony that was ready to swallow him up. But the power of the fire and uncomfortable heat on his posterior made it clear they needed to jump before their seats melted.

"We've gotta go now!" Isaac screamed.

"You first!"

It didn't take but one additional swing for Isaac to ready himself. The current situation was just as, if not scarier than the leap of faith itself. As his next stride propelled him to what he hoped was the pinnacle of his momentum, he slipped his arms around the chains.

As he thrust his body into the air, it felt like time stopped. Isaac sailed through the darkness for what felt like an eternity.

The gap grew smaller.

And smaller.

And smaller.

When he came crashing down onto the concrete, the feeling was a relief punch of intensity that would satisfy the most experienced adrenaline junkie. While the sensation was beautiful, it was a perverse high, the likes of which Isaac hoped to never understand again.

Immediately, he turned back toward his sister.

"C'mon! It's not that bad!" he lied.

Isaac hoped his words of encouragement wouldn't be the last he offered his sister.

Sadie gritted her teeth, emulating her big brother to the best of her ability. The dread biting at her belly was a little more passive because she now knew survival was at least a possibility.

As the swing creaked forward Sadie readied herself. She had to be at her best. She eyed her brother who stood near the edge of the platform with open arms.

"I've got you, Sis!" he yelled.

Just before her momentum hit its peak, Sadie took to the air like a baby bird on its first flight. As it had with Isaac, the hang time felt almost supernatural. The results topped even what her brother was able to achieve.

Because Sadie's body was smaller than Isaac's, the motion pitched her even further onto the platform.

Their bodies collided like a wrecking ball into a skyscraper. They both tumbled and Sadie landed on top of her grimacing brother.

While the pain of their collision left his body aching, it was somehow secondary and almost ignorable when he looked into his sister's watery eyes.

"You did it. I knew you could do it," he whispered.

Isaac curled his back upward and gave his sister a peck on the forehead.

The two had hated each other for nearly the entire duration of their lives. But when everything was on the line, the countless fractures separating them smoothed out. Nothing from their history mattered anymore.

Sadie couldn't find the words, but her face said it all. She didn't realize how much she'd loved him until that moment. All the mean things she'd done to him. All the hurtful remarks she'd hurled. As she looked up at her brother, there was a lifetime of apology in her eyes.

Their moment, and any potential celebration, was short-lived. The noise of the metal squealing on the track suddenly overshadowed their exchange.

Isaac softly slid his sister to the side and rose. He held his breath, hoping that he'd see the others find their way to safety as they had.

Sadie lifted herself off the ground and stood up beside her brother. She hoped the same as Isaac, despite the lingering feeling of anxiety that Bobby conjured.

To their relief, all the other children were working in unison. Even little Donnie seemed to heed Tanya's warnings as she coached him along. The newfound group timing pushed the platform past the second pendulum without issue.

Isaac watched on and let out a deep huff of air, as all four of the kids dismounted their spring riders.

THE FORGOTTEN PROSPECT

Tom and Molly's chests pounded with extreme pacing. Watching Isaac and Sadie have such a close call had set a new threshold of paternal agony. Combined with not being able to watch Sam, at that moment, or ever again, they'd just swallowed enough stress for a full life cycle.

However, victory was short-lived; Isaac and Sadie being currently alive didn't guarantee their protection. Their minds remained active, continuously scanning for whatever advantage they could uncover.

They were still working on the only available option, the muscular goon watching over them. Cracking Rock was the only thing that mattered, but the daunting task was becoming infuriating. They'd had their chance to buzz in and communicate with their children, but the opportunity was useless if they only knew as much about the playground as their kids did.

They'd tested the waters again a few times since Rock's outburst. He remained stable enough that he allowed them to interject a question or two. He didn't always answer, of course, but to Tom and Molly, even just allowing them to speak made it seem like he harbored far more compassion than Geraldine or Fuchs.

"I don't understand what the point of us getting a chance to speak to our kids is, if we don't have any way of helping them. There must be something you can give us?" Tom asked.

Rock said nothing. He continued to stare ahead at the monitor. One by one the big man watched each of the children disappear into the black hole with the oozing word 'SLIDES' above it.

"Even if it's just a small hint, like how the flames appeared under the swings, anything. Nothing that would get you in trouble of course."

Rock gritted his teeth once again and turned his head toward them. He still had a tight grip on Donnie's bloody leash. There was something about the material that helped comfort him when he touched it.

"I'm not worried about getting in trouble. *You* should be worried about getting in trouble," Rock grumbled.

"He didn't mean it like that," Molly said.

"How about you all shut the fuck up? Next game is about to start and we'd like to watch in peace without the background chatter, thank you," Greg said.

He stroked Lacey's pale hand and eagerly diverted his eyes back to the screen.

"Don't you even care about your kids?" Molly asked.

"At this point, why should I? Dead is dead. It's not like I've ever had anyone that gave a shit about me. Didn't need 'em anyhow. Fuck 'em. Taught myself to play ball. Taught myself to drive. Taught myself to pull girls. It's all a game. Life's all just one big game, and I was born ready to play."

Greg's unflinching, casual nature was uncomfortable to be around. The glaring absurdity of his tone and views was wearing on Molly again.

"What do you mean?! Your fucking son is dead!" she screamed.

Trying to get through to Greg was like trying to reach someone on a broken telephone. There wasn't even the slightest possibility of connecting.

"Dead because of your boy! Instead of being a team player and taking his shot like a man, he let it fall onto Kip! And now he's gone! Gone forever!"

It wasn't a coincidence that Greg saw the events the same way his son Bobby did. He'd been imprinting his warped perspective into the boy since he'd left Lacey's womb. Of Greg's entire lot, Bobby had simmered in his philosophies the longest.

"Isaac had nothing to do with that!" Molly cried.

"Your boy's a killer!" Greg yelled.

"No, he's not!"

Tom tapped his wife's arm, trying to steer her away from the pointless argument.

"I don't expect you to admit it, but that's alright. You fuckers wanna play dirty? That's fine. I promise you, the Matthews can play dirtier. You'll see."

"He didn't mean to! It wasn't Isaac's fault—"

"Just stop," Tom whispered. "He's a lost cause. Don't let him drag us down. I need you to stay focused."

As much as Molly hated how Greg saw the event, she knew it mattered very little in the grand scheme of things.

Rock watched on as Isaac guided Donnie toward the dark, unwelcoming hole. His heart felt a sudden strangeness inside, a hurt that was unfamiliar.

As Greg rambled on to himself, Tom calmed Molly and directed their attention back to Rock.

Tom's eyes spied the stained leash in his hand.

"Why does he keep going back to that leash?" he asked.

"I don't know," Molly replied.

While Tom's question wasn't directed toward Rock, his ears still picked it up. A grimace of discomfort found Rock's face. His eyes remained attached to the screen but drifted back down under the sign. He now felt another sensation he wasn't expecting: he was nervous.

His mitt toyed with the leash again as he repositioned his stance. Rock may have been in control of the situation, but he couldn't have appeared more uncomfortable.

223

The cameras had yet to transition and Rock suddenly realized something. It had been in the back of his mind all along, but he hadn't really appreciated the thought until Tom's remark. Not only was he anxiously awaiting Donnie's reemergence, but he cared about the boy.

MONKEY HEAR, MONKEY DO

Isaac was the last one down the slide behind Donnie. They both made it through the plastic channel without issue. When he arrived to face the other four remaining children, he once again felt relief.

He was also thankful that there were no razor blades integrated with this slide or bushels of barbwire to offer them parting gashes. It was just a small victory, but a welcome one.

Isaac moved toward the edge of the new platform and toward a sign they'd now come to expect, which of course read: PLAYGROUND RULES.

The long, multicolor set of monkey bars extended from their platform, all the way over to a separate area. On the other side of the monkey bars, a few yards apart from each other, stood two slides that extended to nosebleed elevation. The nerve-racking height of the towering chutes was all their current vantage point could offer. What came afterward was still anybody's guess.

But before they could worry about what was next, they needed to worry about what was below. It wasn't a surprise to any of the children that the space below the monkey bars didn't contain anything pleasant.

The drop was about twenty-five feet; probably just high enough to break a leg or two. While the fall most likely wouldn't kill anyone, the contents of the gigantic pit surely would.

The odd mishmash consisted of a collection of countless shattered glass fragments. But the broken bottles, cracked windows, and lengthy shards weren't alone.

Within the piles of transparent torture, there was movement. The variety of colors on the scaly exteriors of the countless serpents was beautiful in a way that they'd never be able to appreciate.

Many of the snakes had already cut themselves from slithering against the razor-sharp shards. The gushing effects made the mass below a pulsating monstrosity; one giant moat of horror. The bloody, glimmering rows of reptiles throbbed like they were one with each other. The visual alone of the countless lines of living agitation would've been enough to horrify the children. Never mind the sinister chorus of hisses that seeped up from the pit.

Isaac peered down at the countless knots of reptilian tissue intertwining. Their split, pink and purple tongues ejecting every few moments, ready to unhinge their jaws at the drop of a hat.

He frowned as his heart accelerated; Isaac hated snakes. He didn't know why he had that feeling or how he'd come to find such a particular fear, but ever since he'd seen one on the television, the dread lurked inside him.

Tanya looked at the sign, shaking her head.

"Like a monkey swing all the way, but slip and the fangs will find you today. Should any feet reach the other side, then pick *just* the right moment to go down the slide."

CJ and Tanya looked at each other.

A tiny smirk came across CJ's face; he couldn't help but be proud of his sister. She remained calm and thoughtful even when it felt like they were hopeless.

"What?" Tanya asked.

"Nothing," CJ replied.

"As much as I don't wanna do this, it seems a lot easier than the last thing we did."

"Yeah, but what about the smaller kids? How the heck are they supposed to do monkey bars this big? It's a long way to get across."

"Who gives a fuck? They'll have to figure it out on their own. We can't hang back and help everyone, we need to keep moving forward. Isn't that what *you* said?" Bobby asked.

"But we can't leave them—"

Bobby stepped up to CJ again.

"Look, you were the one that asked me if I wanted to get outta here. Don't make me ask you the same thing."

"We all want to get out of here, but we're not leaving anyone behind."

"Suit yourself."

Bobby pivoted his body to the monkey bars, turning his back on his brother.

"Isaac! Sadie! I love you—and—and your daddy does too. I don't have much time, please just listen."

Isaac and Sadie both looked up where the digital crackle had come from. They couldn't believe their ears. The voice that rang out through the loudspeaker was one that they weren't certain they would ever get to hear again.

Molly sounded terrified.

"Mom?!" Isaac yelled.

Hearing his mother's voice left him utterly confused.

"Mommy! I wanna go home! Mommy, please! Take us home!" Sadie cried.

While it broke her heart, Molly didn't directly answer them. She just continued talking.

Isaac wondered if she could even hear what they were saying. If she wasn't directly responding to them, he knew whatever his mother was saying must've been important.

Isaac put his finger on his lips and looked over toward his sister.

"Shh! Just listen a second," Isaac said.

"Listen carefully, the monkey bars are greased. Look up close at how shiny they are. Don't try to hang from them and swing across, you'll slip right off. See if you can get up on the top of them and—and maybe you can crawl across instead. But whatever you do, don't grab the monkey—"

The speaker projecting Molly's voice cut out.

"They're still alive," Isaac whispered.

A sigh of relief whistled out of Isaac as he squeezed his sister tight. He felt selfish at that moment. Things had been so chaotic since they entered the playground that he hadn't dedicated any time to thinking about his parents and their well-being. Suddenly, the thought jarred him to the core, like the impact of a car crash. His parents, like Sam, could've already been dead.

"Mommy!" Sadie cried.

There was no response.

"I want Mommy!"

A fresh wave of tears started up again.

Isaac looked into his sister's runny eyes.

"We're gonna find a way back to her, I promise."

"Why did she go?"

The question was also puzzling to Isaac. But the distress and dread in his mother's voice didn't sound promising.

"I don't know, but I'm sure they're trying to get back to us, just like we're trying to get back to them."

Isaac made a promise to his sister, but whether he could keep it would be out of his control. But what the fuck did it matter? They were all in anyhow. It wasn't as if Sadie could call him out on it if they wound up dead. To Isaac, it was more fuel to the fire, a promise of more potential energy and motivation.

CJ stepped up beside Bobby and inspected the colorful monkey bars. He noticed thick globs of a slimy, translucent grease had been applied to all of them.

"Your mom's right, these things are all gunky," CJ said.

"Crap," Isaac replied.

Tanya positioned herself back beside CJ.

"She's right then. We're gonna need to get on top of it," Tanya said.

"Fuck!" Bobby yelled.

"What?" CJ asked.

"I'm the biggest one, that's gonna be hard for me."

"We'll figure it out, don't worry. *We're* not leaving anyone behind."

CJ's slight annunciation when he spoke the word *we're* was a subtle way of trying to let his brother see the error of his ways.

Bobby was prepared to leave anyone behind, but now he was looking for comradery to hoist his heavy ass atop the structure. Still, he gritted his teeth, annoyed that he had to depend on anyone at all.

"But since you and I are the biggest, we're gonna have to get everyone up first. Then, I should be able to get to the top and help pull you up myself."

"I've gotta go up last?! No fucking way!"

"Well, how else would you work it, Einstein?"

Bobby thought momentarily. The warped, clunky wheels spinning in his big head soon became his undoing.

"Fine," he said.

CJ found his smile again. He knew his brother wasn't happy to do the right thing, but at least he'd agreed to do it. That was about as much as he could ask for.

CJ nodded his head in Bobby's direction.

"That's the spirit."

CONSCIENCE OR COINCIDENCE?

"How did that little whore know we lubricated the bars?! I know she's pretty young still, but her eyesight can't be *that* fucking good, can it?!" Geraldine bellowed.

"Zhe bars are very shiny," Fuchs replied.

He squinted at the monitor and saw the shimmer with relative ease. Fuchs watched Bobby and CJ hoist up Tanya on top of the monkey bars first, before moving to Donnie.

"But she was so fucking certain about it. It makes me wonder…"

"Wonder what, my lady?"

"You don't think—no he wouldn't…"

"What is it?"

"You don't think Rock would tell them any details that were pertinent to the playground, do you?"

"He has obeyed you since you brought him into zhis house. I highly doubt it."

"Is there a way to get audio from the spy room?"

"I'm afraid not. We can only hear what is conveyed by zhe loudspeakers in zhe playground. Zhere will be a historical recording of zhe cries and screams zhat you may watch for future convenience, but we are not equipped to listen to zhem live."

"Drat!"

She narrowed her eyes at Fuchs. There was nothing in the world Geraldine hated more than being told no.

"At least one of them was supposed to die here! I don't want too many of them reaching the end! That just takes the fun out of it!"

"I zhink zhat you are underestimating zhe rest of zhe playground. We will be lucky to see one remain."

"I can deal with one or two, but anything more is a failure. And we simply cannot accept such failures. Not today."

"Understood. Today shall be a day of triumph," Fuchs concurred.

He returned his gaze back to the monitor and the control panel in front of him.

Geraldine watched the children on the monitor. While she wasn't happy to see all of them safely cross, there was one person she was grateful for.

Tanya had already lowered herself to safety on the other end of the bars. She'd continued to study her scrupulously for the entire day, only growing more impressed as she surveyed.

The girl had served as a cog in the group's survival. The manner in which she continued to strategize and pull the strings of her peers was a spectacle in itself.

The sight of the girl quelled her anger and replaced it with a fuzzy feeling that seemed alien. The cloth that rode her vaginal area grew soggy as she considered a future with her potential new toy. The salacious thoughts of what she might do with such a brilliant prospect caused her hand to slide down over the front of her dress.

As she inspected the image of Tanya, Geraldine used her pruned finger to softly pick at her pussy.

Normally, the urge didn't strike with such intensity. With only a disappointment the likes of Rock, or a static realm of fantasy such as the hall of mirrors, there wasn't much of a point. Those means only took her so far.

But Tanya could be different.

By the day's end, she would find out if there was any merit to her unspeakable inkling.

Geraldine removed her hand from the front of her dress and reached for her drink. There was no sense in getting any more riled up just yet. The girl still needed to prove herself.

Geraldine watched CJ help muscle his brother Bobby up to the top of the monkey bars and considered what was on tap next. Just the sight of the boys annoyed her. They made her think of Rock, which was always a pain point.

Just you wait, Geraldine thought.

A smile exaggerated the wrinkles on her face.

Geraldine watched each of the brothers scale over the top of the structure. It didn't take long for them to crawl their way across. As their feet touched down safely on the other side, she was still hopeful that the next steps they took would be their last.

BLOOD FROM A STONE

A fresh wave of relief washed over Rock when he saw little Donnie standing unharmed on the other side of the monkey bars. But there was still another feeling. A dread lingering on in the background. He knew what came next.

It wasn't pretty.

The boy's chances of survival were slim to none, but somehow Rock still felt like there was a chance.

I saved him just to leave him to the wolves again, he thought.

Rock peeked back at the parents.

Greg sat staring forward like a wide-eyed maniac.

Tom and Molly whispered amongst each other, plotting their next move.

He knew what they were doing; contrary to his cadence and meathead appearance, Rock wasn't stupid. He certainly hadn't let that nugget about the oiled-up monkey bars slip out because they'd tricked or manipulated him. Rock offered it because it was the right thing to do.

The right thing for Donnie and everyone else.

The more he thought about the events of that day, the more distraught he felt. There were countless instances of unappreciation. He was feeling closer to the Grimleys than he did with his own 'family.'

Geraldine's lack of gratitude, praise, and love, continued to pound him over the head. Her outright hatred of his mere existence was obvious enough for even the strangers in the room to pick up on.

It felt like steam was coming out of his ears.

When the day had begun, Rock thought he might finally find acceptance. Even if it was acceptance into the arms of evil, it was still an elusive feeling he'd relentlessly sought. A measly offering of basic emotions might've potentially subdued his rage. Just a taste might've left him a smidge more complacent in his goonish role.

Maybe I am the dummy for thinking it would somehow be different…

He toyed with Donnie's leash in his pocket, recalling the pulpy heap he'd turned his mother into. Liberating the boy, even if it was to his potential demise, was still redemptive. The carrot dangled in front of him; was there more room for redemption that day?

He understood Tom and Molly's actions even clearer now. They wanted the same simple things he desired. When Molly had given the announcement over the speakers, he could see it on her face; the love she had for her children was powerful enough that it still lingered in the room.

They were the kind of people that didn't have the 'class' or bottomless prosperity like Geraldine, but they had heart. When Rock was a child, and even in that very instant, he'd have cut off his own hand to have someone feel that way about him.

Greg, not so much.

His eyes darted back to the king of competition. The deranged, glazed-over gaze on Greg's face was more familiar to him. Greg watched the children closely with a subtle grin curling his lip. It was almost as if he was looking past the images in front of him. Rock wondered what it could possibly be.

Maybe a fantasy?

Maybe a reality?

Whatever it was, it seemed to cloud Greg's spirit. He was like a thunderstorm; he carried an unmistakable darkness with him wherever he went.

Rock's eyes bounced back and forth from Greg to Tom and Molly, before finally returning to the screen.

Within the glass, he saw his reflection.

He'd never been excited by what he saw; the sins of his past came to mind each time. Self-hatred oozed from his pores like a bum-rush of blackheads being purged.

Outside of the hate, he couldn't help but focus on his flesh. The nagging pain from the slices on his face wouldn't allow him to forget.

What am I doing? he wondered.

The many particles of glass that slipped under Rock's stubble served as a smarting reminder of his inferiority. He was at the edge. When he finally fell off, where the tumble would lead, even he didn't know.

Something had to give.

The aches in his face.

The guilt in his gut.

The disappointment in his heart.

The lack of change in his 'family' dynamic after such a monumental moment had left Rock sure of one thing:

He was tired of being abused.

FATHER KNOWS BEST

Deeply disturbed looks latched onto the faces of the kids as they first set eyes on the slides. The stretched jaws and furrowed brows were indicative of a new dread; one that had somehow driven them past the previous zenith.

Each of the slides was positioned at the beginning of a pit of blackness. The long slab of U-shaped metal stretched on for thirty yards over the certain doom. The ride ended on a lower-level platform where an open elevator door awaited. But coasting over the gaping void wasn't even close to the most terrifying aspect of the sadistic stunt.

Beneath each of the slides were clusters of circular saw blades. They were positioned in a way that, upon descent, there was no way to avoid crossing over them. But in a perverse, gimmicky fashion, the machinery attached beneath the slides, pushed the spinning blades through the slits and then backed them out, rotating every few seconds.

The threat of extreme violence faced them, but the timing mechanism allowed a brief window for safe passage. If they slid down at just the right time, they would coast over the slits while the saws were retracted and avoid the hazard. But alternatively, if they chose the wrong moment, the saws would shred them to ribbons.

The severity of such damage would most likely be of the irreparable variety.

Tanya watched Donnie take a step closer to the edge.

"Hold on to my hand," she said.

She wrapped her trembling digits around the boy. The shrill twist of the spinning saw blades made Tanya's body tighten. Her troubled squint found CJ.

"I—I don't know if I can do this," she said.

"It's all about timing, if anyone can do it, it's you," CJ said.

There was even more stress straining his voice than before. Looking back to the rest of the group, he saw each child adorning their own stage of worry.

"We can all do this. We just have to watch the saws. If we can pass over the blades when they're coming down, I think the—"

A loud motorized noise coming from behind them cut CJ off. The pit that lay under the greased monkey bars rumbled.

Isaac looked back to where the commotion was. To his ultimate dismay, the floor of the deadly pit was elevating towards them.

"Oh no! It's coming up! The snakes are coming! It's moving fast!" Isaac cried.

The sight injected him with a new motivation. He ran over to the ladder and propped his foot up on it.

The sound of the hissing heathens drew closer. They couldn't be certain if they were poisonous or not, but they'd been conditioned to jump to worst-case scenarios as of late.

"What do we do?!" Sadie cried.

The sight of the buzzing saws wasn't much more favorable than the horde of reptiles closing in.

"Everybody on the ladders!" CJ yelled.

"C'mon, Sadie!" Isaac yelled.

As the children scrambled, the platform leveled out, and the knotty upsurge of the blood-drenched serpents slithered forth.

There wasn't time to choose which slide they wanted to be on. On one side, Tanya continued to guide Donnie up to the top of the fifteen-foot ladder. She held him steady while CJ climbed up into the space behind his sister.

On the opposite side, Isaac made his way up to the top quicker than anyone else. He peeled his eyes from the scary sight of the saw to check on his sister.

As Sadie pulled herself up, she remained just a short distance behind her brother. The tears found her again and her face crinkled. She felt pain; her skin had grown sore from the continuous expressions of dread.

Bobby didn't have a choice but to be on the same side as Isaac and Sadie. The snakes had come so fast that it was to be his destiny. He was a few steps high, but far enough from the serpents to avoid peril.

When Isaac looked down the massive chute, the sheer length of the ride made his knees buckle. He clenched the metal poles tightly and watched the saw blades repeat their motions.

Up.

Down.

Up.

Down.

Up.

Down.

Across the way, Donnie did the same as Isaac. However, he saw the unforgiving steel with a far calmer poise. While he wasn't as frightened, his unflinching yet blank nature did little to contribute ideas.

CJ was too far below to gauge a strategy. He felt helpless when it came to planning. Donnie surely wouldn't be the one to probe about the topic. He turned his head toward Isaac. CJ hoped he'd be able to rely on him.

"Isaac!" CJ yelled.

"Yeah?!" Isaac answered.

"How many seconds is it between when the saws go down and come up?!"

Isaac waited for the blades to drop, then counted.

"One-one-thousand, two-one-thousand, three-one-thousand, four-one-thousand, five—"

The metal popped up, reclaiming its prior position.

"It's—It's just about four seconds, I think?!" Isaac hollered back.

"You think?" CJ asked.

"Is it four seconds or not, fuckface!" Bobby yelled.

"Stop yelling!" Sadie demanded.

"Shut up!"

"Everyone be quiet! I think I've got an idea!" Isaac interjected.

He pulled his body forward and cautiously balanced himself at the top of the slide. His shaking rump sat on the flat part of the tube just before the dip. Isaac untied his left sneaker and slipped it off his foot. He tested with the shoe, gliding the rubber along the metal that comprised the slide.

Isaac was disappointed when he noticed the material got hung up, gripping against the metal instead of easily sailing down it.

"Dang," he mumbled.

Another idea quickly struck him. Isaac used his free hand to remove the sock over his foot. Upon brushing the soft cotton against the slide, he found it glided against the metal without issue.

"What the heck are you doing?" CJ asked.

"A test run!" he replied.

Isaac unbuckled the brown belt around his waist. Then he slid the leather off, bunched it up, and stuffed it into the shoe hole. He palmed the weighted sneaker in his hand afterward and judged the density. Lastly, Isaac took hold of the sock and stretched it out. Once the material was slacked enough, he slipped the cotton around the entire shoe.

Sweat dripped off the tip of his nose, and his glasses clouded. His eyes darted from the sock-wrapped sneaker over to the blades. He watched intently, waiting for them to return.

He calculated the space between him and the first set of blades. If he slid down while they were showing, by the time he reached them, they should already be back down. The distance between each set looked about the same. If the sneaker made it by the first set of blades, it should also make it past the remaining saws just the same.

"Here we go!" Isaac yelled.

As the blades came up, the sneakers slid toward them. Just as Isaac predicted, the smooth gliding sneaker moved past the first set without issue. Then past the second and third, before arriving safely at the below platform.

"It made it!" Isaac rejoiced.

"What does that mean?!" Tanya yelled.

There was still much worry in her tone.

"It—It means that if you slide down right when the saw blades come up that we should make it through without getting cut!"

"Should?!" CJ yelled.

"I think so. We're all heavier than the shoes so we might go a little faster, but I think there was enough space in between!"

A snarl found Bobby's face, his impatience, anger, and annoyance beamed.

"Then go ahead! If you're so fucking sure then—"

"Bobby, he's trying to help!" CJ yelled.

His brother's antics were wearing on him.

"No, he's right. I should go first. Besides, I don't think we have another option!" Isaac yelled.

"Don't leave me, Isaac!" Sadie cried.

Isaac looked back at his kid sister.

"I'm not leaving you. I've just gotta get down there first. Once I do, then I can tell you exactly when to come down. It'll be alright, I promise."

Since they'd entered the playground, Isaac had made enough promises to his sister to fill up a punch card. She'd earned another free one. Still, nothing had changed. Not a single one of them was guaranteed.

"I'm scared, I—I don't want you to go yet," she cried.

"Well, whether you like it or not, he's going!" Bobby barked.

Sadie's hysterical sobs broke Isaac's heart. He wanted to cuss Bobby out, but he knew it wouldn't help the situation. He controlled his emotions and stared into his sister's eyes.

"Do you trust me?"

When Sadie nodded, multiple tears toppled off her face.

"Then I'll see you down there, okay?"

She could only offer Isaac a horrified nod; her brother had said enough to convince her.

"Alright, here we go," Isaac said.

He looked back toward the meat-wrecking machinery. The lump in his throat grew to gargantuan dimensions as he watched the blades go down.

He couldn't blink.

A big bead of sweat drizzled into his eye stinging it, but it didn't deter his concentration. He clenched the metal bars readying himself, and just as the spiky tips of the saw blades emerged, he pushed forward.

Isaac's take-off was clean. While nothing snagged him initially, that didn't stop the screams of terror from erupting out of his esophagus as he approached the first set of saw blades. He kept his feet angled upward as he closed in, elevating his heels higher. It might very well come down to inches, and if that was the case, Isaac needed to ensure he gave himself the best shake at clearing the saws.

Thankfully, it wasn't as close as he projected it to be. The blades fell into their slits just before the bottom of his feet reached them. The same as his sneaker had done, Isaac sailed safely past each of the perils implanted on the path of malice.

"Yes!" CJ cheered. "He did it! I can't believe he did it!"

The adrenaline coursing through Isaac hadn't allowed him to celebrate or even comprehend the frightening feat that he'd just conquered. As his body thudded against the cold ground, the emotional exhaustion weighed him down.

"Just have a seat on top. You're just gonna go for a little slide now, okay?" Tanya asked.

As Tanya readied little Donnie, he obeyed her, flattening out at the peak of the slide.

As an extra measure of precaution, she held onto the back of his shirt, not trusting that he wouldn't just skip ahead like he'd been known to.

One by one, Donnie, Tanya, and CJ found a way to forget their fear. They trusted the results that Isaac's successful attempt presented them with.

As Isaac regained his bearings, he noticed Donnie standing over him. He was holding onto the sock-wrapped shoe. Donnie thoughtfully set it down in front of Isaac, just as Tanya found her way to safety.

By the time CJ made his way down, Isaac was once again wearing all of his clothing and accessories. While he was happy to see the three of them arrive unscathed, his attention immediately turned back to his sister.

When he looked at the top of the distant slide, he saw Sadie's blonde ponytails trembling and her toothless frown in the distance. She was frozen from the fear; her entire body possessed at a steady rattle.

"Fucking go!" Bobby screamed.

Sadie remained motionless. Her small, shaky arms were clamped onto the metal bars on each side of the slide. Her insides ached as a yellowish fluid exited her body and drizzled down the massive chute.

It only took seconds for the warm trickle to make its way onto the platform in front of Isaac. As the pungent odor of the urine invaded his nostrils, a terrible feeling came over him. He instantly knew that his sister was in deep trouble.

"I—I'm scared, Isaac! I can't do it!" Sadie cried.

"Yes, you can!" Isaac yelled.

"No! It's gonna cut me up! I'm gonna look like Sam!"

A thick string of drool seeped out of Sadie's mouth.

"You just have to slide down when the blades are up! I can watch them for you and tell you when to—"

A grainy sizzle suddenly echoed throughout the room. A voice came over the loudspeaker blotting out any chatter. But the voice didn't project an endearing or frightened tone. It wasn't about concern; it was about command.

"Bobby, I know I've always been down on you for not having what it takes to play ball. But maybe I was wrong. Maybe that skateboarding you do can actually help you. Just think about it, if you find something to ride down on, then you won't get hurt. These little fuckers killed Kip! We can't just let them get away with it! It's only fair. Don't disappoint me, Son. Don't disappoint—"

Greg's voice cut off just as the horrified cries and curses of Tom and Molly exploded in the background.

"Noooooo!" Isaac screamed.

Bobby's mind was already in a dark place. Since he'd witnessed his brother being broken down into shreds, he felt different. Just because he was a disappointment to his father, it didn't change the instincts entrenched in his bodily fiber. If anything, it only amplified it.

He wanted his father's acceptance.

He wanted to make him proud.

Bobby would never be CJ or Kip. He wasn't fortunate enough to be blessed with such a raw knack for sports or athleticism. He could never be what his father wanted.

Until now.

The violence had slowly desensitized him. It made reaching for Sadie's ankle much easier. Before the little girl could understand the macabre nature of what Mr. Matthews was suggesting, Bobby gave her a good tug. She pancaked forward, landing flat on the top of the slide. Bobby elevated himself closer and pinned her back down with his knee.

"Bobby, what the hell are you doing?!" CJ cried.

As Bobby retrieved the forgotten knife from his waistband, he was struck by a moment of brief hesitation. He wondered if he could really go through with it. It was like a thunderstorm inside his head. The electric current struck, and images materialized in his mind.

Flashes of Greg's grinning face—they radiated a proudness the likes of which he'd never been graced with.

Flashes of Kip's brutalized remains—they oozed the faint traces of the life he was robbed of.

Flashes of Isaac finishing hopscotch—the release of relief that he didn't deserve.

"This is for Kip!" Bobby yelled.

"Bobby, no!" CJ cried.

"Stop!" Isaac begged.

The hard point of the blade plunged through Sadie's back, sliding several inches inside her. The depth of the wound went almost up to the hilt, causing her little lung to collapse in the process.

Tanya was shell-shocked by her brother's actions. As she clenched onto Donnie, she recalled Bobby's mean-spirited jabs. It just seemed like a normal sibling rivalry. She never imagined he might be capable of such an atrocity.

But what confused her almost as much as Bobby's unforgivable act, was her father's sadistic directions. It was a side of him that was seething with a vengeance. A sickening dimension of his personality she'd never seen. Did he really believe that Isaac or Sadie had anything to do with Kip's death?

Sadie squirmed and cried out, but her pleas were cut short by a cough. A hot mass of blood and spit rained down the metal slide.

Bobby held Sadie steady as the blade exited her back. It reentered her tissue beside the initial wound just as quickly. He continued to back-stab her repeatedly until the blood was pissing out of the several holes dotting her back with each breath she took.

Bobby slammed the gory tip into her one last time. This poke landed closer to her neck, and the sheer force drove it deeper into Sadie's body than any of the prior strikes.

It was by design.

Bobby yanked it around intentionally, confirming that the knife was securely lodged inside her flesh.

Bobby pulled himself up to the top of the slide and methodically nudged Sadie to the edge where it dipped.

As she choked on her own blood, the red rained down the long chute, tracing over the path of her piss. And just like he did on his skateboard, Bobby secured his footing on Sadie's backside.

He steadied his balance by holding onto each end of the U-shaped slide. Then, Bobby set his right foot close to Sadie's neck, just behind the knife he'd left sticking out of her back. A chiropractor-caliber *crack* erupted from Sadie's spinal column. As he pressed her pale face into the metal, Bobby could feel the bubbling blood in her lungs as she attempted to gasp for air. Sadie's internal rumble continued as he set his left foot down on her butt.

"Just like you wanted, Dad," Bobby whispered.

He used his arms to pull himself forward and soon realized that the amount of blood and piss on the slide had created an even slipperier slope.

Bobby always enjoyed riding fast, so as he rushed toward the blades, his excitement heavily outweighed his fear. He believed there was enough meat underneath him to avoid getting sliced into.

Despite not being academically inclined, his horrific hypothesis proved true. The first set of blades didn't cut all the way through Sadie's backside; she'd caught the tail end of the cycle. The mauling slowed them momentarily while the metal carved out several gaping wounds into her face and neck. Tiny teeth ejected, gums were gashed, and parts of her lips were ripped off. Sadie's chest and bones were sliced through, the revolutions deep enough to almost reach the organs inside her torso.

The immense outpouring of blood offered additional lubrication, accelerating their pace. As Sadie's upper body hit the next wave of blades, the steel shredded into her even deeper. When the pink meat was divided by wild slicing, the flesh was flung in every direction. The act of violence was so devastating, it made Sadie look like human vomit.

Sadie's tongue and nose were destroyed. The blades had unearthed her cartilage, muscle, and bone. The damage was of such a magnitude that Sadie's head now looked like a bunch of fresh slaughterhouse scraps that were randomly glued together.

Below the space where her face had once rested, Sadie's right arm had been viciously gashed. Her tiny bicep was so mutilated that it had detached from her splintered skeleton.

The interior thigh on the same side got slit to the bone, offering a veiny exposure that shouldn't have arrived until the varicose days of the future. Another Fourth of July-worthy explosion of blood splatter painted the already crimson metal.

By the time Sadie's body reached the final set of saws, the meat serving as Bobby's protection was scarcer. He could clearly see the hole that had developed right under her shoulder. Bobby used his left hand and secured his fingers around the handle of the blade wedged in Sadie's back. Then, cautiously, he repositioned his footing away from the cavernous wound.

His actions wouldn't even matter.

The gory heap that was Sadie Grimley breezed through the final set of saw blades. The combination of the prior two slashings and the lubricated track altered the timing. The change was enough that, by the time they arrived at the last trio, the saws had already retracted under the slide.

As Bobby rode the bolting, bloody cadaver to the end of the slide, he and Sadie both became airborne. A sudden halt struck as the messy corpse connected with the stone floor. When Bobby somersaulted forward, his grip on the knife never wavered.

Being familiar with failure, he handled the wipeout with grace. As he rolled his way back to his feet, the first thing he saw was the wrath in Isaac's eyes. But just as quickly as the boy charged him, Bobby raised the blade. When Bobby pointed the steel, slathered in Sadie's final drippings, at Isaac, he knew his aggressor's fury would soon fizzle out.

BOTTOMLESS HATE

Rock couldn't help but cringe. The sound of Molly's vocal cords shredding was like nails on a chalkboard. He could hear the pain, but even more than the pain, he registered the love. The animalistic wailing she'd set free sounded like something from the depths of the jungle. He'd never seen such a display of affection. Such internal destruction couldn't be faked.

The raw reaction displayed an emotional investment far beyond the kind he'd regularly dreamt and fantasized about. It was a notch of intensity Rock couldn't fathom.

Contrary to Molly, who looked as if her heartache might kill her on the spot, Greg's mood was the polar opposite.

"That a boy, Bobby!" he yelled.

A dastardly cackle leaped from his lips as he basked in the joy of the twisted victory. The bloodshed meant nothing to him. The pile of human slop at the bottom of the saw slide didn't disturb him, it devolved him.

The violence was eating away at his humanity.

To Rock, he was no longer looking at the same man he'd ushered into The Borden Estate. Either that, or he just hadn't been around enough people to realize how to spot someone's true colors.

Regardless, the person Greg had become was beginning to bother Rock. When he watched how he'd used his final connection with his boy for evil, it reminded him of something Geraldine would've done. But an even darker question now emerged in his mind: if he'd grown disturbed by what Greg had become, then what about his own collection of sins?

His eyes found little Donnie on the screen again. In spite of the death, violence, and current hostility he'd witnessed, Donnie remained numb.

Rock and Donnie were two peas in a very perverse pod.

An icy shiver ran down Rock's back. He couldn't seem to shake the feeling that he was on the verge of something.

Something big.

He felt the internal agony and self-loathing slither closer to each other. The unavoidable shame and flaring disgust poked their heads out too. The endless cycle of cynicism and decades of guilt were all coming to a long overdue climax. The results could only be volcanic in scale.

The massive amalgamation of uncertainty that stretched from his gullet to his gut felt like a fat serpent slithering inside his torso. But even pondering the distress inside his body and soul wasn't enough of a distraction to make Rock forget about the current situation at hand.

Molly's tear-jerking cries had almost overshadowed her husband. Tom squirmed wildly in his chair like a loon that had been strapped down for electro-shock.

While the metal collar still restricted him, his violent moments had somehow caused the sturdy seating to rattle. The bottom level of hell had manifested inside him and it was ready to burn its way out.

"I'll kill you! I'll fucking kill you!" Tom screamed.

His red, runny eyes burned through Greg until Tom snapped his focus on Rock.

"Let me—let me out of this fucking chair! Let me out now! Is this what you wanted?! Is this what you wanted, you sick fucks!" Tom screamed.

As Rock looked at the destroyed man, the question hit hard. In his beefy heart, he believed he knew the answer. Maybe he didn't before that day, but he certainly did when Tom asked him.

However, it wasn't an answer that Rock was prepared to divulge. Moreover, knowing the answer to the question didn't necessarily change the outcome. But, at the very least, it allowed Rock's wheels to keep turning.

As Rock watched on, digesting Greg's maniacal laughter, he found himself disgusted. On the other hand, the dread and audible anguish of Tom and Molly birthed a sickness and suffering in his chest. He suddenly found himself volleying a question of his own.

Where's the line? he thought.

As Rock looked back to the monitor, he saw young Donnie still fighting and scrapping for every moment. Just as Rock had done for his entire life, Donnie somehow kept finding a way.

The clouds in Rock's skull were fading away. Their dissipation shined a light on the uncomfortable truth that he continued to hide behind.

He could only use his fear as an excuse for so long.

THE CONSTANT CELEBRATION

A fresh cork unloaded from the bottle of bubbly and fizz flooded outward. The leer on Geraldine's face stretched to an uncomfortable wideness.

"Did you see that?! I told you they were turning on each other! He literally stabbed her in the back!" Geraldine yelled.

Her glee only paused while she took another huge slurp from the fresh bottle.

"You are marvelous, my lady!" Fuchs replied.

Fuchs extended his glass, and Geraldine sloppily filled it to the point of overflow. The twist of joy and madness reflecting in each of their pupils was for a job well done. He remembered drawing up the blueprint for the saw slide. It was one of the structures he was most proud of. Seeing the device reach its intended potential for the first time left a warm sensation around his stony heart.

"And zhe boy's father, he told him to!"

As Fuchs continued to laugh, Geraldine grew somewhat somber in her expression.

"I just can't believe that he stabbed her. I never would've imagined that they'd use the knife on each other but…" She composed herself, fighting back a tear. "But today is truly a special day."

Fuchs slowed his laugh, taking notice that Geraldine had moved on from the giggles.

"Zhat, it is," he concurred.

Fuchs raised his glass up to his lips and took a generous swig in celebration.

Geraldine controlled her lip quiver and subtly wiped away the lone tear that showed in the corner of her eye before it could drop.

Her eyes were back on Tanya again. After Geraldine bet on her, the girl continued to advance and show promise. She'd added an *extra* layer of excitement to Geraldine's special day. If all went well, Geraldine could capitalize on their blossoming relationship long after the nefarious events on the playground ceased.

"Don't look so sad. It is not over yet," Fuchs said.

"I suppose you're right," she replied.

Geraldine found her grin again.

"I've still got a few more tricks up my sleeve."

HORROR-GO-ROUND

Isaac paused his charge when he saw the dripping blade just a few feet away from his face. Seeing Bobby regain his footing and stab at the air was enough to force Isaac's reasoning to overtake his emotional outburst.

"Try me, dandelion! I'll leave you looking worse than her!" Bobby yelled.

Isaac couldn't help but let his eyes drift to the goopy, vomitus blend of meat and muscle that was sandwiched within the torn ribbons of skin. The haggard husk that no longer resembled his sister left his spirit trampled in the worst of ways.

He was alone now.

When the harsh realization that he was the last member of his family remaining in the playground hit, snot bubbled from Isaac's nose, and the tears and drool leaked. If he wasn't so angry, he might have fallen to his knees. But instead, he found a promise in his heart.

"You're gonna pay for this," he grumbled.

"We're even now!" Bobby exclaimed.

Isaac didn't need to reply to the absurd claim. It wouldn't change anything. He just wanted to let Bobby know that wasn't the end.

The cold-hearted confidence that he hadn't displayed was something different. His trauma helped recast him in a new role. Isaac sniffed up some of the snot that still oozed from his nose, basking in the thoughts of violence that infected his thought stream.

"Why the hell did you do that?!" CJ screamed.

"You heard Dad! You heard what he said!"

"Did it ever occur to you that maybe Dad's not right all the time?! Especially when he's telling you to kill people?! Maybe they're hurting him too or—or making him say that stuff to trick us!"

"Of course you would say that now!"

"What are you talking about?"

"The second I get some shine, the *one time* when *I* finally get a moment! You can't even wait five seconds to rip it away from me!"

"People are dead! You think I care about that?! What the heck is wrong with you, dude?!"

"It's *your* life. That's all you care about—"

"I don't even like baseball! I hate it! I do it because I have to, not because I want to! I do it because Dad will hate me if I don't!"

"You'd—You'd say anything. You're just mad that he didn't ask *you* to do it! You never did wanna share that shine. You were always a greedy brother."

CJ took a step closer to Bobby until the knife blade was nearly against his cheek. He didn't let the weapon intimidate him. As CJ squared eyes with his big brother, he did everything he could to keep from blowing a gasket.

"Dad's lost his fucking mind… and now… so have you." CJ didn't enjoy swearing, but he wondered if it might help somehow get through to Bobby.

"He's never steered you wrong before! Why should today be any different?! I don't know about you, but I'm not here to lose! Not to this faggot," he pointed at Isaac, "not to those old weirdos, not to anyone! Not even to you! But I sure hope it doesn't come to that," he said.

CJ couldn't believe it; the rhetoric that was typically reserved for his father sitting on the ballpark bleachers on a hot, sunny day was spewing from his brother. He espoused it with such passion because it had been burned into his brain. It was like they were the same person.

Bobby had finally become the young man that he never figured himself good enough to be. He'd finally gotten the overdose of praise he'd thirsted for from his father.

It was all he could see.

"Bobby, please stop, you're—you're scaring me," Tanya said, tears streaking down her cheeks.

"This piece of shit killed our little brother, and you'd just let him be? You'd just... never mind. You're not gonna get it. Neither of you are. It doesn't matter anymore, anyway. That's why Dad picked me. It's time for us to move on."

"You can go to Hell. I'm not going anywhere with you," Isaac replied.

"I wasn't asking. You've got two choices: get in the elevator, or the knife gets in you. Pretty simple, wouldn't you say?"

Isaac ground his teeth and balled his fists, pushing his fingernails into his palms.

"As much as I know you'd like to do your own thing, when we get to the next part of the playground, I think that I'd feel safer having you go first."

A nasty grin manifested on Bobby's face. The thought of using Isaac as a guinea pig not only kept him a step away from death, but it also felt like justice.

"So, get in the fucking elevator. Now."

***

When the elevator completed its ascension and the metallic door squeaked open, two groups of children were revealed. On the right side of the elevator, Bobby stood, holding the knife menacingly. On the left side, everyone else stood, with a profound uncertainty and fear that left them gobsmacked.

As Bobby directed them to exit, they could all smell chemical fumes starting to fill up their nostrils. A short, straight pathway stared back at the children with a lone sign erected at the end.

Just past the sign, sat a sizable, hexagonal platform. The ground within was occupied entirely by a huge, self-propelled, slow-spinning merry-go-round. But this merry-go-round wasn't the carnival standard filled with animals on poles; it was the playground variety.

It was comprised of a mostly wooden exterior except for a few rusty metal bars for each rider to cling to. However, contrary to most of the other creations they'd seen up to that point, the roundabout seemed like it was intentionally outdated.

The iron bars were corroded.

The wood frame was rickety and splintered.

The foundation squeaked with each revolution.

It wasn't a ride designed to derive pleasure; it was a ride of doom.

The roundabout was positioned in such a way that there was no footing on the platform besides the lip of the merry-go-round itself. Beyond that narrow lip was a steep fall that led to a manmade moat underneath.

The malicious moat was occupied with a variety of toxic elements. The ominous, slimy, neon-greenish fluid bubbled and steamed. For anyone unfortunate enough to find themselves clinging to the roundabout, the noxious goop served as the ultimate motivator to hang tight.

Past the roundabout stood another platform, but there was no path that led from the roundabout to the final progress point. The lone doorway on the final platform was adorned with crimson font above that read: THE END?

Bobby glared at his sister Tanya; the eyes in his head weren't the same that she remembered.

"Read it," Bobby demanded.

Tanya stared at him but did as she was told. The sign remained consistent. It read: PLAYGROUND RULES.

"To reach the end you all must play, to see your parents once more today. Hold on tight for the final hooray, or just let go and melt away."

"Shit," Bobby muttered.

He glared at the words 'you all' with aggravation. Bobby would've loved to use Isaac as a guinea pig, but it appeared that wasn't in the cards just yet.

Tanya coughed, her drying throat stinging.

"I don't think these fumes are good for us. It's hard to breathe. They're—They're making me feel dizzy."

"Yeah," CJ said, letting out a cough of his own. "Me too. We gotta get through this as fast as we can."

"Wait, what do we do?" Bobby asked.

The harshness of his tone had died down. The dread had sunk its fangs into his belly again.

"What do you think we do? Like every other merry-go-round, we hold on. You can do that, can't you, tough guy?" Isaac interjected.

Bobby approached him with the blade, pressing it against his throat.

"I can make it so you don't even get a last ride, smart ass. Is that what you want?"

Bobby let out a cough. Despite his thickheadedness, he was beginning to realize each word he spoke was a second he wasted. He knew his poor choices might be inching him closer to his own doom.

"We don't have time to fight," CJ said.

He couldn't even muster anger anymore. The slices in his back still ached, his body was sore, and his spirit was running on empty. More than anything else, he was tired.

CJ removed himself from the argument and grabbed hold of little Donnie's hand.

"Let's go," CJ said.

Bobby eventually dropped the blade from Isaac's throat and gestured with it to move ahead.

Tanya quickened her pace until she was close to CJ.

"What are you gonna do with him?" Tanya whispered.

"I'll just have to keep him in front of me. That's his best chance. There's no telling how long this thing's gonna spin for. Are you gonna be okay holding on by yourself?"

"I think so," Tanya replied.

CJ was scared but didn't make it obvious. The added responsibility of accounting for Donnie did little to boost his confidence. He looked to some small talk with his sister to distract him.

"We never did end up getting to hit that seesaw, did we?"

"It's probably for the best," she replied.

Tanya passed in front of her brother, stepping up to the slim slice of platform that would allow her to board the roundabout.

"Well, I still wanna seesaw with you," CJ said.

He smiled at her, trying to trick his mind.

"I don't think so. After this… if there is an after this, I'm never going to a playground ever again."

CJ's grin warped slightly.

"Fair enough," he whispered.

The merry-go-round was spinning slowly, allowing Tanya to hop on without issue. She grabbed onto the bar in front of her tight, then planted both of her feet firmly on the wooden base.

"You ready buddy? I'm gonna pick you up. When we get on, we've both gotta hold on as tight as we can together," CJ explained.

He still didn't know exactly how much Donnie could comprehend, but it made little difference.

CJ let out another cough as he secured the vertical metal bar. The rusted section he chose seemed the most stable to him; a piece of steel serving as a pillar for the two bars that intersected above it.

He grabbed onto it with one hand and set Donnie down gently with the other. CJ kept Donnie between his legs and they both planted their feet on each side of the steel column. Donnie wrapped his hands around the pillar, and CJ firmed up his grip on the two connecting horizontal pipes.

"Just hug it as tight as you can," CJ whispered.

Donnie remained dumbfounded; hug was most certainly not a word he was familiar with. But when CJ thrust his hips forward and snugged him close against the vertical pillar, his instinct was to wrap around it.

CJ adjusted his left arm, locking it through the pillar until he was satisfied with his position. He tightened up his body and used his legs to hold Donnie in place as best he could.

Isaac jumped on a few yards in distance away from where Tanya, CJ, and Donnie were positioned.

As he'd done previously, Bobby stuck the gore-caked blade back into his waistband. Watching another revolution, he timed his hop so that he could occupy the space right beside Isaac.

The instant Bobby's feet landed on the roundabout, the platform he'd jumped off of rapidly descended. In a matter of seconds, the entire path had completely vanished; the area was now covered by the sickening, shamrock substance in the ditch below.

Isaac snuck a peek back at Bobby. The exaggerated creases on his face formed a look of malcontent. Isaac didn't like being near him, but as the roundabout accelerated in speed, he knew there wasn't time to negotiate or reposition himself.

The gray castle walls surrounding them had morphed into a massive, smoky blur.

CJ flexed his muscles, pinning little Donnie against the steel. As the dizziness set in, he kept them in place without issue.

Tanya coughed again; the potency of the noxious fumes only seemed to increase with time. As each spin dragged them all screaming toward a new spike in their pacing, her stomach rumbled violently. She suppressed the urge to vomit and closed her eyes, keeping her grasp firm.

Bobby, like CJ, was positioned against a column of steel where two of the grip bars connected. Despite having the largest frame, he could still hold himself in place.

Just feet away from Bobby, Isaac hung onto the bar in front of him. But when the metal around his fingers squeaked, he realized his grip might not matter so much as the area he'd chosen to hold on to did.

He'd chosen a horizontal stretch of the bar. Not thinking to align himself in front of a support column suddenly proved to be a poor decision.

The increased acceleration of the roundabout only amplified the amount of stress on the wobbly structure's framework.

Isaac could hear more groans leaving the old wood in front of him. He could feel the unsteadiness of the support bar as he attempted to inch his way closer to the steel pillar for added security. But the pressure of the spin in his face was too much.

Suddenly, the bar in Isaac's hands gave way. The rusted screws that once made the bar feel completely secured, began to detach from the support column. The sudden, jarring separation caused his left hand to slip off the metal. His lone remaining grip came from his right hand as the bar continued to bend and further distort.

Isaac looked down at the bubbling stew of toxicity and chemicals, his pulse jumping, causing his throat to bulge. He fought against the momentum, getting his left hand back on the warped pole, but the stress of the revolutions caused his grip to slacken.

"Isaac!" CJ cried.

He wanted to help, but due to his current obligation with Donnie, moving would create more overall risk than it was worth. CJ's gaze of terror transitioned to Bobby. His brother was within arm's length of Isaac, but CJ was less than convinced he would do anything to help.

"Bobby! Help him—"

CJ's pleas were cut short by a wave of violent coughing. The fit, paired with the roundabout's force, triggered a tiny mouthful of vomit to rush up his neck. The liquid was hot and mixed with a chunky and milk-like texture.

The ride's motion caused the barf to completely miss Donnie's head. Instead, it traveled past him and the hot chunks speckled both Bobby and Isaac.

"Help me!" Isaac cried.

In directing his pleas toward Bobby, Isaac felt a new type of helplessness inside.

"I'll help you alright," Bobby said.

A sinister grin twisted on his face.

Bobby hooked his right arm under the steel pillar and used his free hand to reach back into his waistband. When he retrieved the knife, it was still bloody and caked with bits of Sadie's insides. Bobby didn't hesitate; he extended the steel toward Isaac's knuckles.

"What are you doing?! Wait!" Isaac cried.

"Bobby, no!" CJ said, with puke still sliding off his face.

Suddenly, the loudspeaker in the room crackled. Tom's typically kind and relaxed voice was more enraged and animated than ever. Molly's hysterical moans served as torturous background fodder.

"Leave him alone! If you hurt my son, I'll fucking kill you! But first, I'll kill your dad! I've got him right here!"

Tom wasn't lying, but he was certainly embellishing the truth. He figured a threat to dispose of Bobby's idol would be the only clever tactic left in his arsenal.

To his credit, the words worked well enough to make Bobby hesitate. But Tom didn't account for what came next. His minor oversight put him on a path toward grave consequences.

Greg's seasoned loudmouth boomed enough to push his words to something more than background chatter. His heinous message was projected to Bobby without issue.

"He's bullshitting you, Son! Take that fucker out! Get him good—"

The speaker suddenly cut out.

The question of confidence hindering Bobby evaporated upon hearing his old man's voice. He'd made him proud once before, but now the opportunity to double up had presented itself. The attention-starved teen twitched with fury as he clenched the gory blade with malice.

"I'll get him, Dad!"

The tip of the knife cut through the thin skin on Isaac's knuckles. As the agonizing slicing burrowed deeper, Isaac felt the steel connecting with his bone. The pumps of blood were taken by the spin and slid away behind him.

The crimson fluid splashed over Bobby's body and face, staining the teeth inside his disturbing grin. The splatter didn't deter Bobby, even as it painted him in heavier strokes, it only intensified his devilish persona.

Isaac screamed louder, but his cries had zero impact on the situation. With the knife sawing to a point where it was almost completely through Isaac's fingers, he decided there was only one choice.

Isaac pushed through and thought about CJ, Tanya, and especially Donnie. If allowed to continue in the leadership role he'd highjacked, Bobby's reign of terror wouldn't end with him. Isaac wasn't part of their family, but he felt like he'd been through enough with CJ and Tanya to know they were good people. And he'd been through even more with Bobby to understand that he wasn't. Donnie would be the last person outside of the Matthews' bloodline. There was no doubt in Isaac's mind that Donnie would become his replacement target.

As the blade dug further into his skeleton, Isaac felt the bones in his hand weaken. He wouldn't be able to hold on much longer. His moment of truth had arrived.

Isaac loosened his left hand and pounced, latching onto the instrument of violence. His lower palm grabbed onto the drippy, double-sided blade and Bobby's fingers.

"Hey! Get off me!" Bobby screamed.

But Isaac was done listening to his commands. He slid his right hand off the bar and swiftly wrapped his gory grasp around Bobby's wrist.

"Get the fuck off! You're heavy! I—I can't hold us both up!" Bobby cried, panic now oozing from his tone.

Unable to think of another means of survival, Isaac projected a distant gaze past Bobby's arm and into his eyes.

"I guess we lose together then."

"No! Let go! Let—"

Bobby's appeal was cut short. The weight of Isaac's entire body multiplied by the roundabout's momentum his biceps drained. The tension in the arm he'd interlocked around the rusty pipe diminished until it was no longer strong enough to hold them in place.

The quarrelsome pair that rejected each other with regularity in their brief time together, sailed through the air in a flash. Their bodies landed in close proximity as they went splashing into the monstrous substance below.

As their frames connected, the poignant froth swallowed them whole, completely submerging them into the hellish horror. Almost immediately, the rivals could feel an otherworldly agony as their skin fizzed and blister. Whatever the cruel concoction was, it knew how to attack the human form with unmatched rapidity.

The porridge eliminated their clothing hastily and went to work on their soft exteriors. It was as if the ingredients in the stew were specifically designed to exterminate man.

Upon breaking through and resurfacing, all of the hair follicles on their entire bodies became a memory of the past. Additionally, the minuscule amount of weight that the fluid drizzling off their heads generated, pulled away at their scalps, and their casings began degloving. The sloppy skin gliding off of their skulls made them look like piles of shredded cheese melted in a microwave to excess.

The ultra-aggressive waste had already burned through multiple layers of skin. Upon submerging, each boy had instinctually shut their eyes, but the unforgiving solution liquefied their eyelids. By the time they reached the oxygen, the scorching green liquid had made its way to their pupils. The vision they'd each taken for granted since birth was no more. A streaky wave of sizzling slime was the last thing Bobby and Isaac saw.

In the finale of disassembly, their once ordinary orbs speedily distended. They ballooned outward, expanding to the point of eruption. The vile burst pushed a mushy, off-white material out from their sockets and into the soupy mixture below.

As they flailed about in the marsh, the raw, pinkish meat glistened where their skin had once been. The lethal chemicals were quick to move onto their major muscles. The fluid found crevices, joints, ligaments, and tendons. It soon dissolved enough carnal bondage on their bodies to disconnect the muscles from their bones.

The frantic peddling motions came to a slow, and each of their bodies shut down. Seconds later they were both static—erased into oblivion and forgotten by the surrounding universe.

In life, Isaac and Bobby went together like oil and water, but in death, that wouldn't matter. As the vicious ocean of scorching fluid destroyed the little that remained of their tissues, the opinions and differences they held in life were suddenly of little consequence. Now they were one and the same; a single, all-encompassing soup of sizzling cells, dissolving ambition, and lost youth.

FINDING THE WILL

Everyone was at a loss for words.

When Rock glanced discreetly at Tom and Molly, their frenzy shook him.

The crushing grip that interlocked their fingers reddened the flesh. As the waters of sadness gushed from their heads, toothy, drooling frowns stretched their faces most monstrously.

They were possessed by pain.

Rock could see the parents had reached a grim tipping point on their torturous trajectory. Upon arriving at such an odious finality, it wasn't so much the emotional elements they displayed that puzzled him; it was the absence of them.

There was no rage.

There was no anger.

There was no outburst.

Only the profound pain of loss lingered; the ultimate theft of love, heart, and adoration.

They were broken.

"Fuck!" Greg grunted.

Rock could tell Greg was clearly upset at the loss of his son, but compared to Tom and Molly, it was more annoyance than agony.

"Took a couple with him at least," Greg mumbled, trying to find the 'bright side' of Bobby's demise.

Rock felt disgusted. Greg was like a living representation of everything evil. The opposite of what he saw in the Grimleys.

Tom and Molly didn't view their children like pawns on a chessboard. Even when they'd first arrived, before the kids set foot in the playground, Tom displayed genuine and thorough concern for them. The money Geraldine offered was by no means as important as his family.

Rock wondered how he might've felt if Bobby had done to Donnie what he'd done to Sadie and Isaac. As the thought simmered in his head, Rock imagined the sensation inside him was somewhere in the realm of what the Grimleys were feeling.

But there was something else too.

The fury Tom and Molly lacked budded in Rock. The gory roses of revenge were begging to unfold in his spiritual garden. But as fast as the flowers were ready to bloom, Rock knew Geraldine would be just as quick to snip them at the stem.

As Rock watched the roundabout slow, the moans of Tom and Molly dug into his soul. While the wails fueled the wrath that left his hands shaking inside his pockets, the fear that Geraldine had impressed upon him still kept his heels pinned in place.

THE END?

When the roundabout came to a standstill, CJ and Tanya felt a hammering of devastation. Crying had become the new norm. The fresh streaks of tears they sprouted weren't only for Bobby, but also for Isaac.

They remembered a different version of their big brother. One that existed before the evil and unflinching threats had tarnished him. At times, Bobby had been a prick and a bit of a bully, but nothing the likes of what they'd witnessed in the playground. They each mourned the mostly positive sentiments they knew him to harbor.

There was one other feeling that neither CJ nor Tanya would ever dare admit; not to themselves and not to each other. It gnawed at their hearts, but they ignored it. They each felt a certain measure of relief in knowing that Bobby was gone. His unpredictability and anger issues had made each of them periodically wonder if he would think twice about sacrificing his own family if he could ensure his own survival by doing so.

A single day had changed so much. The dark alterations were glaring. It was as if the playground amplified the absolute best or worst traits of the children imprisoned within it.

On the other hand, Isaac couldn't be overlooked either. After all CJ and Tanya had been through with him, there was no doubt that they'd bonded. Isaac held a similar set of morals. He wasn't above putting others first. He had acted selflessly and abided by their initial agreement. His decency, intelligence, and flashes of unexpected bravery helped to push them toward their common goal of group survival.

Now he was gone.

Isaac had been cast out of existence in horrific fashion, a gruesome fate CJ and Tanya knew he didn't deserve. They could only hope they wouldn't end up victims of a similar exodus. At the juncture they'd arrived at, death by natural causes or old age sounded like winning the lottery.

CJ saddled his sentiments and coughed. The harsh fumes continued to weaken him. He looked forward to the door in the distance that read 'THE END?'

"How do we get off this…"

The exhaustion in CJ's voice wouldn't let him get the words out, but it didn't matter. His question was about to be answered.

The area between the merry-go-round and the progress point rumbled. Through the murky death slime rose a single, straightforward section of the platform that led directly to the last door.

Despite her arms feeling like jelly, Tanya could monkey herself around the roundabout to the section that aligned with the newly exposed pathway. However, there was good reason for caution; the pathway had no barriers on either side. One false move and they could end up dissolving away in the pinkish pool of discoloration surrounding Isaac and Bobby.

"I'm so dizzy," she said.

CJ thought more as he guided Donnie toward the escape route. He shimmied over slowly until they were directly beside Tanya.

"Be careful. Try to stay on your feet, I think there's some of that slime on the ground still," CJ said.

Tanya took his suggestion. She hopped off slowly and landed flat on her heels. Thankfully, there wasn't enough of the toxic liquid remaining to impact her. She held her arms open, and CJ lowered Donnie into them.

"I got him," she said.

Tanya took a few steps back to allow her brother some space to work with. Then she watched CJ drop without issue.

The gases continued to wear on them, burning their lungs each time they inhaled. The trio of survivors urgently pushed forward until they were in front of the ominous doorway that they hoped would be their last.

"You really think it's the end?" Tanya asked.

"Does it even matter? Either way, we've gotta find out," CJ replied.

As they entered the next room, they found it was much tighter than any prior area of the playground. Almost the entire room was occupied by one giant seesaw that extended nearly ten feet in length.

The seats attached to the structure were unconventional. Unlike any traditional seesaw they'd ever encountered, this one offered cushy back support. Below each of the bulky seats sat a large, red coil spring. Should the bottom of the seesaw connect, it would serve to increase the momentum. In the center of the seesaw stood a long metal bar that sprouted up several feet into the air. Affixed to the very top of the pole were two long, chrome propellers that extended the width of the entire seesaw.

Affixed to the wall hung a red digital readout that was currently populated with two zeros. Under the scoreboard display, hung another familiar sign. Unsurprisingly, it read: 'PLAYGROUND RULES.'

Tanya sighed, growing more than weary of reading the riddles that offered them a set of veiled instructions.

"Up and down till the count strikes ten, but not too high to keep your friend. Should you avoid an untimely end, then your parents may see your faces again."

Tanya thought about her father. Would she even want to see him again? His actions were every bit as selfish as she remembered. But it was one thing to be selfish with his time, it was something completely different to coach Bobby into taking lives. The disturbing colors that lay beneath his surface had suddenly bled out. For the first time, she realized, her perception of the man had changed entirely.

Another thought struck her; Tanya heard from several of the parents during their venture through the playground but not from her mother. She wondered if something had happened to her. Tanya hadn't even heard her mother say anything in the background like the other parents. That was very unlike her. She normally *always* had something to say.

She didn't always see eye-to-eye with her mother; more times than not they were at odds. But despite her flaws, Tanya knew that her mother was a good woman. The idea that she might never see her again left an unsettled feeling rumbling in her stomach.

"Looks like we're gonna get to seesaw after all," CJ said.

He was too worn out to properly inflect the dread or cynicism he felt into his tone.

Tanya let out a muffled groan of angst.

"You think Mom's alright?" CJ asked.

It almost felt like her brother was reading her mind.

"I hope so," Tanya replied.

She tried not to get emotional. She understood that with such a daunting task at hand, letting her feelings blur her concentration could result in a fatal error.

"I can't believe they're all gone," CJ said.

"Are you ready for this?" Tanya asked.

Her lip quivered as she intentionally tried changing the subject.

"Do I have a choice?"

Tanya looked over to Donnie. He was far too little and unpredictable to be trusted.

"I guess not."

CJ nodded his head.

Taking Donnie by the hand, CJ led him over to the corner of the room. As he guided the boy down into a seated position, he patted him on the head. CJ felt compelled to recognize him. Donnie was the smallest and disabled to some extent, but the boy had still somehow made it that far. It was an accomplishment too incredible to overlook.

"You're the toughest kid I know. There aren't many kids—heck, there aren't many *people* that could've made it this far. Just let us do this last one, okay, buddy?"

Just as Donnie had done the entire time, he stared forward, void of expression. The fact that he remained seated was good enough for CJ. He rubbed his head one more time before moving back to the intimidating seesaw.

CJ grabbed hold of the diagonally angled support beam of the structure and pulled down on it. It was more difficult to level than he'd assumed it to be, but as he applied more of his weight, he noticed that the lengthy chrome propellers at the top were turning.

"So that's the trick," CJ said.

"What is it?" Tanya asked.

"I guess as we go up and down, that sharp blade at the top is gonna spin even quicker. And if we aren't really careful with how high we go, well… you know."

Tanya bit her lip hard, reconsidering her eagerness to get through the task.

"I really don't feel good about this. Maybe help will come if we just wait here?" Tanya asked.

"The way this has been, more than likely it'll be snakes, or gas, or ants that come for us before any help. I don't wanna do this anymore than you do, but I'm pretty sure something worse is gonna happen if we don't. What do you say?"

Tears welled up in Tanya's eyes again.

"It'll be okay—"

"What if it's not?!" Tanya screamed.

The pressure had found her.

"I—I can't lose you too."

CJ moved in and wrapped his arms around his sister.

"No matter what happens, we tried our best. And no matter what happens, I'll always love you," CJ whispered.

"I love you too."

Tanya let the water leak out, trying to get past the hurt. Moving onto the task at hand wasn't easy. Once her breathing calmed a bit, the two siblings parted.

"We can do this," CJ said.

He moved toward the seesaw and placed both of his arms on his seat to steady it as best he could.

"Go ahead," he said with a nod.

Tanya mounted the seesaw by slipping her right leg over the handlebars; the elevated seat support at the back was too tall for her to reach over. Once she mounted it, she placed her feet on the metal platform below and stabilized the other end for CJ.

Her brother soon followed her lead, lifting his leg over the handlebars and securing a steady balance between the two of them.

"So, I guess we just—"

Before CJ could finish his thought, two hooks ejected from the back support on the seating behind them. Their speed and curves were equally extreme. The steel extensions of the sadistic seesaw twisted and pierced into the soft flesh under both Tanya and CJ's shoulders.

The metal moved inside each of them, and they felt a targeted stabbing pain as the hooks set in deep under their armpits. The blood oozed just as sure as their movement had been restricted.

"Ahh!" CJ cried.

The backboards on their seats retracted downward, aligning with the height the hooks emerged from. There was no support directly behind their heads any longer. It stopped at the back of their necks, surely offering a path of success for the propellers above.

"What's going on!" she wailed.

Tanya's screams and groans meshed with CJ's.

The siblings squirmed fighting like a pair of trout being reeled in. But the more they moved the faster they realized the hooks were set too deep to free themselves.

They weren't going anywhere.

"We—We just need to play! Just make sure you go slow!" CJ yelled.

Fighting through the agony, Tanya found a way to gently push up with her legs. She slowly ascended as the propeller above her head gained speed.

When CJ pushed his seat closer toward the spring on the ground, he looked over at the wall-mounted counter.

"It's still at zero, you have to go higher!" he yelled.

As CJ applied further pressure on the seating, the top of Tanya's skull inched closer to the fierce, spinning blades that were now self-propelling themselves at a blurring rate.

A droplet of sweat drizzled off the tip of Tanya's nose. She watched the scoreboard sign intently, feeling the push of wind from above. The breeze was a constant reminder of the horror that awaited should a mistake be made.

"I'm getting really close!" Tanya cried.

"I think it's almost there," CJ responded.

Now with the top of her cranium just mere inches from being shredded into oblivion, the sign was finally updated. To their unrivaled relief, the number one revealed itself.

"Okay, it's there!" CJ yelled.

"Bring me down! Bring me down!" Tanya begged.

"Sorry, I know it's scary, but it wasn't too bad. I—I think we can do this!"

"I hope you're right!"

Luckily for CJ, despite being two years older than his sister, she'd had an early growth spurt. The advantage of their body weights being close to equal would allow them to angle each other up methodically. If there had been a large discrepancy between them, his strategy wouldn't be possible. They'd have been forced to rely on a far more dangerous variable—momentum.

Tanya followed CJ's instructions and used the same

method he'd found success with. She achieved an identical result, and the counter increased to two.

Then three.

Then four.

Then five.

"We're almost there!" Tanya said.

She elevated CJ again, but as she continued to push him higher, the real challenge was suddenly revealed.

Without warning, flames erupted from the discreetly placed steel gridding attached to the bottom of the seesaw. Fire flooded out toward Tanya's ankles in flamethrower fashion. Not only was it coming from the pivot point on her side of the seesaw, it was also on CJ's side as well.

The flurry of flames was angled low and reached close enough to her feet and ankles that the hairs singed.

"Oh my God! Fire!" Tanya cried.

She reacted to the hazard before thinking it through. Tanya immediately pushed off and vaulted her body upward to escape the horrific heat.

As his sister ascended, CJ was forced to come down and be greeted by the scorching flames on his side. He knew, fire or not, they couldn't escape with the hooks set deep in their armpits. They still had five more revolutions to reach the goal of ten that the Playground Rules specified. A long road of agony lay ahead.

CJ tried to tolerate the heat and block out the pain. The fire didn't hit his flesh, but it was just close enough that his leg hairs turned to dust and his skin dried.

The blazing discomfort that covered his shins didn't force CJ to lose his concentration. He kept on and continued his effort. As he angled his sister closer toward the top, he released intermittent grunts of agony.

CJ juggled his focus. He kept one eye on the top of Tanya's head, ensuring the sharp propeller was far enough away to avoid decapitating her. The other eye remained on the makeshift scoreboard affixed to the wall.

Sweat beaded off his face as he cried out, "C'mon!"

"CJ, be careful!" Tanya begged.

Donnie watched from the corner, mystified by the ungodly seesaw. He remained frozen, in awe as he watched the number on the wall increase.

Six.

When the count jumped a tick, CJ finally hopped up off the ground, allowing his scorched shins a much-needed rest. But as he watched his sister sinking closer to the inferno on the floor, he could already sense that his breather would be short-lived.

Tanya planted her ankles firmly and held her breath. But as she angled her brother up toward the propeller blade, the anguish on her legs became too distracting.

"I—I can't do it! I can't take it!" she cried.

Tanya tried to squirm out of her seat, but the metallic hooks cinched in deep under her armpits screeched the action to a halt.

"Yes, you can! I know you can! You—You have to!" CJ responded, trying to motivate his sister as best he could.

"I'm sorry, CJ."

Tanya continued to cry and pushed herself back up from the flames licking at her legs.

CJ gritted his teeth; he knew what needed to happen for them to survive the seesaw. When his legs once again entered the path of the fire, it was far worse for his flesh than before. As he struggled through the anguish to position his sister high enough to earn another point, his hardened casing cracked.

Seven.

Watching the tissues on her brother's legs become even more damaged pushed Tanya. The sense of responsibility for CJ's horrific burns unleashed a shot of guilt to go along with her fear. She knew she needed to reattempt to earn a point herself. As Tanya replanted her legs on the ground, the meat on her bones braised. She ground her teeth and continued to elevate her brother.

Tanya dug deeper than she'd ever had to. She wasn't

about to watch her only remaining brother burn away in front of her. As Tanya released a hellish shriek, she found the will to hang on. She powered through the few additional seconds required to raise CJ up high enough.

Eight.

By the time the counter went off, Tanya's pain was unbearable. She shot back up from the floor, getting her extremities out of dodge as quickly as possible. But the damage had already been done; her legs were roasted.

CJ hadn't even been able to cheer her on or offer support during the moment of superhuman ability. He was too busy trying not to pass out. His vision had grown blurry and his body was rattled. The accumulation of his hurt had finally reached a questionable threshold. For the first time, he wasn't sure if he'd be able to continue.

As CJ's legs were reinserted into the blaze, the barbeque continued. But as the skin began to char over the blisters, miraculously, he harnessed the power to angle Tanya upward. The crisping over of his meat triggered a transition in color; CJ's eyes begged for the counter to turn.

Nine.

The smoke and scent of over-cooked human flesh filled the small room. CJ's floating particles had made their way over to Donnie. The boy's eyes watered and he let out a few coughs. He still observed the ghastly conditions without fail.

When CJ made his ascension again, his sweat-soaked head suddenly went limp. His body remained up straight because of the hooks under his arms, but for all intents and purposes, his lights had gone out.

When Tanya's seared legs returned to the infernal atmosphere, she wasn't ready to resume the pain. Her sensitive flesh returned to the torturous temperature, and she tried again to tough it out. But before she could get him to the proper height to register the final point needed, she vaulted back up again.

"It's too much, CJ! I—I just need another minute! My legs feel like they're melting!" she cried.

She'd focused on the top of CJ's head while attempting to avoid the propeller, but not his facial expression. But as Tanya bounced back up, it suddenly became clear that her brother had fallen unconscious. The resounding bell going off in Tanya's head knew the results were going to be horrific, but because of her panicked state, she hadn't been able to calculate just how horrific.

CJ was going down full speed toward the one part of the demonic structure that had slipped both of their minds. The part of the device that hadn't really been relevant since the harrowing adventure had commenced—the massive spring coils below their seating.

Under each of their seats sat a single, thick spiral. Each time they'd descended to the surface previously, they were both planting their feet firmly on the ground and controlling the pivot. Fully aware of the menacing blade ripping through the air above their heads, neither Tanya nor CJ had let the other person get too high too quickly. But as Tanya launched herself up with CJ incapacitated, that resistance wouldn't be there anymore.

His dead weight was headed right for the spring.

As Tanya ascended, she quickly did the math in her head: one propeller plus her face equaled zero future. In her mind, she had only one option to leverage, and she had to act on it quickly.

Kicking her legs up on top of the handlebars, Tanya forced her body deeper into the hooks under her arms. She wailed out in horror as the stabbing, curved metal dove deeper into her gushing wounds. The cruel material was in so far that it had reached her bones. As the human hooks scraped against her skeleton, Tanya was offered a little more space to turtle her head down.

There were only a few inches of the metal backrest above her head when the chopper blade hit. The blow made the structure shake, and the balance bar hyper-extended sideways. The vibrating blow jarred the seesaw and pushed the pain in Tanya's armpits up another notch.

Ten.

As the last update occurred, suddenly, a room that appeared to not have an exit sprouted one. The wall behind the seesaw opened up. Sliding stone crumbled and a golden glow emanated at the end of the dark cove.

Donnie looked at the golden opportunity for several seconds, before returning his gaze to the huge seesaw.

Upon connecting for the second time, the propeller slid off the top of Tanya's back support and sent her end of the seesaw rocketing back to the ground. The launch occurred with such speed, and the armpit hooks were so deep, that Tanya didn't have a chance to readjust. When her end landed on the spring below, it lifted CJ to his pinnacle.

He still hadn't regained his bearings when the propeller took the top of his skull off. The unflappable steel sloshed through the scatter-brained boy making him just that, absent-minded. The harsh, circular hack left the brain split into two pieces and CJ's cranial juices erupted in every direction. He'd become the embodiment of his favorite fruit snack, Gushers. A treat he'd never enjoy during school recess again.

CJ's young mind had been switched off permanently. An organ that had crept out of CJ's infantile stages of life with bottomless potential, would now never reach it. Not that his mind was destined to create revolutionary gadgets or beak barriers in the scientific realm. He was intelligent, but that wasn't his greatest asset.

His nature was loving.

His purpose was caring.

His destiny was to unify.

No matter how selfish, uncooperative, frightened, or flawed a person could be, CJ always found a way. He sifted through their sins and shortcomings until he uncovered the common ground. Whether they liked it or not, CJ always brought the best out of people.

The boy who'd brought so many people together had done so until fate chose to tear him apart.

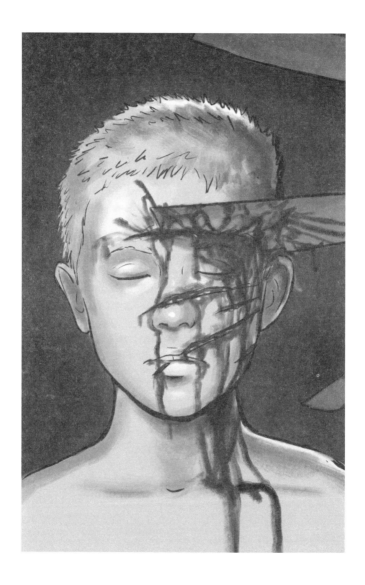

The swiftness of the propeller steel cut off another section of his head, this time at the jawline. The horror offered a momentary window into a new pink slab of runny gore, just before the final revolution came for his neck.

As the chop hit his throat, it opened up all of CJ's major veins. The fountain of carmine fluid fled his once energetic frame, as the lower fractions of his face and neck dropped onto the fire dancing on the floor below.

Tanya screamed as an overload of dread blew up inside her. She vocalized her living hell, as a jumble of the wonderful memories she'd shared with her brother flooded into her head.

She knew how special of a person CJ was. At times she'd wondered what they might look like hanging out later in life once they were grown. Tanya never imagined that she might not find out. She'd taken that much for granted.

While she wasn't nearly as close with Kip or Bobby as she was with CJ, Tanya found herself wondering the same about all of them. But the brain fodder was pointless now; all three of her brothers were dead.

CJ's seat elevated to the max. This time, as the propeller connected with the metal back support, instead of just nipping the top and sliding off, it slammed into the side full-bore and knocked the entire structure over.

The power of the propeller loosened the bolts at the pivot of the seesaw, sending the end with CJ's headless body crashing into the wall. The other end, where Tanya remained, fell back into the hell path of the ferocious flames at the base of the ride.

The sudden violence of the fall caused the hook buried in Tanya's left armpit to dislodge. Left in its wake was a gaping slash with a blend of gummy, violet meat seeping out. While the rip had freed one side of her body, the other side was in a far more precarious situation.

As the hook in her right armpit jerked out and up, the ghastly result left another cavernous tear in her cavity. Upon exit, the steel re-hooked itself into her triceps muscle.

She was like a fish with her fin hooked. But unlike a fish that might've been doomed to dangle in agony, the worst part wasn't over. The side of her face and right arm were directly in line with the flames bursting from the base of the seesaw.

When Tanya's bloody body roasted and her hair wilted away, she screamed something fierce. She prayed and begged, but she'd already faced the reality of her situation. If God had been planning on saving them, he'd have done it long ago.

Both her arm and face were sizzling. Fresh blisters rose as the final traces of hope escaped her. She accepted the extreme pain, understanding that it would be all that she had until the end came.

Then, out of the blue, she felt a tiny hand wrap around her wrist, and another around her elbow.

As Donnie tugged on Tanya's leaking limb, the scorching flames burned his hands and arms too. But if there was one person who could stand the heat inside the kitchen, it was Donnie.

As Tanya continued to shriek in agony, Donnie's eyes widened to hypnotic dimensions. His flesh still burned, but he continued. Donnie yanked at the hot, buried hook until he'd done the impossible and slipped Tanya's arm free.

He kept hold of Tanya's wounded arm and dragged her away from the dangerous flames.

She was in shock still, but upon stabilizing, Tanya grabbed at the dead tissue on her face. The pain was crippling, but when she looked into Donnie's eyes, she was able to muster the gas she needed. She watched on in amazement as the young boy squatted down beside her and willed her to her feet.

As the salty tears dripped down Tanya's burnt flesh, her gaze drifted to the golden light at the end of the tunnel.

THE TRANSITION

"Bravo! Bravo!" Geraldine yelled.

"Ha-ha!" Fuchs rejoiced.

"That boy was quite spectacular, but I knew it was just a matter of time until he stretched himself too thin."

"He truly was, my lady."

Geraldine was pleased, but a faint sourness still puckered her face. CJ's death didn't make her feel better, but it did make her feel equal. Equal to the unworthy, peasant parents on the secondary screen. Their dread was legendary. Gorging on their sorrows filled her with overflowing gratitude; she was like a spunky tick that had latched onto a dog's belly.

A giant grin creased Geraldine's face as she watched the severely burned Donnie, and blood-roasted Tanya limp away from the seesaw. They continued to struggle but were now just a few yards away from the tunnel.

"Zhese two will never make it through zhe last part of zhe playground alone. Prepare yourself, zhe final fatalities are upon us," Fuchs said.

As Geraldine watched the mad scientist pull down on a lever, the ceiling ventilation triggered and the flames at the base of the seesaw deactivated.

But the wicked flames in Geraldine's heart still burned something fierce.

"We shall see," she whispered.

Geraldine's dark horse might've gotten maimed on the seesaw, but Tanya was still in the running. There was a spiral of unfamiliar emotions swirling inside her when she'd watched the propeller twist above her darling's pretty little head. The bizarre blend of fear, hope, and horniness brought her to a boil. Then, just when she figured her head would be split, fate spared her and took CJ instead.

It was meant to be, my darling. You shall be mine. There is just but one final test, Geraldine thought.

Tanya had shown her everything she desired. Geraldine knew the girl's wounds were severe, but that was part of the test. If Tanya could find enough reserve to make the impossible possible, then the girl was undeniably the one.

In her best-case scenario, where Tanya triumphed past the final part of the playground, Geraldine would dispatch Fuchs to offer her constant care. She would heal and mend to full strength, then Geraldine could play with her new toy.

As Fuchs adjusted the camera, it transitioned to show the next area. Tanya and Donnie once again appeared on the screen.

"Ugh, hopefully this is the last we see of that little brat," she scoffed.

"I don't imagine he has zhe capacity to continue on without zhe help of others," Fuchs replied.

The boy's death could serve as the cherry on top of Geraldine's picture-perfect day. Watching him fail in the final area and seeing Tanya thrive would provide her a regret-free outcome.

Geraldine lifted the bottle and took another sip of the bubbly. She looked back to the screen that was occupied by the parents trapped in the spy room.

"I certainly hope you're right."

FADING HOPE

When Greg's laughter finally stopped, he applied a crushing grip to Lacey's dead hand. His crown jewel was gone. Seeing CJ's head get sliced into slim slivers of ultra-gamey deli meat was the most traumatic visual he'd ever faced.

"Took my shining star…" Greg mumbled.

Greg was in a state of disbelief. Uncharacteristically, a tear welled up in his glossy eye. As he thought about CJ and the ceiling-less potential his once active frame contained, a tiny bead of water slid down his cheek.

With his pride and joy lost, it was beyond difficult to understand that the game was still on. Yet, somehow, Greg's immorally competitive instincts superseded all else within his broken mind.

"But we still got one more, baby doll," he whispered, waiting for the screen to transition away from CJ's mutilated corpse. "We're gonna win this thing. Just like I told you before, Tanya's better than you think. She's sure as shit better than that little retarded boy."

Rock clenched his mammoth fist as Greg's babble found him. He was witnessing a depraved reality, the one Greg projected tirelessly in his heinous hemisphere. All of his boys were dead, but he could give a shit less.

Somehow, it was all still about 'winning.'

It was his only obsession prior to entering The Borden Estate, and it was his only obsession currently. Winning the pointless challenge that would see everyone dead at the conclusion was all that mattered.

It was all he had left.

The man represented the dark side of the world, the only side that Rock had been shown. Everything felt hopeless again until he shifted his focus to Tom and Molly.

All of their children were gone. The two of them had been gushing tears without fail, entangled in their suffering. But even though they'd lost their skin in the game, they found a way to carry on. When the Grimleys presented their most recent pleas to Rock, they weren't the requests he'd expected.

Rock would've assumed since all three of their kids were dead, that they'd begin begging for their own lives to be saved. He was wrong.

The other half of the world had been unlocked. The brighter side that had been tucked away from his sight by Geraldine's decades of programming and decadence.

The Grimleys hadn't made it about their own potential escape; it was still about the children. The two that remained. The two that they didn't even know from a hole in the wall.

"Please, sir, the little boy and girl, you can still stop it. They didn't do anything wrong. You—You have to stop this," Molly cried, between sobs.

Rock didn't answer.

He couldn't.

As far back as he could remember, everything that Geraldine had shown him, was always about her own importance. Other people had never been a part of the equation. Creating circumstances to accommodate her was what nearly every action Rock had taken in his life amounted to. If only he'd had a woman like Molly around when he was younger.

Someone to advocate for him.

Someone to protect him.

In a way, that's what she was trying to do for him now. Because, as the monitor screen transitioned to the last patch of the playground, and little blood-soaked Donnie entered the picture, Rock finally accepted it.

He and the boy were one.

THE SECRET SILENCE

The smell of burnt flesh hung in the stuffy air of the tunnel. As they approached the light, Tanya thought about the signage in the prior room.

Is it really THE END? she wondered.

The question was rhetorical. She didn't know the answer, nor did she feel comfortable speculating. However, deep inside, she still feared the worst was yet to come. Nothing had gone according to plan since she'd taken that long slide all the way down into the bowels of the devious castle.

Why should anything change now?

Tanya pushed past the raging pain spreading over her seared skin as little Donnie continued to help her advance.

The boy's smooth baby face projected the idle emotions of youth; it looked like it could've been any other day for him. The bubbled, red, and white flesh where his arm had been burned was of no consideration to Donnie.

When they both made it to the end of the tunnel, the gloomy but unsurprising realization found them; their journey wasn't over. While the new room's dimensions in width were a bit bigger than the seesaw space, the height was a far different story.

There was a sizable, rectangular sandbox with various lettered blocks sprinkled within the fine dirt, but that wasn't the concerning part. Beside the sandbox, towering up at least fifty yards in height, stood the most intimidating, sadistic structure they'd seen yet.

Even at first glance, the gigantic rope climber was beyond problematic. The structure ascended so high into the dark space that it was difficult to locate the apex. If it weren't for the shiny golden bell with a pull string at the top, Tanya might not have been able to find it.

The altitude of the climb wasn't the only peril present. Within the metallic stabilization pillar at the center of the massive web of red ropes, dozens of retractable spikes thrust in and out from the center pole. The long spears re-erected themselves in every direction, pushing outward, ready to skewer anything in its circumference. Then, just moments later, the shiny spits collapsed in on themselves like magic. The deathtraps were spaced every few feet and seemed to project with no particular rhythm. The randomness of the device made it quite possibly the riskiest structure they'd encountered.

I guess they saved the best for last, Tanya thought.

Her body and mind were too damaged to even conjure the strength to get worked up. But she knew the difficulty they faced was legendary.

Instead of a sign like all the previous rooms had, Tanya peered in the sandbox. A message had been laid out via the order of the multi-colored building blocks inside. There were countless wooden squares scattered about within the entire sandy rectangle, but the ones in the center clearly held a very specific message. The first set of letters had naturally been arranged to read: PLAYGROUND RULES.

Tanya struggled to keep her focus. An ordinary task as simple as reading now seemed like an epic challenge. But she hadn't come that far to just pass out. Tanya looked beneath the heading for the challenge details and read them aloud to Donnie.

"No time for the sand, just climb to the bell. Only after the chime will you get a final farewell."

Without warning, Tanya fell over into the sandbox. She no longer harbored the bare minimum of energy it took for her to stand.

"I—I don't think I can do it…" Tanya mumbled.

She still sounded like she was in shock from her injuries. When she looked up at the diabolical tower of rope and thrusting spikes, her body locked up.

Somehow, Donnie seemed as if Tanya's reading had registered with him. He pointed up at the bell all the way at the top of the structure and then pointed to himself.

"You think you can make it?" Tanya asked.

Donnie could see that Tanya was afraid for him. He hopped over the short wooden wall into the sandbox. Looking down at the many blocks lodged in the grains, Donnie fished out several letters. He placed them so that they faced Tanya, arranging them in a specific order.

The blocks read: I CAN RING IT.

The arrangement was more than a message to Tanya. Donnie had just revealed himself to be more capable than he'd let on. Instantly, she wondered why he hadn't chosen to speak with anyone the entire time.

She had to know.

"Why don't you just talk?" she asked.

Donnie thought about his response for a moment, then snagged a different variety of building blocks and placed the response in front of Tanya.

The blocks read: MOMMA SAY I TALK TO MUCH.

"But that doesn't mean you shouldn't talk at all, right?"

He quickly shifted the letters around again.

The blocks read: I CAN'T.

"What do you mean you can't?"

Donnie slowly unhinged his jaws to reveal the sad, slimy truth. A tiny nub sat toward the back of the boy's throat; the sizing was all wrong.

Almost all of Donnie's tongue had been lopped off.

Tanya's eyes popped.

While nothing surprised her anymore after their ghastly journey, it suddenly became clear to her why the boy had been so daring the entire time. He was probably better off not making it home.

As sadness entered her sore guts, Tanya watched Donnie reset the letter line-up.

The blocks read: YOU HELP ME, NOW I HELP YOU NOW.

Her salty face was too roasted for emotion.

Donnie reshuffled the cubes one final time.

The blocks read: I BE BACK.

Donnie turned away from Tanya and pulled himself out of the sandbox. He dusted off the many dirt particles that clung to him, then took hold of the ropes at the bottom of the colossal tower.

"Be—Be careful," Tanya said.

She was unsure what other words she could offer him. While she didn't like the idea of him climbing up the sadistic structure, who was she to stop him?

Donnie turned to her and nodded his head. Looking back to the rough rope in his hand, he readied himself. But before he could pull himself up, the crackle from the loudspeaker gave way.

A gruff voice manifested, giving Tanya and Donnie a stern pair of instructions.

"Don't climb it. Just stay where you are," Rock said. "The game's over. I'm gonna let you out."

BREAKDOWN

Rock lifted his finger from the blood-drenched button beside Lacey's mangled neck. He knew there would be rapid repercussions for his actions, but he didn't care. He just wanted to see Donnie get through the ordeal. Maybe he was young enough to salvage. Maybe he wouldn't have to become the diabolical tool that Rock had. His view had shifted; if nothing else, Donnie's sheer perseverance showed he deserved to have a chance.

Rock was finally looking past his fears. He was no longer in a box and realized the walls erected to confine him were weak. He could've broken through them long ago.

Better late than never, Rock thought.

Outside of the disturbing domino effect that was surely unavoidable, setting them free was all that mattered.

There was a shift in the curled expressions of agony on Tom and Molly's faces. The wrinkles flattened, their bodies perked up, and a surprising heartbeat of hope flickered within them.

"Thank—Thank you," Molly said.

Part of her couldn't believe he'd seen the light, but her skepticism had been disproven by the undeniable actions unfolding before her.

292

Tom and Molly both instantly transformed; the tears dried up, and the adrenaline was pumping. Change was afoot, but they understood they needed to ready themselves. They weren't out of the woods yet.

While the loss of their offspring still weighed heavily on the Grimleys, there was an unavoidable survival instinct that continued to power them. The hatred and horror of the day's events floated within, but they knew the mammoth man in front of them wasn't the source of their agony.

The damages inflicted on Rock's psyche and soul had left him open to manipulation. The man had been piloted by the dominant forces who created the playground. But the spell he was under had finally been lifted.

Tom and Molly clung to the arms of their chairs stiffly, astounded at the mere possibility of getting out of them.

"It's over now," Rock whispered.

He hung his head. A shower of shame encompassed his giant frame. The realization that he'd merely been a tool since he could remember was a bitter pill to swallow.

"It's not over! What the fuck are you thanking him for!" A sudsy shot of spittle flared out from Greg's lips. "My boys are dead! *Dead!* You took away my prospects! You took my future! You took everything! And for what?! Not to finish?! We always finish! The Matthews always finish Goddamnit!"

"Shut your fucking mouth!" Tom roared.

The wounds of Greg's murderous instructions still fermented freshly in Tom's brain. He was the reason his Sadie was sawed into slivers. He was the reason that Isaac was dissolving in the chemical pool.

"Why don't you fucking make me, tough guy! You're all talk! All talk!"

"Let me out of this chair! Let me out of this Goddamn chair!" Tom wailed.

His malicious glare shifted to Rock. His eyes pleaded with him to release them. It was a look he'd given the big man before, but now it actually seemed feasible.

"That's not going to happen," Geraldine said.

Rock's gaze drifted to the dark doorway where the outlines of two familiar figures stood. Their stoic postures and matching grimaces meant all business.

"The children haven't finished playing yet! This is the best part! And it isn't over until I say it is!" Geraldine screamed.

"Don't listen to her," Molly pleaded.

"You've always been a bad boy, but this is a new low, even for you. I've given you everything! More than most simple minds could even imagine! And you betray me?!"

Geraldine's gawk was transfixed on Rock. The subtle but reliable tremor to his texture that she spotted with regularity was oddly absent. There was something different about Rock's demeanor. Something that left a micro mouth of fear nibbling at Geraldine.

Rock didn't respond to her query. He would no longer entertain the mind games. He would no longer obey the wicked, wormy words that had previously penetrated him with such normalcy and ease.

He walked toward them with a purpose.

"What are you doing?! You can't listen to her! She's— She's just a peasant! She's beneath us!" Geraldine wailed.

In registering that Rock didn't plan on breaking his stride, Geraldine looked to Fuchs.

"Adolpho!"

Fuchs reached into his hazelnut vest and retrieved a Luger pistol.

"Don't test me, boy!" Fuchs threatened.

Rock's fury could no longer be controlled. He saw Fuchs for what he was: a malignant extension of Geraldine.

Fuchs had stood by willingly while atrocities unfolded. He'd watched Rock devolve into the scared, abused animal he finally realized himself to be. The Nazi was fueled by an evil that should've been snuffed out ages ago. Fuchs may have been able to sidestep his horrific war crimes, but it was clear that he'd grown too long in the tooth for the dance Rock aimed to have with him.

Just as Rock's hand wrapped around Fuchs' wrist, the gun barrel aligned with the big man's beefy bicep. When Rock cranked back on the old Nazi's frail joint, his pruned finger squeezed down on the trigger.

The sound of Fuchs' rigid forearm snapping and the bullet blasting happened simultaneously. Their extremities now each offered a certain degree of overlap. Rock's smoky suit tone was now overrun by the cranberry cascade rushing from his arm, but the brute force of Rock's wrath caused a cringe-worthy compound fracture, a break so severe the skeletal fragments had opened a gaping portal.

"Ahh!" Fuchs cried.

His wrinkled hand flopped sideways, losing all function. The 9mm left his touch and landed on the floor below. Fuchs remained stupefied as the outpouring of blood continued to sprout from the meaty chasm.

The bullet buried in his bicep didn't faze Rock. While he grunted in agony and projected a scowl, the pain that resulted from the shot paled in comparison to his robust history of accumulated tortures.

Rock used his uninjured arm to muscle his mitt around Fuchs' saggy neck. He clamped down on the German's windpipe but soon realized strangulation was an exit too pretty for a father of such evils.

He keyed in on the black and red buttons affixed to the wall just feet away from them. Powering through the pain, Rock mustered the strength to palm the sides of Fuchs' head with his hands. He aligned the elder's graying scalp with the controls and unleashed his rage.

The explosion of energy sent Fuchs' liver-spotted head smashing into the buttons. The action caused the steel neck collars that subdued Tom, Molly, and Greg to retract back into their chairs. Additionally, the many screens on the viewing wall were swiftly covered by the crimson curtains.

"Shows over," Rock grumbled.

Geraldine's mouth gaped with horror as she watched her faithful architect crash into the control panel he'd designed.

The back of Fuchs' ripened cranium quickly conformed to the steel switches. Two gushing hollows bore into the back of his skull, busting through the bone before sliding downward toward his brain stem. The bloody hunks painted the wall behind the mechanism, while flocks of sparks arched upward around Fuchs' head.

The electrical explosion jolted Rock, but he was able to pull himself away from it. He watched as Fuchs' skull and frame rattled. His body language wasn't something typically seen among the living.

The spark count and their intensity increased, causing the gray follicles on Fuchs' scalp to catch fire and his eyes to warp outward. The pressure of the thrust from Rock's hands had also left a heavy stream of blood raining hard from Fuchs' bent beak and busted mouth. He had become a representation of the many messes that he'd created.

Tom and Molly slipped out of their chairs, taking cover behind them from the worsening horror. As much as they'd have wanted to make a move, the time was beyond risky.

Just behind them, Greg did the same. He looked up at Lacey's lifeless corpse and tugged her arm toward him.

"Stay low, baby doll," he whispered.

Then, like a porn star positioning for the money shot, the final surge of electrical current pushed through Fuchs' destroyed dome. Each of his eyes transitioned to appear more like a pair of runny eggs as the liquefied lens and sclera leaped out of his sockets. The sudden departure of his eyeballs was accompanied by a thick, gory reservoir of red and pink humanity.

The scent of burning flesh was distinct. It was an aroma Rock had smelled under undesirable circumstances before. One that brought him back to when his witchy guardian had seared her brand upon him. A memory of the period when he was just a piece of property.

In his new mindset, the idea only served to insatiate his bloodlust. The translucent drool of morbid but somehow moral delinquency dribbled out from his mouth.

It doesn't stop here, Rock thought.

Fuchs' undoing pushed a feeling of elation through Rock. But as the motion subsided and the flames on the Nazi's head dwindled, the excitement for what came next possessed him. But as he turned toward the doorway, somewhat obscured by a thin veil of vaporized humanity, he realized he was late to the game.

Several flashes of white light accompanied by loud *bangs* manifested in front of him. The hot metal made its way into Rock's gut repeatedly. The streaks of utter agony that ripped deep into his abdominal tissue, even with the compliment of his adrenaline, couldn't be ignored. One of the paths the pair of bullets created died inside him, while the other made its way out of his lower back.

The stabbing pain brought Rock to his knees and left him clenching at his gut while blood spewed out of it. As he tumbled backward, the last barrage of bullets flew over his head, lodging into the wall behind him.

Groaning on the ground, Rock looked up at the smoke toward the silhouette in the doorway. The elderly, evil maiden of the manor's outline was unmistakable. Geraldine continued to pull the trigger, but the hollow chamber of the Luger only produced a clicking noise.

"I think she's out of bullets! We—We need to make our move now!" Tom yelled at Molly.

As Tom jumped up and took his wife by the hand, Geraldine's outline disappeared from the doorway. But her presence, or lack thereof, suddenly was no longer the most menacing factor.

"Like hell you are!" A voice from behind them yelled.

Greg wrapped his firm arm around Tom's neck before he was able to slip away.

"Leave him alone!" Molly screamed.

Greg muscled in his chokehold as deeply as possible. He stared at Molly with a grin of total depravity as Tom's face rapidly transitioned to a dark shade of cherry.

"Like to talk a lot of shit, don't you, sissy boy!"

Molly slipped around to Greg's back and balled her fists. She flung her hands wildly as Greg tried to dodge the blows and choke Tom at the same time. Her knuckles bounced off the sides of Greg's thick head, not producing the desired effect.

"Get off of him!" she shrieked.

Molly continued the rain of feeble shots like a pesky gnat until she finally got swatted.

Tiring of the repeated jabs, Greg transitioned his choke into a single arm submission but cranked back even harder on Tom's throat. The adjustment allowed him to launch his free fist right at Molly's ear.

The stiff blow landed on her temple, sending her reeling backward. The back of her skull crashed into the wall and her body skated down to the floor.

"Let the men settle it!" Greg said.

As the words came out of his mouth, Greg realized he was about to get what he wanted. However, he was not getting it in the way he'd hoped.

Greg didn't even get to close his mouth before Rock's bloody, sausage fingers pushed their way inside it. As Rock stood at Greg's side, he pushed his fat digits deeper into his air hole. Rock's mitt clasped around Greg's jaw, as sweat secreted from the big man's brow.

Rock wasn't going to let the hurt he was feeling hinder him. As much as his belly killed him, he wasn't dead yet. He wasn't going to just stand by and watch while Greg slaughtered Tom and Molly.

He wasn't that person anymore.

Greg was such a foul and familiar piece of shit. One that Rock felt like he housed hatred for long prior to meeting him. One he was eager to flush down the toilet.

Greg tried to bite down and keep his grip on Tom, but he soon realized that his jaw was no match for Rock's power and will. His bulky fingers had become immersed knuckle deep in his mouth. Using the blood-like lubrication, Rock's digits slithered deeper into the back of his throat.

Greg finally released his stiff grip, and Tom dropped to the floor. His arms flailed wildly, but he wasn't capable of avoiding Rock's power.

Rock's mammoth mitt remained wedged firmly between Greg's jaws as he drove his body into the ground. It wasn't a secret that Greg had a big mouth. It was only fitting that, as Rock mounted his body and applied more pressure, the flesh in the corners of Greg's mouth tore. His most obvious character wart had finally shown itself.

Greg punched upward and kicked his legs about madly to no avail. Rock's weight kept him pinned, and his lengthy arms covered enough distance to keep him above Greg's striking distance.

The bleeding facial skin only continued to rip wider until Rock was wrist deep inside his head. His entire fist had found refuge inside Greg's mouth.

Rock's buttocks could sense the vomit and bile that was bubbling up from Greg's gut. As his torso tremored, Rock could feel his bodily slime on his hand. His fingernails scraped against Greg's moist uvula and extended into the sloshing vomit that had accumulated in the back of his throat. The pool of regurgitation didn't deter Rock. On the contrary, it motivated him, letting him know just how close Greg was.

Lifting his other hand up, Rock took his thumb and index finger and clamped them over Greg's nose. While he still attempted to emit an inaudible plea, Rock ensured that the request would be his final.

The big man's dominant fingers sprung with the speed of a mousetrap, twisting sideways and snapping Greg's nose bone. Rock watched the pathetic man as he continued to choke on his fist and the bum-rush of blood welling up in his nasal cavity. His glowing eyes adored what they saw.

Greg gagged like an old car trying to turn over until a lethal limpness found his frame. As movement in his body stalled out, the fight he always liked to talk about and use as motivation, was all but gone.

The father who viewed life as a constant competition had officially lost.

Rock pulled his blood and puke-drenched fist out of Greg's reamed opening. He dismounted the dead body and rolled himself toward the wall. The anguish on his face was overly obvious as he bit down on his lip and clenched his belly. While he was focused on killing, the gunshot wounds didn't seem to bother him so much.

Good thing. I ain't finished yet, Rock thought.

Across the room, Molly remained smushed against the wall. While the violence she'd just witnessed was highly disturbing, the dreadful expression she donned wasn't alone. Along with the horror came a forbidden feeling.

A dirty but irrefutable sense of satisfaction.

It sickened Molly to consider the notion. It was a result that felt impossible. The collective tragedies she'd experienced were enough to somehow justify the inhuman pleasure she took while watching Greg slowly choke to death.

She stared blankly at Greg's demented-looking corpse, finally able to exhale a sigh of relief. Suddenly, it was like her brain was plugged in again. She snapped out of her trance and Molly's attention immediately shifted over to Tom.

"Oh my God! Tom! I—I can't lose you too!" she cried.

She shimmied over to his body and checked for a pulse.

"I think he's okay. At least, I hope he is," Rock said.

When Molly turned him over, Tom's face was purple. Her trembling fingers hesitated before tracing over his neck.

"He's alive!" Molly yelled.

Her mind was racing at breakneck speed.

"We—We've gotta get the hell out of here! Before she comes back!"

"It's not safe yet. She's ain't gonna let you live. You need to stay here," Rock replied.

"What about the kids?"

"They're trapped in the playground still. She won't go for them until she's dealt with us. Business before pleasure."

"What are we gonna do then?"

"*We* ain't doing anything. I'm gonna take care of her. You and your husband just gotta lay low until I get back."

Rock brandished an extreme grimace as he forced himself to his knees.

Molly watched the blood ooze out of his abdomen with uncommon generosity.

"You're bleeding. It looks really bad."

"It's nothing," Rock lied.

"Let me at least try and stop the bleeding for you first."

Rock thought about it for a moment and nodded. He needed to keep as much blood inside of him as possible, otherwise, he might not even reach Geraldine.

Molly didn't have any prior medical training and even considered herself a bit squeamish, but the ghastly events of the day didn't care. The situational struggle forced her to tap into locked-away knowledge, and run head-on into the things that made her uncomfortable.

Rock grunted in pain as Molly helped him remove what was once his fanciest attire.

With his blood-drenched jacket, white-collared shirt, and undershirt off, Molly could see a pair of small holes in his belly. She also took notice of a larger exit wound on his backside. But despite being confronted with the grisly violence, Molly couldn't avoid the elephant in the room.

The bubbly flesh.

The hidden torment.

The insidious branded letters that ran across the top of his chest that read: 'MINE.'

Before Molly had even seen the shocking stamp, she wanted to believe Rock was different. During the time he'd watched over them, Rock never actually appeared invested in the horrible things happening to the children.

The subtle aspects of his character seemed to indicate he might not have had a choice in how the events unfolded. She had no idea how long he'd had the scar, but Molly knew with an instinctual certainty exactly who'd branded his chest.

As the red ran out of Rock without fail, there wasn't any time to expound upon her thoughts. Molly balled up the white-collared shirt and set it on the exit wound on Rock's back where the most blood was leaking.

After the first layer was applied, Molly took his suit jacket and wrapped it around the wounded area, securing the collared shirt against Rock. She placed his undershirt over the smaller bullet holes on his front side and tied the arms of his jacket together, tightening the clothing around him as snugly as she could.

Rock moaned in pain but didn't shy from making his way back to his feet. He staggered forward, using the wall to brace himself.

"You're in terrible shape. Are you sure this is the best way?" Molly asked.

"It's the only way," Rock replied.

Molly nodded her head. There was a stark sadness and dread squirming inside her.

"Just hang tight. I think I know where she is."

"Where's that?"

"Where she feels safest."

"What are you gonna do when you find her?"

Rock slowed his stride near Fuchs' dead body. He looked down at the sick old bastard and watched as a bit of smoke continued to fume out from his ear holes.

He looked back at Molly.

"Something I should've done a long time ago."

THE FINAL REFLECTION

Rock's instincts served him well. He stared down the hallway that led to Geraldine's room and the door cracked open ever so slightly. Geraldine's door was *never* left open. It was always shut and locked. If the door was open, it was open for a reason.

The passageway beckoned him.

The insatiable lust to end his warped, lifelong odyssey possessed him. It was a desire that had unexpectedly arisen. Rock was living through a day he'd dreamt about, but he never believed his dreams might actually come true.

As the pain reminded him of his own mortality, Rock had already had a philosophical conversation inside his head. He'd accepted that he probably deserved to die. But in that same thought, he knew what was left of the families that remained definitely didn't. His longing to achieve that small victory compelled him forward.

While Molly had stopped the rapid blood loss from continuing, the effects of what Rock had already lost began to haunt him. The sweat slid out of his pores and a stabbing sensation attacked his brain. His legs were tired as hell, but Rock forced himself down the hallway until his stride broke the threshold.

The room was empty all but for another partially open door opposite Geraldine's bed.

To Rock, Geraldine's bedroom was only an incubator for sin and trauma. One that had hatched so many mental and physical scars that it caused him to become confused. Confused as to the purpose of his existence, and, more broadly, confused as to the purpose of man as a species.

Upon entry, the room where his perverse perception of reality bloomed made his skin crawl. Rock could still smell the stench of Geraldine haunting the air around him. Her rotten, glaze-gushing cunt and the fermented hole below it remained as hideous as it was the day he'd first stuck his face into them.

He wanted attention, but not *that* way.

He wanted to be held, but not *that* way.

He wanted to be loved, but not *that* way.

Geraldine had turned him into the saddest kind of damaged goods. The kind that's too fucked-up to realize it. When horror isn't quite horror anymore, it's just normal. And when awful isn't quite awful anymore, it's just life.

He looked back over to the fireplace. It remained an eerie reminder of when things had gone off the rails. When he'd become a marked man. He'd never asked for any of it, but it wasn't like he had a say.

From the blackened fire pit that carried fragments of burned wood, Rock's eyes glided up to the mantle. It was an area they'd drifted to many times before. While ensnared in the foulest of Geraldine's sexual fantasies, Rock had been busy subduing his own.

The sweet thoughts of an otherworldly relief; he recalled them vividly.

The daydream always began with him stumbling upon Geraldine's room unlocked. Then he'd somehow get his hands on the vintage Winchester rifle, Geraldine's prize gun mounted over the mantle. While he admired the cocking lever and style of the firearm, the gun was far more than just an antique showpiece in his eyes. It was an escape.

The visions of methodically loading the rifle up and sticking the long barrel inside his mouth always ended the same. When he pulled the trigger, Rock felt the elusive relief that he'd sought wash over him. But having that fictional liberation ripped away each time he withdrew from the fantasy almost made the entire charade more trouble than it was worth.

He'd never found the willpower to snatch the rifle off the mantle before, but today was different. There was just one problem: the gun was nowhere to be found.

For Rock, in that very instant, everything had finally come to a head. The suppressed compilation of volatile emotions. The decades of second-hand decadence. The crippling sense of self-loathing. It all pointed in one direction: the secret closet.

He twisted his head away from the mantle and toward the belly of the beast. It was a place that Rock, regrettably, was more than familiar with. The dark realm of vanity that Rock knew to be Geraldine's sanctuary. A place where her narcissism bred with her perverse infatuations to spawn her abhorrent moments of bliss.

She's so predictable, Rock thought.

Geraldine had forced him to pleasure her among the innumerable mirrors on many different occasions. The hall of reflections was never an area Rock was able to find peace. He didn't like the things he did inside. They felt wrong, but they were all he knew.

It seemed the more Geraldine grew to worship her own reflection, the more Rock grew to detest his. Only one good thing had come out of the torturous duration he'd spent between the mirrors: familiarity.

During his time inside, he'd become well acquainted with the layout. Focusing on the room itself helped to distract him from the more upsetting aspects of his time inside it. It was only a small nugget of information, but in the end, it might very well be the deciding difference in who walked out of that room.

Before Rock even entered Geraldine's chambers, he'd felt weary, but upon crossing the entrance into her wicked walls, the feeling vanished. As he pushed his way into the hall of mirrors, Rock's anger and urgency only inflated. He'd become the embodiment of wrath.

***

Geraldine remained tucked away in a small black cove at the rear of her maze of mirrors. It was a unique vantage point; one that placed her in a blind spot. The room filled with countless reflective surfaces remained blank. The imagery inside each mirror stretched on for what appeared to be infinity.

She patiently waited.

The only disadvantage of Geraldine's strategy was that she wouldn't be able to see if anyone entered the halls. She was relying on her other senses to hint at when the most opportunistic moment to pounce would be.

The faint sound of the door creaking echoed throughout the halls.

Geraldine cocked the lever of the rifle as quietly as she could. The mechanical noise still bounced around the room more than she would've preferred, but she knew, in just a matter of moments, the sound would be of little consequence anyway.

When she peered around the edge and caught a glimpse at the reflection, she saw her failure. The mountain of man that she'd botched. His bloody body was covered with Molly's makeshift patching and his boxy face was adorned with slices that had just enough time to congeal. The puffy scar tissue on his chest displayed the capital letters that she'd violently engraved upon him to initiate their bitter bond.

She thought about Rock's recent revolt and the anger inside blinded her. Now, the four letters couldn't have held less significance.

Mine… he's supposed to be mine! she thought.

Geraldine whirled around the corner lowering the rifle back at his wounded mid-section. She let a round rip off, but the bullet failed to penetrate Rock. Instead, his entire body fragmented and fell crashing to the floor.

"Son-of-a-bitch!" she yelled.

Geraldine stepped out into the hallway as a trail of smoke drifted from the barrel of the rifle.

"You said it, not me," Rock mumbled.

His gruff words boomed around the space. The echo attached made it difficult for Geraldine to pinpoint his exact position; maybe Rock wasn't as stupid as she'd perceived him to be. The raunchy memories of her relentless sexual escapades in the bizarre room reentered Geraldine's mind. The absurd amount of time they'd spent there *together* was incalculable.

Another loud crash of glass clanged against the floor.

The noise only confused Geraldine. She hadn't fired another round; she could only assume Rock was responsible for the sound of the damage.

"Silence! I made you who you are, you damn well better believe that I can ruin you just as fast!"

Geraldine popped around another corner of the maze and sized up her injured servant. She reloaded, cocked back, and continued the assault.

Blam! Blam! Blam!

Another three ripped out of the chamber in succession, but only yielded a disappointing mini-mountain of glass.

"You never did see me for who I was," Rock said.

This time, when his voice boomed, it felt even closer to Geraldine. The creepy, sudden shift in location caused her to whip back around.

Before Geraldine had even aimed the rifle, another pair of back-to-back shots left the barrel.

Blam! Blam!

More shattered glass with the same lackluster results.

"Oh, I know exactly who you are!" Geraldine yelled.

"Do you?" Rock asked.

"You're Rock *Stanley!* Not a Borden! Not a son! You're nothing but a mutt! A worthless pile of misery! A defect! I tried my damndest to fix you, but it's time to cut my losses!" Geraldine screamed.

As the chilling words left her wrinkled lips, Geraldine heard a heavy footstep. She pivoted back around holding the rifle steady, but Rock's reflection was nowhere to be found in the mirrors. She took another step in the direction his voice had last come from, knowing he couldn't be far.

She was right.

***

Having just heard the shots close enough to make his ears ring, Rock knew it was time to take *his* shot. His hand gushed blood from the mirror he'd punched through, but the wound was worth the advantage.

Geraldine had let her own familiarity and fondness for the hall of mirrors overshadow the most important detail of the room: Rock was the person who built it.

While she might've fashioned the blueprint, it was Rock who worked on the project night and day. It was Rock who spent months positioning the mirrors to gain Geraldine's ultimate approval. It was Rock who knew of the rectangular stretches of dead space that separated the isles within the wicked hall.

Punching through the mirror had left several deep gashes on his right hand, but being able to slip behind the reflections gave him a chance. He didn't have a gun, but the element of stealth allowed him to craft a strategy that might present Rock with the opportunity to neutralize Geraldine's firepower.

Rock listened intently; Geraldine was light on her feet but heavy on her shit-talk. Each hurtful word she hurled inched her closer to violence. She might've been rich in the pocketbook, but Rock was tired of listening to the old hag write checks with her mouth that her ass couldn't cash.

It was time to pay the piper.

The plan wasn't an exact science, but Rock had her location measured up to the best of his ability. He was feeling even weaker than before. The new gushing cuts on his hand had fostered further blood loss. But nothing was going to prevent Rock from finally getting his hands on Geraldine.

"Remember that word on your chest! You're mine! And no matter what happens, until the day you die, you will *always* be mine!" Geraldine yelled.

The familiar insults rang out in Rock's ears. The pitch and volume of her words confirmed it; she was standing right next to him. The perverse lust for the countless daydreams of carnage he'd fantasized about now owned him. He wanted nothing but to ensure Geraldine's hollow words would be the last she ever spoke.

Rock wound his good arm back as far as the tight space permitted. His yellow teeth ground against each other as his massive arm blasted through the black coating on the back of the mirror. Shards rained down slicing into his bare flesh, but it didn't matter; he was a man possessed.

"Ahh!" Geraldine shrieked.

"Unless you die first!" Rock yelled.

The entrance was simple but spectacular. Rock bull-rushed his way through the void and knocked Geraldine's brittle frame into a mirror on the opposite side of the hall.

Geraldine's hip *cracked* against the floor, and the rifle slipped out of her grasp. The ensuing hail of reflective spikes showered her, creating various cuts through her dress and triggering blood to expel from the gashes on her face.

Rock kicked the gun away and watched it slide several yards toward the end of the hall.

When he looked back at Geraldine, she still hadn't gotten her bearings back, but seeing her bleed was about the prettiest fucking sight he'd ever encountered.

Rock took pleasure in watching the instant confusion and fear as it suddenly conquered Geraldine.

She tried to shake off glass and shock. With her weapon out of reach, Geraldine knew she needed to leverage the only tool she still had at her disposal, her tongue. And with the wit of a magician unveiling a trick, Geraldine was suddenly a different person.

For the first time in their storied history, the evil hag of The Borden Estate spoke to him with a soft cautious approach. Wielding a calculated comfort the likes of which she'd never offered Rock before, Geraldine spoke as if she was talking to another person.

"Please, I—I was just upset. I didn't mean what I said," she begged.

The untruths were spewing in abundance, but Rock had known her long enough to understand the game. Her abrupt change in character was too convenient. The proof was in the actions. More than anything the witch could say, Rock trusted his gut; it reminded him that the bullets that burned inside it, were the ones that Geraldine had fired.

Rock bent over and clamped his mitts on each side of her skull. He savored the dread in her eyes as he lifted her quivering body off the floor. He'd made her body quiver many times before but never had he felt such satisfaction. The sweet sound of Geraldine's rickety spine and old bones *cracking* echoed through the halls.

"But, I'm—I'm your mother!" she cried.

"And I'm a motherfucker," Rock grumbled.

Rock hurled Geraldine forward, once again shattering the replication of the image she obsessed over. The force of the toss projected her so far that, not only did she explode the mirror she connected with, but she also burst through the one behind it.

As Geraldine hit the floor, a fresh peppering of razor shards sank deep into her facial tissue. The damage opened the floodgates, causing blood to rapidly pool under her head. Her shoulder was wrecked; an abnormal bulge inches from the joint signified its dislocation. The socket itself had shattered, and the fragmented bone lay divided inside.

Rock stepped through the opening behind her and back into the initial hallway. Just as they had when he'd entered the room, the collection of crusty dildos suctioned to the various mirrors sickened him. The mere reminder of her pleasure relit his rage.

His meaty fingers intertwined with Geraldine's grayed locks. When Rock gripped the follicles, he did so with all of his might. He lifted Geraldine's mangled body off of the ground only by her hair as she sputtered a mixture of groans and incoherence.

He positioned her at the midpoint of the mirror where she could gaze upon her brutalized face.

"This is what you wanted, isn't it?" Rock asked.

As Geraldine's wicked mouth shuddered, blood poured with a vengeance. But just before she was able to get a word out, Rock beat her to it.

"That was a rhetorical question," he mumbled.

Rock smashed her face into the glass with unnecessary force. But it wasn't as if he was thinking strategically any longer. He was now only powered by bitter emotions.

The slivers stabbed into Geraldine's face, opening up her cheek. A hearty hunk of skin was left flapping on the side of her head. New glass shards pierced into her skull and were sandwiched between the ruined flesh.

But Rock wasn't done.

He latched onto Geraldine's slippery neck again.

Rock propelled Geraldine through the prior mirror with such excessive power, it caused new lacerations to cut his hand all to hell. One of his knuckles found daylight, revealing a bony whiteness amid the crimson. But the gruesome injuries changed nothing. Rock's grip was true.

Without hesitation, he dragged Geraldine down to the next mirror beside them. As if she were a puppet, he propped her on her knees in front of her reflection.

Aimed between her eyes, a lengthy, orange dildo projected out several inches. The dried, cakey remains of her pleasure still littered the plastic shaft.

"There you are again, and look, one of your friends too," Rock said.

Geraldine attempted to speak, but when she opened her mouth, a waterfall of warm red was her only response.

"It's the love of your life, right? She probably deserves another kiss," he said.

Rock sent her face into the mirror again.

Geraldine's raspberry-lubricated lips aligned with the girthy toy. The hard plastic penetrated her mouth with such might that it knocked her dentures loose. As the dehydrated flakes of climax melted into the blood in her mouth, the tip of the toy stabbed her throat nearly reaching her tonsils.

With her oral cavity occupied by the phallus, the front of Geraldine's raining face turned the mirror to pieces. The glass offered new slices, the extreme violence pushing her closer toward un-recognizability.

Once the dust settled, Rock acted with the haste of a marathon runner pushing forward with the finish dangling just a short distance away.

He dragged her to the next mirror and immediately put her head through it. The blood-slathered dildo suctioned to the glass pushed its way into Geraldine's mouth, causing her dentures to eject from her mouth.

Rock hardly even noticed. The destruction of the room was music to his ears, just as the demolition of Geraldine's face was candy to his eyes.

After several additional mirrors came crashing down, Geraldine's face looked like a pork pin cushion that had been slashed to ribbons. It was now just a collection of meaty, wet globs that were randomly positioned.

In achieving the ghastly results, Rock had become the definition of red-handed. While even more of his blood drained out of his limb, he gawked at the broken mirror in front of him. Rock couldn't help but notice the unique break calling out to him. Fate had seen to shatter the glass in such a way that left only a single, long shard of glass positioned upward like a stake.

Rock looked down at what was left of Geraldine's head. The red oozed or squirted from nearly every direction. But he could still see that the well of blood that covered part of her face was bubbling.

Still hanging in there, Rock thought.

His lips twisted into a grin of gratefulness.

He was excited to see she was still fighting. A feeling of joy buzzed, knowing that Geraldine had stuck around long enough to feel what he had in mind.

"I know how much you love yourself. I'm gonna make your dreams come true," he whispered.

Rock reached underneath her dress with his red hand.

It was difficult at first for Rock to get hold of her panties because of the surplus of blood coating his mitt. But after a moment, he was able to get around the elastic end and tear the crusty cloth clean off.

Rock could've never imagined a scenario where he'd be removing Geraldine's underwear with genuine excitement. The vile symbol of his horrors smelled the part. The fetid aroma infecting the panties was like a big plate of rotten flounder and eggs left out in the sun for several days.

She'd taken everything from him. It was only right that he took everything from her.

Rock lifted Geraldine's leaky, motionless body off the ground. He parted her haggard legs with such care and intention. When her body let go and Geraldine's bowels emptied, it didn't dissuade him in the slightest.

"Hurry now," he whispered.

Once Geraldine's rancid release concluded, Rock aligned her puckering pussy just above the spike. He tried to look into her eyes but couldn't find them. Her face was too destroyed to make heads or tails of her anatomy any longer.

"I ain't good at goodbyes," Rock said.

He let his grip on her fail.

To Rock, it wasn't just Geraldine's body that he was letting go of, but the totality of his demons as well. All of his insecurities. All of his torment. All of his hate.

He'd found the unfathomable freedom of his dreams.

Rock watched on solemnly as the long spear of glass carved into her curdled meat curtain. As the shard carved deeper into her tunnel, Geraldine's demonic hole swallowed it up. It was symbolic in a way. The reflective spike suffered the same fate that most everyone who came into contact with Geraldine Borden did.

The blood vacated her pussy in jailbreak fashion before the shard snapped off three inches inside her. But the glass that remained at the base of the mirror burrowed into the back of her thighs deep as a creep in heat.

When her body hit the floor, she fell onto her side.

While death wasn't the ideal conclusion Geraldine sought that day, her life ended in a way that even she herself might've seen fit. Despite the rosy muddle she'd devolved into blurring out almost her entire field of vision, from the mirror across the hall, Geraldine was still able to get one final gander at herself.

SALVATION

"Wake up, sweety," Molly whispered.

As Tom's eyes fluttered open, she watched him let out a deep cough. His breathing didn't sound quite normal, but it was still magic to her.

Molly wiped the tears away from her cheeks. She'd lost more than she could've imagined, but the tiniest part of her was eternally thankful that she hadn't lost it all.

Tom rubbed his throat with his hands. His neck was still incredibly sore from the chokehold that Greg had snagged him in.

"What… what happened?" Tom said.

"He saved you," Molly replied.

"Who?"

"The big fella. He stopped Greg," she explained.

Molly gestured over to Greg's body.

Tom sat up, and his eyes found his rival. Greg's destroyed mouth offered a grotesque sight. The divot of congealing blood that covered his snapped nose offered Tom traces of the mayhem he'd missed while unconscious.

"What about the kids?"

Asking the question brought a slur to the delivery of his words and caused a lump to manifest in Tom's throat.

He suddenly remembered his indisputable reality. Tom wasn't asking about his own children; he was asking about someone else's. Still, despite his own horrors and heartache, the other innocent kids remained on his mind.

"We have to wait. He said he'd be back once he's dealt with that old… woman."

Molly knew how she'd described Geraldine wasn't a lie, but the word seemed too good for her.

She wasn't a woman; she was a monster.

"But he's been gone for a while now and I just," Molly paused fighting to keep herself from breaking down.

"Just what?" Tom asked.

"I just hope he finished it. I just need it to be over."

The loud sound of a heavy thud on the ground suddenly filled the room.

Tom and Molly's eyes widened in unison.

"Don't move," Molly whispered.

She placed her hand on Tom's chest and felt the panic racing inside.

His heartbeat was everything.

She slowly ascended so that her head was just peeking over the chair. Molly squinted into the darkness and saw the massive heap of blood-soaked man on the floor. She was beyond relieved to see Rock return, but his condition had declined even further.

"It's him, c'mon," Molly whispered.

She rushed back to Tom and helped him to his feet.

When they reached Rock's body, he was still breathing. But the substantial outpouring of blood from his abdomen and backside didn't serve as a good omen. Additionally, his right arm and glistening hand stuck out. These parts were riddled with at least a half-dozen deli-style slices.

The exposure of his enormous paw's massive knuckle made Tom and Molly cringe.

"She's gone," Rock said.

"You're—You're sure of it?" Molly asked.

"Positive."

The weight of dread and sense of impending doom lifted off Tom and Molly's aching shoulders; they suddenly felt light enough to float.

But Molly's reprieve was short-lived. There were injured children that needed medical attention, and, to her surprise, she also found herself thinking about Rock's well-being.

"We need to call the police and an ambulance right—"

"No," Rock interrupted. "I—I just need you to help me to the elevator."

"But you've lost so much blood."

"Just forget about that."

It took a lot out of him just to speak, but the sternness in his tone didn't allow Molly to mistake his urgency. However, Rock's demeanor abruptly transitioned. When he spoke again, his gruff voice sounded like a tired old dog.

"I just…I wanna see the kid."

Tom and Molly couldn't argue. They were in agreement; the most important task that still remained was getting to the children.

The Grimleys each got on one side of the gentle giant and managed to get him back on his feet. They pulled him forward like an injured football player being helped to the sideline, and they all exited the doorway of the spy room together.

***

When the elevator came to a stop, the exit didn't open. Rock had a silver skeleton key ready and inserted it into a hole in the elevator panel. After twisting it sideways, the elevator doors parted and unlocked access to the subterranean level.

"Go right," Rock managed.

A drizzle of blood fell from his mouth after uttering the directions.

"Okay," Molly said.

Tom and Molly helped Rock out to the basement level and escorted him down the long vestibule.

The Grimley's reckoned the channel they were heading through served as the backside of the demonic playground. An unsettling sense came over Tom and Molly as they neared the end of the tunnel. The feeling was unexplained; a nightmarish awareness only the parent of a dead child would pick up on.

Their babies were near.

A pair of double doors came into focus at the very end of the dim tunnel. Additionally, to the left of the double doors, another lone metal door stood.

Tom and Molly noticed the singular door at slightly different times. But they both shared a similar, nauseating rumble in their stomachs post-discovery.

They couldn't deny the truth; they were forced to absorb the grotesque details as they played out on-screen. But it was still hard to believe that any of it was real.

When they approached the entrance, Rock found his footing and held himself up with the wall beside the threshold. He took hold of the massive deadbolt at the top of the door and pulled it out of the wall.

Rock reached back into his pocket and extracted a keyring. After sifting through the blood-stained metal, he finally located the key he was looking for. He stuck it into the lone hole and twisted.

As the lock popped, Rock looked down at the second deadbolt lock that ran across the bottom of the entrance.

"I—I don't think I can bend down. Can you get the other one?" he asked.

Tom squatted down and pulled the metal bar until the second mechanism was deactivated.

Rock placed his gushing hand over the handle and turned. Due to his injuries, and the weight of the metal barrier, he struggled.

Tom stepped up beside Rock and helped muscle it open.

As the path to the children was finally unveiled, Molly held her breath. She still didn't want to accept what she knew to be the truth.

In her heart, Molly wished that Isaac, Sadie, and Sam, through a miracle or otherwise, would be standing safe and sound behind the door. That the horror she'd been forced to swallow on the television was just the cruelest Hollywood special effects gag known to man. If it was, she'd gladly take it in stride. She wouldn't even be mad. But inside Molly's twitching gut, remained the reality.

As she took a look inside the playground, the fading flares of her pipedream were indefinitely extinguished.

No Isaac.

No Sadie.

No Sam.

She expected the hurt to resurface, but that didn't make it any less devastating.

Tanya remained in the sandbox beside Donnie. The young boy's burned arm was slung around the shoulders that now held up a disfigured face. The charred skin and melted flesh that covered Tanya's grisly exterior looked disgusting, but they were both still alive.

The sound of the massive metal spikes shooting in and out from the rope tower offered a slight audible distraction. It was the only one of the diabolical devices Geraldine and Fuchs had created that would never see any use.

The looks on Tanya and Donnie were that of relief and exhaustion. But there was still a certain measure of fear and distrust that wouldn't be erased until they saw daylight. They were grateful that the attitude and emotions Tom, Molly, and Rock carried weren't of a malicious nature.

As they read into them further, Tanya and even Donnie seemed content to see people come to their rescue. While they shared a pool of similar emotions, they also held their own unique variants within.

Donnie was glad that he didn't have to see his mother again. He didn't fully comprehend the finality of death. For the entire duration of his time in the playground, he debated if they might eventually reconnect, or if the hurt that the big man had put on her would keep them separated forever.

He was grateful that it was the latter.

On the other side of the spectrum, Tanya understood her parents were far from perfect. She was evolved enough to comprehend that what her dad told Bobby to do was evil. Not just evil, but evil beyond anything she believed him to be capable of. But when she only saw the three of them standing at the door, she bawled.

"Where's my dad and mom?" she howled.

Donnie stroked her shoulders delicately, attempting to ease her anguish.

Molly's bottom lip quivered. What kind of answer could she possibly give her? Ignoring the question seemed like the only reasonable reaction.

"We've—We've got to get out of here," Molly said.

Tanya broke down into a hysterical outpouring. She was overcome with the emotion she'd been forced to subdue for most of the day.

Donnie continued rubbing her shoulders, trying to comfort her to the best of his ability. Then he slid his arm around her hand and helped Tanya to her feet.

***

When the double doors opened, the five of them were confronted with a tall set of concrete steps. They sluggishly ascended them together and made their way up to the grass.

It took a moment before any of the visitors realized that they were standing in the backyard of The Borden Estate. They were all just a stone's throw from the harmless-looking playground where the disturbing day began.

They had come full circle.

A somber silence had fallen over the entire group. No words were going to change the horrors that had transpired in the bowels of The Borden Estate that day. They would all now and forever be missing pieces; pieces of their hearts and pieces of their families. No matter how dysfunctional or difficult they could be, they were still family.

But in a way, when the mishmash of misfit bloodlines stood beside each other, it almost felt like their collective horrors and heartaches had fused them together. And as the waning sunlight shined upon them, the broken stood as one. Just because the scattered fragments had been drawn together in Frankenstein fashion didn't change the result. If anything, the extreme suffering and severe trauma made them closer to a traditional family.

The bond they all shared was odd and unintentional, yet, still, undeniable.

Rock staggered over to the wall, continuing to lose blood from his belly, back, and hand. He turned his attention to the gray electrical box with a single keyhole on the side of the stone exterior of The Borden Estate.

He inserted a key into the box and twisted it sideways. A variety of switches were revealed. Rock scanned the labels inside until he located the one marked 'FENCE.'

His bloody finger coated the white plastic, and he pulled the tiny lever downward.

"What is that for?" Molly asked.

"The gates out front, they're electrified. Geraldine had it installed so if things went haywire, no one could get off the cliff," Rock replied.

A moment of awkward silence arrived once again.

Rock looked over to the fenced-in, beautiful playground that the sun was now setting behind. He summoned the strength to get a few more words out.

"You're free now."

Tom looked over to his wife, unsure what to say next. He was thankful, but still emotionally destroyed.

A strange, untranslatable sadness found Molly. The quiet, blood-drenched man in front of her had been part of the worst day of her life, yet somehow, she still took pity on him. She now understood that monsters weren't born, they were created. In Rock's disastrous case, anyway. It was a complex goodbye, but what her soul wanted. Molly finally found a way to put it into words.

"We need to get you to a hospital. There are two cars. Tom can take the kids in ours and I'm—I'm going to take you in the other one," she stammered.

A coating of gloss welled up in Rock's eyes accompanied by a subtle curl at the corner of his lips. There was an acceleration in his pulse and a vibration in his soul.

During his entire life and times, Molly's words were the first to make him feel like someone was actually concerned about him. He was grateful to finally be able to appreciate what someone's care felt like. Even if it was coming from a stranger. Even if it was fleeting. He was still thankful.

It was the greatest gift he'd ever been given.

It was a feeling that was warm and wholesome.

It was a touch that he knew he'd never taste again.

"I'll be alright. Just take care of the kid for me," he said.

The tears trickled down his face as Rock stared into the boy's lost eyes.

His own eyes.

Again, Rock saw himself in Donnie. The endless accrual of hurt and sorrow that he'd endured didn't have to be that for the kid. Rock knew he didn't have another chance in him, but more than anything, he felt that he didn't deserve one. But when he looked at the burned little boy, he knew that Donnie did.

"No, you—you helped us. I know you didn't want this. We need to get you—"

"Just go!" Rock roared.

He didn't have much energy to yell anymore, so he hoped that Molly would just listen to him.

"And what are you gonna do?! Just lay here and die?!"

Rock glanced back past the playground toward the sagging sun. There was still an hour or so of daylight left.

"No. I'm gonna do something—"

Rock coughed up more blood. He used his forearm to wipe his lips, but his arm was so bloody, that it only made his face more of a mess.

"I'm gonna do something I never got to do before."

The tears gushed from Molly's eyes. She didn't want to ask him. She didn't want to hear or see anything else that hurt. Her jaw chattered as she barely got the question out.

"What's that?"

Rock looked away from the picturesque area and locked his eyes with Molly's.

"Play."

LIKE A KID AGAIN

Blood pooled at the top of the slide. There was so much it had even started to run down. The long streaks of warm red had already coated the yellow plastic at Rock's feet. He looked over the fence at the dead dog wrapped in a tee shirt on the other side.

It felt like ages ago when he'd released the hounds on the children. The sight of the broken pup disgusted him. After shaking free from Geraldine's cocoon, the act felt alien to him. The person who had walked up to the sandy cage, the puppet of evil, had officially died.

As his gaze shifted from the animal corpse to the slide, Rock realized his frame was far too massive to squeeze through the hole.

"Rats," he grumbled.

Still clenching at his gut with his gory hand, Rock turned away from the hole to the long, winding set of monkey bars. The deluxe version easily stretched on and on.

Rock clamped his mangled hand and good one onto the bar in front of him. As he swung forward a groan escaped him. Upon reaching the next bar, a stabbing pain surged across his entire mid-section. Still, he swung forward again, grabbing the next pipe with his blood-drenched digits.

When he tried to hold on and swing to the third bar, his gory grasp gave way. Rock was already too big for the toy so the fall was brief. But when his wounded back smacked into the sand, he still felt it plenty.

"Ahh!" he wailed.

He couldn't help but let out another growl of anguish and annoyance. But as Rock lay on his back, looking up at the sky, his initial curses were followed by something else. Something unexpected.

A giggle.

He fell into another coughing fit, drool and blood splattered over his lips and dribbled down to his chin. The pain still reverberated inside him, but he'd never let that stop him before. Rock forced himself to sit up. The surprising crimson smirk remained on his face, glowing in the fading beams of sunlight.

He eyed the swing set and mumbled to himself, "That might make a little more sense.

Limping over toward the black, rubbery seating, Rock couldn't help but think about Molly and what she'd offered him. As he swung back and forth, the red rained into the tiny pit of soft sand beneath him. Rock didn't stop to think about the bleeding. Instead, he just thought about how grateful he was.

As the metal chains and steel bolts above his head creaked, Donnie entered his mind. Suddenly, an unusual comfort crept up inside him. Even though he'd just met Molly and Tom, he was certain they were going to make sure the boy was cared for. That he was given the chance at the future he deserved.

A loud snapping noise blared out from above as the bolts that attached the chains to the swing set exploded. Again, Rock tumbled a short distance, this time landing flat on his ass and pinning the limp swing to the sand.

There was more pain that accompanied his fall, but it wasn't as severe as it was previously. Another chuckle fumbled its way out of his mouth.

"You gotta be kidding me," he laughed.

Clearly, Rock had missed the boat on all the playground structures that might accommodate a man of his unique dimensions. But he found himself enjoying his bungles more than he would've enjoyed a smooth ride. It fit perfectly; nothing about his life had ever gone smoothly.

Rock willed himself to his knees, despite the blood oozing out of his abdomen. Despite his physical activity, his heart rate had begun to slow. He found himself not only feeling nauseous but also dizzy. However, he didn't allow his illness and pain to sour his attitude. It was both the first and last time he'd ever get to enjoy the playground and he didn't plan on squandering it.

Rock looked over to the roundabout that was just a few yards away.

"Merry-go-round," he grunted.

He'd never had anything to feel merry about in his past, but that day… that day was different.

Lacking the energy to stand, Rock crawled. He dragged himself through the warm and comforting sand, and under the rope tower. When Rock arrived in front of the merry-go-round, the moist, gummy sand had mixed into his bloody wounds.

He had nothing left in the tank, but somehow, he forced himself up to his knees again. Grabbing hold of the bar, Rock slung the circular, orange platform as hard as he could.

The counter-clockwise revolutions increased in their pacing. Each time his hand touched the next bar, he pushed it forward a little harder. Even when the roundabout had picked up a healthy amount of steam, Rock continued to push it faster. Until the blurring speed was finally enough to satisfy him.

Rock willed himself to his feet.

As each of the spaced-out bars whizzed by, he figured he was only going to get one shot at it. Usually, people spun the roundabout while the kids were already perched in their position of choice, but Rock didn't have that luxury.

He studied the speed and plotted his pounce. Believing he saw a gap big enough to accommodate his huge body, Rock dove forward. As he crossed into the path of the merry-go-round, one of the thick, steel bars crashed into the gaping exit wound on his lower back.

"Son-of-a-bitch!" he yelled.

His curse began as a cry but transitioned to a cackle.

"If you didn't have bad luck, you wouldn't have any at all," Rock griped through his runny grin.

The shot to Rock's lower back slowed the roundabout's momentum. But like a gift from God, when Rock landed in the center of the toy, there was still enough energy in the structure to keep it spinning round and round.

A new pool of leakage puddled around his body. The velocity of the ride spread the red around the circular platform in various directions. But the mess wouldn't grow much larger; there wasn't a lot left inside him anymore.

Rock opened his eyes and looked up at the cloudless blue hue that painted his entire blurry perspective. He felt the coastal breeze on his skin, and as he stared into the sky, he wondered if anything was actually up there.

A strange sensation of discomfort was stretching across his face; Rock Stanley wasn't accustomed to grinning.

The pain wasn't the worst he'd felt. It was a different hurt than the kind he'd come to know. A hurt that, under different circumstances, he could've definitely gotten used to.

The beauty of the day had about dried up.

The darkness was priming itself to set in.

Rock's pulse slowed to a crawl as if it was mirroring the pace of the creeping merry-go-round. As his oversized frame finally gave way, he had almost no feeling in his tired body any longer.

Except for the fading flicker of elusive happiness Rock had finally found a way to bottle.

ABOUT THE AUTHOR

Aron Beauregard is a Splatterpunk Award-Winning horror
author and weirdo. He is the writer of over 20 despicable
books and counting. He believes he has many more tales
floating through the holes in his brain that he created in
his 20s. In the event Playground didn't make it clear, he's a
sucker for 90s nostalgia. It was just a simpler time for him.
One he wishes never had to end. Aron lives in the woods
with his wife, dog, and deep personal traumas.

FOR SIGNED BOOKS, MERCH, AND
EXCLUSIVE ITEMS VISIT

ABHORROR.COM